Mexican Hat

Also by Michael McGarrity

Tularosa

Mexican Hat

Michael McGarrity

W. W. NORTON & COMPANY

NEW YORK LONDON

For information about permission to reproduce selections from this book, write to Permissions,
W. W. Norton & Company, Inc., 500 Fifth Avenue, New York, NY 10110.

The text of this book is composed in Bodoni Book
with the display set in Birch.
Composition and manufacturing by the Haddon Craftsmen, Inc.
Book design by BTD/Beth Tondreau.

LIBRARY OF CONGRESS CATALOGING-IN-PUBLICATION DATA
McGarrity, Michael.
      Mexican hat : a novel / by Michael McGarrity.
         p.   cm.
      ISBN 0-393-04063-1
      I. Title.
   PS3563.C36359M49   1997   96-35735
813'.54—dc20   CIP

W. W. Norton & Company, Inc., 500 Fifth Avenue, New York, N.Y. 10110
http://www.wwnorton.com

W. W. Norton & Company Ltd., 10 Coptic Street, London WC1A 1PU

1 2 3 4 5 6 7 8 9 0

Once again, for Emily Beth and Sean Eli, with love, and for HH, with my highest regard for his friendship, support, and wise counsel.

Author's Note

Some of the historical events, people, and places described in this book are based on fact, while most are pure fiction. My sincere thanks go to Ms. Elizabeth "Betsy" Reed and Ms. Ana Marie Ortiz of the New Mexico Department of Environment for their technical assistance.

Quemado

PADILLA CANYON

MANGAS MTNS.

Magdalena

Socorro

Luna

Old Horse Springs

Reserve

NEGRITO CREEK

BLUE RANGE

SAN FRANCISCO RIVER

GILA

Glenwood

DRY CREEK

WILDERNESS

GILA RIVER

Silver City

RIO GRANDE

STATE OF

★ Santa Fe
Albuquerque

NEW MEXICO

DETAILED AREA

Deming

FLORIDA MTNS.

Las Cruces

TRES HERMANAS MTNS.

ARIZONA

0 10 20 30 40
Scale in Miles

TEXAS

El Paso

Juarez

MEXICO

1997 SEAN MC GARRITY

1

A thick cloud broke and rolled toward the distant hogback. Sunlight pierced the narrow canyon, casting long shadows and soft morning colors into the ravine. Pale green cottonwoods, shimmering in a gentle breeze, bordered a dry, rocky streambed. Driving into the sun, Kevin Kerney dropped the visor to block the glare, slowed the truck, and grunted in frustration. He was lost. In front of him juniper and piñon trees climbed steep slopes to a ridgeline that slashed abruptly above the canyon and pointed directly at a serrated peak. From the lay of the land and the piss-poor condition of the forest road, it was unlikely the route would take him to the Slash Z summer pasture.

He stopped and consulted the quadrangle map. Three private

ranches straddled Dry Creek Canyon, deep in the foothills of the Gila Wilderness. He'd passed the first two at the wide mouth of the canyon where rangeland and cactus flats spread to the breaks and dipped down to the San Francisco River. Kerney was a good mile beyond where the third ranch should be.

He glanced at the radio and rejected calling the Glenwood ranger station to ask for directions. He might be new to the job and a seasonal employee to boot, but he was capable of getting oriented without any help. He backed the truck down the road to the cutoff, got out, and found a Forest Service sign that had been ripped off a post and tossed in some underbrush. The spur he'd taken was closed to vehicles. That solved the problem. Kerney backed farther down to the fork and rattled over an equally primitive route that traveled away from the hogback.

After a steep rocky climb, the road leveled as he entered a thick stand of old-growth ponderosa pines that peppered the north face of the mountain. Deep shade made it feel like dawn instead of full morning. He topped out at the crest and stopped the truck, letting the engine idle. A saucer-shaped park, sprinkled with oak and pine, stretched for several miles in three directions. Smack in the center a cabin sat in a small grove of pine trees. A windmill and stock tank were nearby. A barbed-wire fence encircled the cabin to keep away the grazing cattle that moved slowly through the tufts of long grass.

Kerney took in the view, his thoughts turning over the ways he could restore the abandoned homestead and revive it into a year-round cattle operation. There was a perfect cove at the far end of the field where a house, horse barn, and feed shed could be sheltered. The old cabin could easily be converted into a repair shop, to be used when winter came and all the things that needed fixing could be attended to when the weather made outside work impossible. The road to the cabin was in sorry shape and needed to be graded and packed with base course so it could be used year-round. New fences would have to be thrown up to segregate the land into pastures to prevent overgrazing, and a new corral and loading chute were necessary, but all in all, one man could handle it, if he was willing to work sixteen-hour days and forgo time off for a couple of years. With federal grazing rights, he could run several hundred head of cattle and maybe make a small profit, once the operation was up and running.

Kerney shook off the daydream. It was foolish to think that he could ever raise enough cash to buy such prime land, and the owner would be an idiot to sell. He would have to settle for a lot less when the time came to put his money down and get back to the business of ranching. He popped the clutch and drove over the rutted tracks that led to the cabin.

FROM HORSEBACK on the ridge, Phil Cox watched the lime-green Forest Service pickup as it traveled across the field, bouncing in the deep furrows of the ranch road. The driver slowed several times to keep from spooking the cattle that wandered into his path. That was enough to tell Phil that Charlie Perry wasn't driving. Whenever possible, Charlie used his horn with perverse pleasure to run a few pounds off Phil's beef. Charlie believed cattle grazing was destroying the national forest. He wanted the Gila pristine and pure from boundary to boundary; no cattle, no private land, and no ranchers to mess up the wilderness.

Phil didn't recognize the man who parked next to his horse trailer and limped to the cabin fence. After a dozen or so steps his gait smoothed out a bit. Phil hollered, got the ranger's attention, and nudged his horse down the trail, leading a saddled gelding. He wondered who in the hell the Glenwood station had sent to meet him. The ranger waved a greeting as Phil approached.

Phil dismounted, hitched the horses to the back of the trailer, and walked to the ranger. "I don't believe we've met. I'm Phil Cox."

"Kevin Kerney," the man replied, grasping Cox's hand. "You're a hell of a way off the beaten path."

Phil nodded. "True enough. The Forest Service would love to buy me out and retire my grazing rights." He judged Kerney to be in his early forties. His features were strong and his skin was weathered, with fine lines at the corner of deep blue eyes. "I won't do it."

"Neither would I," Kerney replied, as he looked around. With no evidence of a holding pen or a loading chute in the shallow valley, there was only one way to get the cattle in and out. "Do you move your stock on the hoof?" he asked.

Phil smiled. Maybe the ranger wasn't a complete idiot. "That's right. I use the Triple H pens down on the flats for loading. It takes a couple of days to herd them out, but it's fenced most of the way, so we don't have to chase a lot of strays."

"About two hundred head?" Kerney guessed. Phil Cox, a slender man with bushy eyebrows and light brown hair, matched Kerney's six-one frame, minus about ten pounds. His eyes were slate-gray and he had a dimple in his square chin. He was in his late thirties, but his voice sounded younger.

"Give or take a few, with the new calves," Cox agreed. "I could run more on land higher up, if I had a mind to, but when the Forest Service raised the grazing fees, I cut back. I was expecting Charlie Perry to show up."

"He's supervising a prescribed burn in the Blue Range, so you're stuck with me."

"New to the district?" Cox asked.

Kerney nodded. "They sent me down from the Luna station to fill in until Charlie gets back."

"I thought I knew all the Luna rangers."

"I'm temporary help."

Phil nodded to encourage more of an explanation. With the cutbacks in funding, hiring seasonal help was now standard operating procedure for the Forest Service, but commissioned rangers were usually career employees.

Kerney didn't volunteer any additional information. "What can I do for you, Mr. Cox?" he asked instead.

"I'm not sure you can do anything at all," Phil replied. "I found a bear carcass I thought Charlie Perry would like to take a look at."

"Poachers?" Kerney asked.

"Maybe," Phil allowed.

Kerney nodded. He limped to his truck, opened the door, took out a small day pack and a hand-held radio, and returned to where Phil waited. "Let's go take a look."

Phil Cox gestured at the gelding as he swung into the saddle. "We have to ride in. Climb aboard."

Kerney lengthened the stirrup straps, tied down the day pack, and eyed the size of the saddle before swinging himself onto the gelding. "Who's riding with you?" he asked with a slight smile.

Cox smiled back. "PJ, my oldest son. He's thirteen. I've got him posted at the carcass to keep the coyotes away."

Kerney adjusted his rump in the undersized saddle. Riding with a saddle that didn't fit jarred the back and jolted the tailbone. "How far do we have to go?" he asked.

Phil looked a bit sheepish. If Charlie had been sitting on the gelding he never would have known why his tailbone was sore at the end of the ride. Charlie preferred helicopters to horses.

"Not far," Phil replied.

Kerney nodded. "That's good."

Phil took the lead across the grasslands. There was something familiar about Kerney that he couldn't pin down. He was left with the feeling that he knew the man.

PJ COX HAD HIS FATHER'S EYES and the same dimple on his chin. He cradled a varmint rifle in his arm. Lean and deeply tanned, the boy wore a battered cowboy hat pulled down tight on his head. Phil introduced Kerney, and PJ stuck out his hand.

"Glad to meet you, sir," he said politely.

"Same here," Kerney replied, shaking PJ's hand. "Thanks for looking after things while your dad went to fetch me."

PJ glanced up at Kerney, pleased with the expression of gratitude. "No problem," he said.

The carcass was twenty feet away. Kerney took a long look at it. "When do you think the bear was killed?" he asked PJ.

"Yesterday," PJ answered promptly. "It hasn't even started to smell bad yet."

Kerney nodded in agreement. "Did you take a close look at it?"

"No, sir." PJ glanced at his father. "My dad said to leave it just the way we found it."

"That was good advice," Kerney replied with a smile.

He gathered up some twigs and walked an ever-tightening circle around the bear, staking each track and sign that he saw. He could feel Phil and PJ watching him as he worked. Ten feet from the carcass he found the discarded, eviscerated bowels of the animal. Close by were tracks of bear cub prints and the imprint of a boot heel in soft sand. He finished the circle, returned to the horses, got two cameras from the day pack, and started taking pictures. Phil Cox and PJ remained quiet as he shot Polaroid and thirty-five-millimeter photographs of everything he had staked as evidence. Finished with the perimeter search, he walked to the carcass.

The black bear, a female, had been skinned and beheaded, and all four paws had been cut off. Coyotes had been at her, ripping into the soft underbelly, but the animal had not been fully gutted. The ground, swept clean with the branch of a cedar tree to remove footprints, was stained with the juices and blood from the coyote feeding. Kerney took more pictures, gathered some hair samples, and scraped dried blood out of the cavity into a plastic bag before returning to Phil and PJ, who were perched on a boulder. Both stood up when he walked over.

"What do you think?" Phil asked.

"Trophy hunter," Kerney speculated. "Knew what he was doing, from the looks of it. Took out the bladder and bowel before he started skinning. One clean entry hole through the chest from a high-powered rifle. Minimum damage to the pelt. Have you seen anything like this before?"

"Heard about it," Phil replied. "It happens every now and then. A royal elk or a buck deer with a good set of antlers gets taken, or a cougar or a bear like this. Charlie can tell you more about it."

"What would Charlie tell me?" Kerney prodded.

"That some people pay big money to hang a bear skin on their wall," Phil answered.

"Like who?"

"Nobody I know," Phil replied shortly. "There isn't a rancher in the county who would kill a bear that's mothering cubs unless it was marauding."

"You saw the cubs?"

Phil shook his head. "Just the tracks. That's my boot print you took a picture of."

"How long have you and PJ been up here?"

"We camped down at the old cabin last night and came up before dawn looking for strays. When we found the bear I called for Charlie on my cellular phone."

"Have you lost any stock?"

"Not that I know of," Phil replied. "I wouldn't shoot the damn bear and call the Forest Service to come and fetch it, if that's what you're getting at. That would be pretty stupid."

"That would be stupid," Kerney agreed. "Have you seen anyone in the area?"

Phil answered with a tight shake of his head.

"Did you hear any shooting?"

"No."

"Did you pass anyone on the road when you came in?"

"No." Phil stiffened and his eyes narrowed. "I already told you I didn't shoot the bear."

"I'm not accusing you, Mr. Cox," Kerney replied.

"It sounds that way to me."

"Maybe we should back up and start this conversation over again," Kerney proposed.

Phil gave Kerney a slight shrug of his shoulders. "Hell, I'm sorry I sound so gruff. It's not you. I guess I've got a knee-jerk reaction to anything that smacks of criticism. Nowadays it seems like us ranchers get blamed for everything that goes wrong in the national forest. At least you're not giving me a Charlie Perry lecture about how my cattle are destroying the forest."

"Is Charlie a hard-core environmentalist?" Kerney asked.

"And then some. He's one of those back-east, urban conservationists. A big-city fellah who wants to save us from ourselves. I take it you haven't met him."

"I haven't had the pleasure."

"Well, you're in for a treat," Phil said sourly.

Kerney nodded vaguely, his eyes studying the mesa. From what he could see, the tabletop mesa fell off sharply on all sides. It was a rock-strewn piece of ground, no more than half a mile long and a quarter mile wide, with wide beaches of shale broken by clearings of grass, wildflowers, and clumps of piñon and cedar trees.

"Is the trail the only way in?" he asked.

"Unless you're a mountain goat," Phil answered.

Kerney smiled in agreement, took the hand-held radio from his pack, made contact with the Glenwood office, and gave a brief report. He was told to stand by until relieved.

"Charlie's on his way," Phil predicted.

"You think so?"

"Bet on it."

"While we're waiting for Charlie, would you and PJ like to lend a hand and help me look for the cubs?"

Phil found himself liking the ranger's manner. "Might as well," he replied with a smile.

They searched the mesa in sectors. Phil and PJ were good trackers. The boy found recent claw marks on a piñon tree near a cow path, and Phil found fresh bear scat by a rotten log. They fanned out, working between the trees, and Kerney discovered a shooter's nest behind a cedar tree. In the spongy, needle-covered soil a small blind had been constructed of branches and dirt, just large enough to conceal a prone rifleman. There were tracks of a four-wheel all-terrain vehicle in a sandy hollow off to one side.

PJ called out in an excited voice just as Kerney finished photographing the tire tracks. Kerney jogged to catch up with the boy and his father, who stood looking down into a rock crevice. A bear cub, huddled behind the dead body of a sibling, whimpered as PJ bent over with his hands on his knees for a closer look.

Phil turned to Kerney and said something that was lost in the sound of an arriving helicopter.

"What did you say?" Kerney shouted.

"I said it's a damn shame," Phil Cox shouted, as they walked to where the chopper landed.

The pilot shut down the engine as a man disembarked and ran, head lowered, through the dust cloud kicked up by the rotor wash. He nodded at Phil Cox and turned his attention immediately to Kerney.

"You're Kerney," he snapped. He was a man in his early thirties, with a serious face and sharp brown eyes. Sand-colored hair flapped over his forehead. He wore a yellow firefighter's jumpsuit and hiking boots.

"That's right," Kerney replied.

"Charlie Perry," he said, brushing his hair back into place. A strand fluttered back down his forehead. "I sure hope you haven't fucked everything up."

The helicopter blades slowed to a dull thudding sound. "That would be embarrassing," Kerney replied.

Charlie's eyes narrowed at the sarcasm. "What have you done so far?" he demanded.

"Staked evidence. Took photographs. Did a field search."

"Show me the carcass," Charlie ordered, as he started walking away from Kerney.

Kerney didn't move. After a few steps Perry turned to face him.

"There are two cubs over where PJ is standing," Kerney said, motioning toward the boy. "One is dead. The other one looks sickly."

Charlie walked back to Kerney and gave him a sour look. "Why didn't you call it in, for chrissake?" he demanded. "I would have brought my wildlife manager with me."

"We just found those cubs," Phil interjected. "Get off your high horse, Charlie."

Charlie gave Phil a tight smile and looked at Kerney. "Wait here," he ordered, as he turned on his heel and went to the chopper.

As he talked to the pilot, Phil nodded his head in Charlie's direction. "Now, isn't he a piece of work?"

"I like his warmth," Kerney replied.

Phil chuckled. "He sure puts a man at ease, doesn't he?"

Charlie returned carrying a canvas duffel bag. "I'm sending the chopper back for my wildlife manager after you've shown me what you've done," he said to Kerney. "The pilot will drop you off at your vehicle. I'll take it from here."

Kerney gave Perry a tour, while Charlie fired questions at him, each one more terse than the last, his tone peevish. When Charlie finished grilling him, Kerney turned over the Polaroids, exposed film, and evidence and stepped back to take another look at the man. Perry had close-set eyes and a pinched nose. His fingers were long and nervous. Almost skinny, Perry stood just under six feet tall. His shoulders sloped a bit.

Charlie flipped through the Polaroids without comment and stuck them in the breast pocket of his jumpsuit. He looked up at Kerney without any change in expression. "You can take off. Get back on patrol."

Dismissed, Kerney nodded wordlessly, gathered up his gear, and headed for the helicopter.

Phil Cox walked along with him. "It seems to me you did a damn good job out there."

"Thanks. This was my first case where the victim was a bear," Kerney admitted.

"What other kind of cases have you had?"

"The two-legged variety," Kerney said as he climbed into the helicopter. "But that was some time ago."

The pilot cranked up the engine. Phil stuck his head through the open door into the cockpit as Kerney strapped on the seat belt. "I didn't mean to sound so pissed off at you." He finished the apology with a shrug of his shoulders.

"You didn't. Thanks for your help. And thank PJ for me."

"I'll do it. Stop by for a visit when you have the time."

"Be glad to," Kerney answered.

Phil waited for Kerney to ask for directions. "I'm over by Old Horse Springs," he finally added, when Kerney remained silent. "Turn off at the Slash Z sign on the highway."

Kerney smiled. "I know where it is."

THERE WAS NO ANSWER to Kerney's knock at the door of the Triple H ranch house. A station wagon with an Albuquerque car dealer's decal on the tailgate was parked in front of a double garage. He knocked harder and waited. The limbs of an old cottonwood at the back of the house overhung the roof. The home, a contemporary single-story ranch-style, was neat as a pin on the outside. The landscaping, apple trees bordered by a moss rock planting bed filled with flowers, was carefully tended. Against a small hill within hailing distance stood a weathered horse barn with a corral and a loading chute built out of old railroad ties nearby.

Kerney knocked again, got no answer, and gave up. On his way to the truck, he heard a woman's voice calling from the backyard.

"Cody, you get in here right this minute! I mean it, young man!"

He turned the corner of the house in time to see a shirtless, shoeless boy scoot up some steps and fly through the open door of an enclosed screened porch into an old stone house set back against a ridgeline. The screen door slammed closed behind him. It must be the original ranch house, Kerney thought. Square and chunky, it had a big stone chimney at one end, a rock foundation, and old-fashioned casement windows.

Kerney knocked at the screen door. The porch floor was stacked with moving boxes in various stages of being emptied. From inside the house he heard two children, a boy and a girl, arguing over who had been given permission to feed a puppy. The animal, a short-haired mongrel no more than twelve weeks old, answered Kerney's knock with a wag of its tail, pushed the screen door open with its nose, sniffed Kerney's boots, and wandered down the steps into the yard.

"Hello," Kerney called out.

The children's chattering stopped, followed by their rapid arrival at the porch door. They were attractive kids with brown hair, fair skin, and bright, inquisitive faces.

The girl, about eight years old, had long braids that she twisted absentmindedly with her finger. She gave Kerney a shy smile. "Hi," she said.

"Hello. Are your parents home?"

"My father doesn't live here."

"Can I speak to your mother?"

"We're very busy right now," the girl replied.

"I won't take much of her time."

"I'll ask her." The girl retreated into the darkness of the front room.

The boy, about five, dressed in cutoff jeans, stood directly in front of Kerney, squinting up at him. He peeled an orange with his fingers, stuffed a wedge into his mouth, and dropped the rind on the floor.

"What kind of policeman are you?" the boy asked as he inspected Kerney's holstered handgun and the badge pinned on his uniform shirt.

"I'm a ranger with the Forest Service."

The boy swallowed the orange slice. "I'd like to be a policeman when I grow up," he said. "Or a rancher like my grandfather."

Kerney hunkered down to get at eye level with the boy. "Which job do you think you'd like best?"

"Ranching," the boy replied. "You get to ride horses and drive trucks. I like driving the tractor best. My grandfather lets me sit on his lap and steer. That's fun."

"I bet it is."

The boy held out his orange. "Want some?"

Kerney pulled off a portion and thanked the boy.

A woman wearing shorts and a peach-colored sleeveless jersey stepped through a side door that led from the kitchen to the porch. She glanced at Kerney, who rose to greet her, and paused to look into some open boxes. "That's where my saucepan is," she said to herself, taking it out of the carton. "Cody, pick up that orange peel and go help your sister. I see Cody has been feeding you," she said to Kerney as she approached.

"He gave me a piece of his orange," Kerney answered.

Cody gathered up his litter, stuffed it into a pocket, and refused to budge. He wrapped his arm around his mother's leg as soon as she moved into striking range. Her hand dropped gently to his bare shoulder. "Your fingers are sticky," she said.

Cody smiled up at her.

"My parents are in Silver City for the day," the woman said. "Is there something I can do for you?" She didn't wait for an answer. "It's not a forest fire, I hope. That damn helicopter flew over twice this morning."

Kerney shook his head. "No." With creamy skin, cobalt-blue eyes, and black hair that spilled against her shoulders, the woman was very good-looking. The bones of her face, fine and delicate, were set off by a strong mouth that hinted at toughness. Late thirties, Kerney guessed. He looked down at the boy, who still had his arm firmly wrapped around his mother's thigh. Slightly above average height, the lady had long, well-formed legs.

"Somebody killed a black bear on the mesa," Kerney explained. "I'm looking into it. Have you seen any unfamiliar vehicles go by recently? Or any strangers?"

"Why do people do that?" she demanded, stomping her foot. "That makes me so mad." She shook her head in disgust. "Just a minute." She pried Cody's arm from her leg. "Go," she ordered, in an even tone of voice.

Cody didn't move.

"Right now, young man," she added, with the hint of a threat in her voice.

Cody groaned, gave her a dirty look, and shuffled off to the kitchen.

"I've been so busy moving in, I haven't noticed anything except this mess," she answered, gesturing at the boxes. "Besides, that damn house my parents built blocks my view of the road. I swear I'm going to tear it down after they die. I just hate it. If they want to live in a house like that, they should move to Albuquerque."

"It looks well cared for," Kerney noted, trying to remain neutral.

"My father prides himself on keeping things in perfect order. But the house belongs in a subdivision, as far as I'm concerned."

"It does seem a bit out of place." Kerney took out a business card and wrote his name on the back. "Could you have your father call me?" he asked, handing her the card.

The woman studied the card. "Kevin Kerney," she said, looking over his shoulder. "Bubba, get over here!"

Kerney turned. The puppy was busily digging up a flower bed. It took one short leap, then wheeled and trotted off toward the house the woman hated.

"Cody. Elizabeth. Go get Bubba before he destroys all of Grand-mother's flowers."

The children tumbled down the porch steps and started chasing Bubba.

"I named him Bubba because he's so damn stupid," the woman explained.

She looked at the card again, then back at Kerney and caught him staring at her legs. Her eyes measured him directly. He was tall, with square shoulders, brown hair with a hint of gray at the side-burns, and calm blue eyes that looked back at her without flinch-ing. His features, angular and strong, were offset by a mouth that seemed on the verge of a smile.

"I'll give Dad your card."

"Thank you," Kerney said, smiling in earnest now.

She watched him walk down the flagstone path with a limp that threw him slightly off-center. She switched her attention to her children, who had chased Bubba back into the yard and were trying to tackle the puppy as he barked and ran between their legs. She smiled as the chase turned into a game. She tapped the business card against the back of her hand and looked at it once more. Kevin Kerney. She liked the name.

She stuck the card in the frame of the screen door where she wouldn't forget it and went inside. There was an incredible amount of unpacking still left to do.

STOPS AT THE LAST RANCH in the canyon and at the bar, store, and two restaurants in Glenwood yielded no information on possible suspects. Kerney drove the short distance down the highway to the district ranger station, checked in with Yolanda, the secretary, found an empty desk in a back office, and started writing his report. He was almost finished when Charlie Perry came in and stood over the desk, looking down at him. Kerney glanced up, said nothing, and returned to his writing. The expression on Perry's face was enough to tell him that Charlie was steamed.

"I don't recall giving you permission to continue the investigation," Charlie said sharply.

"You didn't," Kerney allowed.

"That's right. I understand you have some law enforcement experience. I relieved you on the mesa and sent you back on patrol. You should know what that means."

"I do."

"Are you always so fucking insubordinate?"

"Not always."

Charlie scowled. Kerney locked his gaze on Perry's face and settled back in his chair to wait the man out. Charlie blinked first.

"Okay," Charlie finally said, "you're new and you're seasonal, but this isn't the Luna office. I handle all the investigations in the district."

"I understand from Phil Cox that you're good at it," Kerney replied.

"That's nice to hear, but it's not the point," Charlie shot back. "Poaching and illegal trophy hunting are a way of life for most of the people in this district. It's part of their culture. They do it to feed themselves, to make money, or just for sport. There are twenty-five hundred people spread out over almost seven thousand square miles in Catron County. A hell of a lot of them are poor as church mice, and they know the forest better than any ranger. Catching them isn't easy.

"You're wasting your time canvassing. You got two kinds of people who live here—the minority who want poaching stopped, but who aren't going to snitch on their neighbors, and all the rest, who see it as a birthright. Folks poach depending on how hungry they get, how broke they are, or how bullheaded they feel. You can't approach it like a criminal investigation. It doesn't work that way. And the locals aren't going to talk to some newcomer they don't know or trust."

Charlie was still scolding. Kerney didn't want to make it worse. "I understand," he said.

"Good. I'll be at the Blue Range burn for the rest of the day. Finish your patrol shift and report back to the Luna office in the morning. Leave your report with Yolanda. I'll read it later."

Kerney tapped his paperwork with the tip of the ballpoint pen.

"Do you have any poaching files I can look at?" he asked. "I'd like to learn more about it."

"You don't have the time."

"I'll do it after work," Kerney countered.

Charlie considered Kerney. He hoped to God he was never in the man's predicament. He knew Kerney was a medically retired cop from Santa Fe hired on an emergency basis by Samuel Aldrich in the Albuquerque Office to fill in for a permanent employee on extended sick leave. The rest Charlie could see for himself: a hobbled-up, middle-aged man in a temporary job that would end no matter how hard he worked or how much he tried to please—not that placating people seemed to be much of a concern to Kerney. There were simply no permanent staff vacancies, with all the budget cuts.

"Catching poachers isn't your job," Charlie said. "I thought I made that clear."

"You did." Kerney leaned back in the chair and smiled at Charlie. "Explain something else to me."

"What is it?"

"Why are you pulling my chain? I don't think asking a few questions has damaged the investigation."

"That's your point of view," Charlie replied bluntly.

"Is there more to this case than meets the eye?"

Charlie exhaled loudly through his nose and shook his head. "You don't get it, do you? It's not your case. It's not your business. End of discussion."

"Whatever you say."

Charlie left, and in a few minutes Kerney heard the helicopter lift off to take Perry back to his fire. As he paper-clipped the report together, Kerney wondered why Charlie had stonewalled him about the case. It made no sense, and dismissing Perry as an arrogant, hard-nosed son of a bitch wasn't a completely satisfying explanation.

Kerney walked down the hall and gave his report to Yolanda for typing. She promptly dumped it on the top of an overflowing tray. A heavyset, slow-moving woman with expressionless eyes, she held Kerney back from leaving.

"Charlie said for you to work a double shift," she informed him.

There was a bite to the announcement. Charlie had obviously made his feelings about Kerney known to Yolanda.

"Did he really? What does he want me to do?"

"Campground patrol." She pulled open the desk drawer and handed him two keys on a chain. "For gasoline and the office," she explained. "Just leave your paperwork on Charlie's desk."

"Anything else?"

Yolanda shook her head and turned back to the typewriter.

It looked like the dead black bear was going to be the high point of his day.

THE DISTRICT OFFICE WAS DARK and locked when Kerney returned from his double shift. He sat in Charlie's office reading closed poaching cases he'd found in the bottom desk drawer. It was meager stuff; mostly small-fry poachers who had been snitched off, caught taking game out of season, or found spotlighting prey at night. A few trophy hunters had been busted while transporting carcasses out of the forest.

Charlie's open cases were stuffed in a file cabinet and consisted of a mixture of poaching and trophy kills, with no solid leads, witnesses, or hard evidence. All of Charlie's attention seemed focused on game-taking within the Glenwood District. Kerney wondered about similar activity in other areas. He scanned through a stack of game-kill bulletins from other agencies. One bighorn sheep had recently been taken on state land by a poacher using an ATV, and several exotic ibex from the herd in the Florida Mountains east of Deming had been harvested earlier in the year. An all-terrain vehicle had been seen in the vicinity by a Bureau of Land Management officer.

With the bear kill on the mesa, that would make at least three cases where an ATV had been used to get to the killing ground. It was enough to raise Kerney's interest. He went to the map posted in the front lobby and studied it. Aside from Forest Service land, there were large parcels under the control of the Bureau of Land Management and smaller sections owned by the state. Maybe Charlie Perry had tunnel vision.

Just for the hell of it, Kerney decided to query every state and federal park and conservation agency in the region and ask for information on kills where an ATV was used. He typed fax messages at Yolanda's desk and sent out the inquiries, asking for responses to be sent to him at the Luna office. As he fed the messages through the fax machine, Kerney wondered how ticked off Charlie Perry was going to be when he discovered this most recent act of insubordination.

He got home to Reserve late. His trailer, painted a bright blue by his landlord in a desperate attempt to rent it, sat in an empty field across from the high school. Inside it was hot, stuffy, and smelled like mouse piss. He opened all the windows. Across the field the parking-lot lights at the high school burned pale yellow. He heard the deer mice under the floor—much more established tenants of the trailer than he was—scurrying around, upset by his arrival. He would put out some traps on his next day off.

The trailer was a dump, but Kerney didn't mind. A single-wide furnished with a bed, kitchen table, couch, ragtag easy chair, and several lamps, it served his temporary needs. He was banking all his paychecks and living on much less than his retirement pension. Along with the money the Army had paid him for the recovery of the stolen artifacts from White Sands Missile Range, he just might finish the summer with enough cash for a down payment on some land. Not much, and certainly nothing as extensive as the Slash Z summer grazing acreage, but something that could get him started.

Kerney really didn't give a damn what Charlie Perry might do. Four weeks on the job was long enough to convince him that he could never permanently return to patrol work. Not even the beautiful landscapes and startling sunsets in the Gila could ease the boredom of long hours in a vehicle. Maybe a wilderness assignment would be different, but that was a plum job reserved for forestry and wildlife specialists.

It had been years since he'd worn a uniform, and he had never liked them—not when he had served in the Army nor when he had started out as a street cop. He stripped off the garments, dressed in his sweats, and limbered up the knee for his nightly run, wondering how long it would take Phil Cox to figure out who the hell he was.

As he jogged away from the trailer he thought about the good-looking woman he had talked to at the ranch house. He didn't even know her name. Even the rawest rookie cop on the street knew enough to ID all possible witnesses. It was a dumb blunder, and his appreciation of the lady's splendid legs didn't justify the mistake. He laughed out loud at himself as he picked up the pace.

2

ector María Padilla had heard the story of his family's history many times from his grandfather. He listened to it again as he drove through the mountains north of Silver City on a winding two-lane highway. The trip from the border through the desert had gone smoothly, but in the high country of southwestern New Mexico he felt less confident behind the wheel. He drove a new four-wheel-drive Ford truck Grandfather had bought specifically for the journey, and towed a travel trailer they had rented in El Paso.

Grandfather finished the story of how his ancestors had settled the Mangas Valley soon after the end of the American Civil War, and now embarked on the tale of his arrival in Mexico City as a young man.

"My father wanted all his children to be educated," Dr. José Luis Padilla said, continuing his narrative in Spanish. "He decided the village needed a doctor. So, I first went to the university in Albuquerque and then to Mexico City to study medine."

"And that's where you met Grandmother," Hector said, keeping his eyes fixed on the road.

"Yes." José Luis Padilla signed inwardly. He missed his dear Carlotta, dead these past three months. "She was the only woman enrolled in my class at medical school. All the men pursued her. I was amazed that she took notice of me. Her family opposed our marriage."

"Because you were not from Mexico," Hector noted, slowing the vehicle as a car approached them from around a curve.

José Luis Padilla chuckled. "Yes. I was unacceptable—a nobody from the United States."

The road was clear. Hector glanced with a worried look at his grandfather, who sat with a road map on his lap. Since they'd entered the mountains, Grandfather's breathing had become more labored. He looked for signs of oxygen deprivation. Grandfather's skin had good color, and his lips were pink. Reassuring signs. He decided to inquire anyway. "How are you feeling, Grandfather?"

Dr. José Luis Padilla turned his head and smiled at the young man. His dark brown eyes were clear and lively. He was rail-thin, with wispy gray hair that curled up over the tip of his ears. His skin, heavily wrinkled, was tight against his skull. "I am fine, *jito*. You must remember that until your graduation next year, I am the only doctor on this journey."

"Your breathing is rapid," Hector observed.

"As well it should be at my age, with so much activity at this altitude. If I require rest, you can park the truck so that I can take a siesta in the trailer. Pay attention to your driving."

Of all his grandchildren, Hector pleased José the most. He was a serious, hardworking young man who would one day be an excellent doctor. Hector reminded him of Carlotta. He had his grandmother's beautiful olive-black eyes that always seemed lively and amused, a resolute spirit, and a sound intellect.

"You never came back to New Mexico after the death of your father," Hector said. It was part of the story Grandfather always seemed to skirt.

"I brought your grandmother here for my father's funeral, and she hated it. It was too isolated and alien to her nature."

"But it was your father's wish that you should return home to practice medicine," Hector reminded him.

"There was nothing to come home to. Pull over to the side of the road."

Grandfather's answer surprised Hector. "Nothing?" he questioned. He stopped the truck on the shoulder of the road next to a cluster of cabins surrounding a tourist lodge. They were in Glenwood, a small mountain town strung out along both sides of the highway. The town—a few businesses, tourist cabins, and small houses fronting either side of the road—perched in a wandering valley cut by the course of a river.

"My father lost everything in the Great Depression," José replied, as he unsnapped the seat belt. "My brothers had already left home to find work, and the village was dying. Gringos from the Dust Bowl moved into the valley and took most of the public works jobs. Building roads. Logging. Drilling wells. All my father had left was his land, his sheep, and a few herdsmen willing to work on the promise of future wages. All was lost after he was murdered."

"Murdered?"

"Yes, murdered. Your grandmother and mother made me promise never to speak of it to the family. But I think I owe it to my father's memory to uncover the truth."

"Sixty years is a long time, Grandfather," Hector replied. "Perhaps it is too late."

José Padilla opened the passenger door. "I think not," he said abruptly. "I have a letter we must deliver. I will ask for directions at the store. Wait here."

"I'll go," Hector said hurriedly.

Dr. José Padilla waved a finger at his grandson as he stepped carefully out of the cab. "I am an old man, not an invalid."

When José returned, he guided Hector to a dirt road off the highway that bisected a small valley, pierced a series of arroyos, and climbed into the foothills. Hector maneuvered the truck and travel trailer cautiously, especially where the sides of the road dropped off into the arroyos. Grandfather had him stop in front of a ranch house and gave him a sealed envelope.

"This is for Mr. Edgar Cox," José said.

"Do you wish to see him if he is home?"

"Not yet."

Mr. Cox was not home, but a very pretty Anglo woman, who said she was his daughter, took the letter and promised to deliver it. Grandfather simply nodded his thanks when Hector returned and gave him the message.

Back on the highway, Grandfather navigated with a road map on his lap. Hector continued north, climbing steadily through mountain passes covered in dense pine forests.

Well past the town of Reserve, Grandfather spoke. "The turnoff to Mangas is not far ahead."

"What kind of road is it?" Hector inquired.

"The map shows it to be an all-weather road. If that is so, it has been much improved over the years."

"A dirt road," Hector corrected. "Unpaved."

José laughed. "You worry like an old woman who has left the barrio for the first time in her life. You are driving very well. I would be lost without your help."

Hector slowed the truck and pulled to the shoulder of the highway. "I think we have traveled far enough for one day," he said.

"But the day is still young, and I want you to see those beautiful mountains." Jose nodded at the peaks that rose up before them. "If I can remember the way, perhaps I will be able to show you Mexican Hat."

"It's not on the map," Hector reminded him.

José waved off the comment. "Not every place is named on a map."

"And not every day has to be spent driving from morning until night," Hector said, stifling a yawn. "Today, I would rather stop and stretch my legs for a while. Please look on your map for a campground."

"Of course," José said. "Will I be allowed to explore tomorrow?"

Hector saw the twinkle in Grandfather's eyes, nodded his head, and laughed. He checked for oncoming traffic, saw none, turned the truck around, and started driving back toward the town of Reserve.

KERNEY LEFT THE FOREST SERVICE TRUCK in front of the old schoolhouse, now the Luna District Ranger Station, glad to be finished with the Glenwood assignment. In the high country, no matter what the season, early morning was chilly, and across the valley plumes of wood smoke drifted from the chimneys of the homes that were still occupied. Over the years many houses had been abandoned, and the village presented a neglected face to the world.

The former classroom that served as an office for the commissioned rangers was a snarl of desks, file cabinets, map cabinets, and office chairs. The walls were plastered with posters, maps, memorandums, and aerial photographs of the Apache National Forest, which was managed as part of the Gila east of the Arizona border. There were several responses to Kerney's fax inquiry on the top of his desk. Clipped to them was a note for him to see the boss. He didn't have a chance to read the replies. Carol Cassidy, the district supervisor, came into the room and stood in front of the blackboard that stretched along one wall. A quotation from Edward Abbey, written on the board with a warning not to remove it, read, "The idea of wilderness needs no defense. It only needs defenders."

"What are you doing?" she asked, nodding at the fax papers on Kerney's desk. Carol's full lips accentuated her round cheekbones. She brushed her short blond hair back from her forehead. Her oval light brown eyes, usually impish and cheerful, were serious.

"Nothing, yet," Kerney replied, waiting for more.

"Are you trying to give Charlie Perry a heart attack?" she asked, walking to him. She picked up the thin sheaf of fax papers and let them float down to the desktop one at a time.

"From what I've seen, he doesn't need any help from me," Kerney answered. "He's wound up pretty tight." He scanned the replies quickly. No hits on his inquiry so far.

"He's hyper," Carol agreed. "But Jesus, Kerney, it's his investigation. I don't need any grief from Charlie."

"Why would he give you grief?" Kerney asked.

Carol leaned back, hand on her hip, and stared at him. She was short and blocky—the legacy of a Nordic grandmother—but carried herself with poise. In her late forties, she was delighted to be running the Luna office and planned to keep doing exactly that until she retired. "This will be a turf issue for Charlie," Carol answered. "It's his district and his case. You did your part. The rest is up to Charlie. Did he put a burr under your saddle?"

"No burr," Kerney replied. "I'm just following up. I plan to pass along whatever comes in."

Carol liked Kerney, which was a pleasant surprise. Often the temporary personnel hired out of the regional office in Albuquerque either lacked a strong work ethic or couldn't adapt to the rural culture of the area. Self-contained yet easygoing, Kerney fit nicely into the team. "What's the issue?" she finally asked.

Kerney hesitated.

"Come on. Give," Carol prodded.

"From what I can tell, Charlie's wearing blinders. He isn't coordinating his investigations with other agencies or looking at trends. I thought it might be worth a shot to see what else is out there."

Carol gave Kerney's assessment some thought before responding. "You can make that same criticism about every district in the region," she replied. "The whole system is understaffed, underbudgeted, and under siege. Top *that* off with the Sagebrush Rebellion and the People of the West movement, and what we've got here is a damn near explosive situation."

"I understand," Kerney replied.

"Perhaps you do in a general way," Carol responded, "but you haven't been here long enough to know the depth of the anger that's out there. Logging has been curtailed because of the Endangered

Species Act. Mines have shut down because of water pollution. Grazing fees have been raised. Everybody blames the environmental movement and the government. People feel that nobody outside the county gives a damn about their survival.

"In the last twelve months, four homemade bombs have been found on hiking trails in the wilderness. *Bombs,* for chrissake. Some people are more than angry."

"Any ideas of who is responsible?"

"Nobody has a clue."

"Not even rumors?"

"Some think it may be the county militia, but nobody is talking to me about it."

"Who knows about the militia?"

"I haven't the foggiest. Some time back, when the first bomb was found, I asked to have an investigator assigned from the Inspector General's Office to look into the situation. Instead the acting regional forester referred the request to Alcohol, Tobacco and Firearms."

"And?"

"And *nada.*"

"Do you want me to drop the poaching research?" Kerney asked.

Carol took a minute to think it through. "No, you can follow up, as long as it doesn't cut into your other duties. Charlie won't like it. He's been handling all the Luna District cases, as well as his own, for the past two years. But it's my call to make, and I'd just as soon put your experience in law enforcement to good use. Remember, you're a ranger, not a chief of detectives in a police department anymore."

"I know that," Kerney replied dutifully. He wished he could

avoid the never-ending sermons that came with being a rookie new-comer.

Carol's expression softened, and she laughed. "I'm lecturing, aren't I? Sorry about that."

"It was more informative than what I learned from Charlie," Kerney allowed, grinning at her. "Tell me about him."

Carol's smile was half a grimace. "He's a golden boy. Can't seem to do anything wrong, as far as Sam Aldrich, our acting regional forester, is concerned. Charlie transferred here about two years ago. He's single and not very social. Keeps pretty much to himself. There's not much to tell."

She wiped the piqued expression off her face. "Like him or not, he does a good job. He's a Young Turk on a fast track. There's nothing wrong with that, I suppose. Are you ready to do something different for a while?"

"What do you have in mind?"

"We're finishing up a new campground at the foot of Mangas Mountain. It's nothing fancy. Parking for vehicles. A well and water line. Some picnic tables. An outdoor toilet. New hiking trails. I can use you there for a couple of days."

"No problem," Kerney answered with a smile. "Any special instructions?"

"Amador Ortiz will put you to work. Keep the area closed until the job is finished. I don't want anyone camping there until it's ready to open."

"You got it, boss," Kerney said, getting to his feet.

"Take a horse and trailer with you," Carol added. "When we open the campground it will be on your patrol route. Get to know the lay of the land."

They parted in the foyer, at the counter where generations of children had presented notes from parents to the school secretary. Carol's office, once the principal's domain, sat at the far end of the building with a clear view of the hallway leading to the classrooms.

Kerney drove a mile down the road to the housing and district maintenance compound, where Carol and her husband and family lived, along with several other senior staff. Tucked away under some full-growth pine trees, the area contained living quarters, horse barns, tack rooms, repair shops, a heavy machinery lot, a garage, and storage buildings.

The Luna Valley dipped away to the south, a shallow, wide depression of grassland ringed by deeply forested mountains. The spire of the Mormon church, prominent in the little settlement, caught the morning sun like a beacon. The highway cut through the valley, past a small cluster of vacant commercial buildings that once served the settlement and occasional tourists driving the scenic route to and from Arizona.

Kerney walked to the corral and inspected the small herd of horses. He took his time before settling on a white-stockinged chestnut stallion with strong legs that stood sixteen hands high. It was a powerful-looking animal with a prominent chest and solid legs that promised good balance. Kerney smiled as he hitched the trailer to the truck and led the horse out of the corral. It was going to be a good couple of days. Anything was an improvement over patrolling campgrounds filled with temporary refugees from urban America.

EDGAR COX sat at the table sipping his morning coffee and looking at the row of Royal Copenhagen Christmas plates carefully arranged on a long open shelf above the double kitchen windows. He didn't have to count them; there were forty. One for each year of their marriage. Margaret had bought the first plate as a Christmas gift to herself when they were newlyweds. After that, he made sure she got another plate each holiday season. It always pleased and delighted her. Edgar wondered if he'd get to give Margaret any more. It didn't look promising. He heard the hinge of the back door squeak, looked over, and smiled as Karen came into the kitchen.

"Hi, Daddy. You got home late," Karen said.

"You know how your mother is when she gets to visiting," Edgar replied, a smile easing across his face. "Are Elizabeth and Cody up?"

"Just barely. They helped me with the unpacking. I think the chaos is under control."

Karen walked to the counter, got a cup and saucer from the cupboard, and poured some coffee. Barefoot, in shorts and a loose undershirt with no bra, she was only just dressed. Edgar was used to it. At the age of three, Karen had started taking off her clothes and running around buck naked. His daughter hadn't really changed much over the years, especially when she was at home. The funny thing about it was that Karen was absolutely stunning when she got dressed up, which wasn't often enough to Edgar's way of thinking.

He waited for her to join him before speaking again. "Are you going to enroll the children in school?"

The question made Karen sigh. "We've talked about this before, Daddy, and the answer is still no. I'll tutor them at home for now. You know how I feel about public schools."

"You've got a teaching certificate and a law degree," Edgar countered. "That's not bad for a country girl who went to public schools."

"I want Elizabeth and Cody to learn how to think, how to love ideas and books. Then they can go to school. Besides, my job with the district attorney's office is only half-time. The kids will get lots of attention from me."

"What does Stan think about it?"

Karen made a sour face at the mention of her ex-husband's name. "It's not his decision to make."

"He's still their father."

"He couldn't care less. In fact, I think he's delighted to have us out of Albuquerque and far enough away to be conveniently forgotten."

"That's a pretty harsh judgment."

Karen laughed. "No, it's an honest one. The harsh judgment came from the court when I was awarded sole custody."

"You didn't tell us that."

"There was no need to drag you or Mother into the messy particulars of my divorce."

The look on Karen's face made it clear that further discussion was closed. "You start work on Monday?" Edgar asked.

She smiled. "Bright and early. I can't wait."

Her father smiled back at her. His gray hair was thick and curly, cut short and combed with a severe part, and his eyes were as blue as her own. Edgar Cox was a big, lean man with a strong chin, a deeply lined face, and an easy grin. He reached over and patted her hand. "I know you'll do a damn fine job."

She smiled at the compliment. "Thanks. What's on your schedule for the day?"

"I'm going to put out fresh salt licks, patch a hole in a water tank, and round up a cow I spotted that looks like it has a touch of foot rot."

"You need to slow down, Daddy."

"Why should I? I only turn seventy-five this year, and God willing, I got another good ten or fifteen years left in these old bones."

"Well, I think you need some more help. Two hired hands aren't enough."

Edgar laughed at the suggestion. "Find me somebody who knows just a little bit about ranching, is willing to work in bad weather, and doesn't expect to get paid more than he's worth, and I'll consider it."

"Sell the place." Karen's smile was devilish.

"We've had this discussion before. The ranch stays in the family. That's what I want, and that's what your mother wants."

Karen laughed. "In that case you'd better make sure that Cody and Elizabeth learn everything you forgot to teach me, so they can help me run this place after you and Mom finally decide to slow down. Think of it as home schooling."

"Touché," Edgar replied.

"Oh, I almost forgot. You had visitors yesterday."

"Did Phil and PJ stop by?"

"No." She reached in the pocket of her shorts, took out an envelope and a business card, and put them on the table. "A poacher killed a black bear on the mesa. A ranger wants to talk to you about it. Charlie Perry was here too, asking the same questions."

Edgar shook his head sadly, picked up the card, looked at it, turned it over, and read the scribbled name. "Kevin who?" he asked.

"Kerney."

"Don't know him. He must be new. This card says he's working out of the Luna station. I wonder what he's doing in Charlie's neck of the woods." He put the card on the table. "I'll talk to Charlie." He picked up the envelope. "What's this?"

"A young Hispanic man left that for you. Very polite and well-spoken; based on his accent, I'd say he was from Mexico," Karen dded.

"Nobody we know?"

Karen shook her head. "I never saw him before. He was with an older man."

"Were they looking for work?"

"I don't think so."

Her father tore open the envelope, read the contents quickly, and grunted to himself. The smile in his eyes faded.

"Is anything wrong?" Karen asked.

Edgar shook his head. "No. Nothing. Some old business, that's all."

"Is it something I should know about?"

The smile on her father's face was forced. "Don't worry, Peanut. It's not important."

She wrinkled her nose in distaste at the childhood nickname.

He stuffed the letter and envelope into a shirt pocket, pushed his chair away from the table, and stood up. "Your mother is sleeping in," he said. "She had a long day."

Karen didn't know that her mother might have cancer. It wasn't going to be discussed until the test results came back. Margaret had made him promise. It would be an anxious wait before their next appointment with the doctor.

"I'm going to town to see Charlie Perry and pick up supplies," Edgar announced. "Do you need anything?"

"No, but I'm sure Cody would love to go along with you."

"Not today. Tell him I'll take him and his sister horseback riding before dinner." He came around the table, put his hands on her shoulders, and kissed her gently on the cheek. "It's good to have you back home, Peanut."

"You and Mom are going to be stuck with us for a long time, Daddy," Karen answered, patting his hand.

"That's just what we want to hear." He kissed her again and walked into the living room. When she heard the front door close, Karen got up and followed, watching him through the window. He got behind the wheel of his truck, took the letter from his shirt pocket, and read it again before driving away. It worried Karen. Something in that letter had upset him, and she didn't have a clue what it might be.

She returned to the kitchen, rinsed out the coffee cups, and quietly left the house. There were still tons of books to unpack.

EDGAR COX absentmindedly waved back at the folks he passed on the highway, his anxiety growing. When he turned off at the Slash Z sign at Old Horse Springs, his heart pounded in his chest and his mouth was dry. He stopped in the middle of the ranch road and looked at the Mangas Mountains. It had been sixty years since he'd been back to the Slash Z. Six decades since he rode his horse to the old highway, left it at the gas station—now boarded-up and abandoned—hitchhiked to Albuquerque, lied about his age, and enlisted in the Army. He shook his head in disbelief. A lifetime. A fifteen-year-old kid running away as fast as that damn pony could carry him.

He knew what was waiting for him. His nephew, Phil Cox, kept him informed, even brought him snapshots from time to time, trying hard to keep some family ties going—at least on the surface. But

Edgar suspected that what really interested Phil was getting first crack at the Triple H if he ever decided to sell it.

Hands sweaty, he took a deep breath, touched the gas pedal with his toe, and started down the ranch road. It felt as if he had stopped breathing when he coasted to a halt in front of the two-story ranch house. The old trees around it were gone, replaced by young willows and a row of poplars in the front yard. Painted white, with green trim, a pitched roof, and a small covered porch that served as a balcony for the second floor, the house looked the same as when he was growing up. The red brick chimney on the north side with wild ivy still clinging to it; the old wooden sash windows; the rose bushes bordering the low rock wall that surrounded the front yard; the picket fence and gate painted white to match the house—all the same.

Slowly, Edgar got out of his truck, turned, and looked across the large horse pasture where, half a mile away, the home Phil Cox had built for his family stood. A low adobe structure with a portal across the front and lots of windows, it faced the Mangas Mountains. Phil's pickup truck was parked outside. Edgar wouldn't have much time alone with his brother. Phil would come running out of sheer curiosity once he spotted Edgar's vehicle.

He walked quickly up the wheelchair ramp and entered the house without knocking. It was quiet inside. He went down the long hall past the closed front-room door and staircase. In the kitchen he found Eugene with his back turned and his arms propped up on a table. He was reading a magazine and drinking a cup of coffee.

"Is that you, Phil?" Eugene asked, without turning around.

"It's Edgar."

The man in the wheelchair froze, the muscles of his neck tightening. "Get the fuck out of my house," he said harshly without turning around.

"Not this time," Edgar said evenly. "Not until you read what I've brought."

"You've got nothing I want to see," Eugene replied.

"Turn around, Eugene," his brother demanded.

Eugene's hands dropped off the table, and he swung the wheelchair in Edgar's direction. "What do you want to show me, little brother?" he asked sarcastically.

For the first time in six decades, Edgar looked at his identical twin, older by three minutes. Eugene's pasty complexion and the stubble of a day-old beard made him look ill. His watery pale blue eyes were filled with loathing. His hair flopped over his ears, white, shaggy, and uncombed. He's old, Edgar thought. We're both old. He took the letter out of his pocket and handed it over. "Read this."

Eugene read it quickly and gave it back, his outstretched arm shaking. "So what? José Padilla wants to talk to you about his dead daddy. It doesn't mean anything," he snapped.

"Don't be stupid," Edgar replied. "He wants to know the truth."

Eugene laughed. "The truth. That's something now, isn't it? Tell you what—you write him back and tell him anything you damn well please. There's nobody left alive except you and José Padilla that gives a rat's ass."

Edgar put the letter away and stared at his twin brother. The nastiness was still there. The bullet in his spine that had crippled him hadn't subdued the bully in Eugene. "You've turned into a mean old son of a bitch," he said.

Eugene pushed the wheelchair suddenly in Edgar's direction. His laugh was as violent as the movement. He stopped short of running into Edgar, and looked up at him. "And you're still a weak-kneed pussy," Eugene retorted, color rising in his face. "José Padilla sends you a letter and it puts you in a tailspin."

"He's here," Edgar explained, "and he wants to talk to us."

"So send him over to see me if you don't want to handle it. Now get the fuck out of here and don't come back."

Edgar Cox, Lieutenant Colonel, United States Army Retired, a man with two wars, six major campaigns, and more than enough military decorations under his belt to prove his courage, bit his lip for a long, hard moment, turned on his heel, and walked out of the house. He got back on the ranch road just as Phil started the short drive over to his father's house, and tore the hell out of there, throwing up a smoke screen of dust behind him. Of one thing he was certain: Eugene wouldn't say a damn thing to Phil about what had made Uncle Edgar come to visit after all these years.

He stopped at the highway, got out, shredded up the letter, and burned it. When the last charred fragment curled and turned black he ground the remains under his boot and scattered the ashes.

AMADOR ORTIZ watched Kerney remove the horse from the trailer, run a string line between two trees, and snap a come-along on the chestnut's halter. Kerney walked toward him with a stiff gait and nodded a greeting. Amador wiped the vexation off his face with a tight smile. What in the hell was Carol Cassidy doing sending him this busted-up seasonal who couldn't pull his own weight? He needed an able-bodied man on this job, not a reject from some police department.

He nodded curtly when Kerney drew near. "Anybody else coming?" he asked hopefully.

"Not that I know of," Kerney replied.

Amador grunted with displeasure. "Too bad. What did Carol tell you to do?"

"Whatever needs doing," Kerney answered, looking over Amador's shoulder. A crew of four Hispanic men stared back at him from a half-completed trench that ran from a wellhead to a water spigot. He didn't know any of them. Eight-inch plastic water pipe lay in a line next to the trench. A small backhoe idled nearby. Off to one side of the construction site a temporary chain-link enclosure protected construction supplies, bags of concrete, a stack of cedar fence posts, and some new picnic tables.

Amador looked down at Kerney's leg. "What can you do?" he demanded.

"Whatever," Kerney repeated.

"Get a posthole digger from my truck," Amador Ortiz said flatly. "I need fence posts set in concrete every eight feet. It's all staked out where I want them." He swung his arm in an arch. "From the well to the trailhead. Can you handle that?"

Kerney smiled. "I think so."

Amador's expression remained skeptical. He scratched his armpit and grunted. A stocky man with arms that were too short for his body, Ortiz was broad in the chest and sported a beer drinker's belly.

"I need the posts in by lunchtime," Amador said in an ill-tempered tone. "That's three hours from now. Be finished by then."

"Okay," Kerney answered, walking away, counting the small red flags that marked the locations for the postholes. Twenty-four holes to dig, two feet deep, a like number of posts to set, and three hours to do it. He poked the ground with the toe of his boot. Not much topsoil to speak of. Mostly hard-packed gravel and basalt. There was no way it could be done by one man in the allotted time.

When Amador and his crew quit for their noon meal, Kerney worked on. There was no offer to help and no suggestion that he break for lunch. The men were grouped in the shade of a stand of trees, speaking softly in Spanish, but loud enough for Kerney to hear the insults and the jokes about how much fun it was to watch the crippled gringo sweat like a pig.

The day was hot and getting hotter. Kerney stripped to the waist and kept working. Grunting with every thrust of the digger, he kept a steady rhythm, finished a hole, and moved on while the ridicule behind him continued. The group was debating his sexual prefer-ences as he started digging the last hole. Ortiz walked slowly toward him, checking the depth of each hole with a tape measure. He made a rude comment over his shoulder about Kerney screwing sheep that got a laugh from the men, and approached with a smirk still on his face.

Thoroughly pissed off at the unnecessary ill-will from Amador and his boys, Kerney stopped digging and waited for the foreman. His back ached and his arms were sore.

"I needed those posts set by now," Amador said, looking at the nasty scar on Kerney's gut. Kerney's stomach was flat. His chest and arms were muscular. There was no fat on the man. Self-consciously, Amador sucked in his beer belly.

"I'll get it finished," Kerney said flatly.

Amador smiled thinly. "Take your meal break. My crew will set the posts. You get that in Nam?" he asked conversationally, nodding at the ugly scar. Carol had told him Kerney was a Nam veteran.

"No."

"What happened?"

"It's a long story."

"Don't like to talk about it?"

"Something like that," Kerney said.

Amador shrugged. "Go eat. The boss wants for you to get familiar with the area. I'll mark the new trails on a map."

Kerney nodded in reply and dropped the posthole digger on the ground at Amador's feet. "Do you need me back here today?"

Amador looked at the tool with half a thought to tell Kerney to pick it up, and decided against it. The gringo's smile was somehow challenging. "Come back in the morning," he said, retrieving the tool. "We've got to pour footings for the picnic tables. If they aren't set in concrete and bolted down, they get ripped off."

"I'll be here," Kerney said. "Anything else?"

"That's it."

"Another six inches and this last hole is done," Kerney remarked, kicking some loose dirt back into the opening and covering Amador's boots with dust. It was a childish thing to do, but it felt good anyway. He grinned at Amador, barely containing a desire to bust the man in the chops, hoping Ortiz would give him an excuse. He didn't like bigots of any nationality. Amador looked at his boots, raised his glance to Kerney's face, and said nothing.

"Think you can handle it?" Kerney asked.

Amador didn't answer. Watching Kerney walk away he thought maybe the gringo wasn't somebody to fuck with.

IT WAS MIDMORNING when Hector returned with his grandfather to the Mangas Mountains turnoff. José's insistence that they stop every so often so he could reminisce made the drive through the mountains slow but enjoyable. Hector relished listening to Grandfather's stories of his childhood and youth in the vast and beautiful land of western New Mexico. And today there was no mention of murder.

The road was good, there was little traffic, and Hector had no trouble pulling the trailer up the grades and around the turns. They passed a campground construction site and paused at a beautiful lake to watch fishermen casting for trout on the shore and trolling from small boats on the water. After leaving the lake, they traveled in a wandering circle that took them to a mountain village called Quemado, which was Spanish for "burned," then east through a hamlet named Pie Town. Hector found the names amusing.

It was afternoon when they arrived in what had once been the village of Mangas. To the east, a high, lone peak, at least ten thousand feet in elevation, rose in the distance. To the west, mountains filled the skyline. The narrow valley where José had been born was thick with grass. A small herd of cattle grazed along a fenceline near an abandoned adobe church with a wooden spire. A single cross was nailed on the cornice below the steeple.

Hector parked well off the road and walked quickly to catch up with José, who had left the truck when Hector had paused at the church. Most of the mud plaster on the building was gone, exposing eroded adobe bricks. The roof drooped crookedly on the melting walls. Near the church a small cemetery, shielded by a row of cottonwood trees, sat enclosed by a rusted wrought-iron fence.

In the cemetery José stopped at a tombstone, obscured by weeds and tall tufts of grass. He stared silently at the grave before dropping to his knees to clear away the vegetation. Hector helped. Soon the name of Don Luis Padilla appeared. Grandfather ran his fingers across the chiseled letters, a strand of wispy hair falling down his forehead as a light gust of wind rolled across the valley.

Finally, Dr. José Luis Padilla rose, smiled at his grandson, and spoke. "It is a beautiful valley," he said, his eyes fixed on the mountains.

"Yes," Hector responded. "It is sad to see it abandoned."

Jose looked at the little row of buildings across the road, all in various stages of decay. Someone had nailed chicken wire over the empty doors and windows of the old schoolhouse to protect the structure. His father's hacienda was gone; only the thick rock foundation marked its location. He took Hector to the site and described the layout of the old hacienda, room by room.

"None of this was given up willingly," José remarked. "After my father's death, the government took much of the land for the national forest. There is a high, wonderful valley where I would tend sheep each summer when I was old enough to be left alone."

"Mexican Hat?" Hector asked.

"It is near the valley. A hidden amphitheater that falls away in heavy timber. Not many people know of it."

"Are you glad you came back?"

"Very glad," Jose answered, as he began to walk to the truck. "Come. We can unhitch the trailer and leave it behind. This will be a good place to camp tonight. We have time for a drive to Mexican Hat. I will take you on the wagon road my father and his brothers built. It starts behind the school."

"What kind of road?" Hector asked dubiously.

José laughed. He was refreshed and enjoying the day. While he would never admit it to his grandson, he was grateful for the early end to yesterday's drive. "There you go again, *jito*. Always worrying. It should not be a problem. At first, it will be nothing more than a trail through the rangeland into the foothills. It climbs gently. After that, if I remember correctly, it is a hard rock surface in the mountains. Let us explore, *qué no?* As you promised when you forced an end to yesterday's adventures."

"Am I to be constantly reminded of my decision?"

"Only as it becomes necessary."

Hector found the rutted road easy to follow, and the truck, with its high suspension and four-wheel drive, handled the hard-packed terrain without difficulty. He began to relax and enjoy the excursion. As they entered the foothills, the road changed to a mild incline that snaked over ridge tops. The forest, a dense mixture of piñon, cedar, and pine trees, intruded over the road when they reached the mountains. Low branches brushed against the windshield and scraped against the sides of the truck. As they climbed, the road got steeper and more narrow. Hector's uneasiness returned. He wondered how far they must go to find a turnaround. Soon he was driving in low gear up a cutback in the mountain, with a deep drop less than a foot away from the truck tires. He stopped where the road forked and ran in both directions toward the summit. Here he could turn around.

"Shall we continue?" Hector asked anxiously.

José chuckled. "Had we come here yesterday, this part of our journey would be over. But we stopped and rested, as you desired."

"I see that I need more reminding," Hector noted.

"We're almost there," José replied, pointing to the left fork in the road.

Hector nodded, put the truck in gear, and eased it slowly up the road, over jagged rocks that occasionally forced him to weave much too close to the drop-off. The road seemed to top out up ahead. He glanced at Grandfather, who smiled reassuringly.

"Just a little bit farther," José said.

Hector breathed a sigh of relief as he reached the top, then the front suspension of the truck slammed into a deep washout that cut across the road. *"Dios!"* he said.

"What happened?" José asked, startled.

"I'll check and see."

Hector cursed to himself as he stood at the front of the Ford. The front wheels dangled in the air, and the driveshaft was broken. Even if he could free the truck, he could not drive it. He shook his head and told his grandfather the bad news.

"What do we do now?" he asked.

"I will stay here and you will go for help," José said, calming himself. "There's a horse trail up ahead—a shortcut—that goes back to Mangas. You should be able to walk out easily."

"I don't want to leave you alone."

"I'll be fine. I have water. The truck heater will keep me warm. Believe me, I've spent many nights in these mountains in much less comfort than this. We have no choice," José added. "I do not think it would be wise for me to try to walk out. Here. You take one canteen and I will keep the other."

Hector took the canteen from José's hand. At that moment, the sound of a rifle broke the silence. "Perhaps we are lucky," he said, his spirits lifting. "Someone is nearby."

"Be careful, *jito.*"

"I'll be back soon," Hector said, smiling with relief. "Don't worry."

Hector jumped the gully and followed the road around the last bend. Below him a vast, high valley of grassland stretched finger-like into the forest. At the top of the next summit he could see a radio tower and the faint outline of a building. He scanned the forest for a road to the peak. There was no discernible access. He saw movement in the tall grass at the center of the meadow. A man stood up and bent back down again, doing something Hector couldn't make out. Too far away to be heard, he squinted against the harsh afternoon light and waved to get the man's attention, but without success. Relieved that help was close at hand, Hector walked into the meadow until he was within hailing distance. He cupped his hands around his mouth and called out. The man stiffened and turned.

Hector closed the gap with hurried strides until he could see the man's face. *"Hola!* My truck is disabled," he said. "Can you help me, *por favor?"*

The man nodded and gestured at him to come closer.

JOSÉ RESTED in the truck, half asleep. The effects of the altitude were wearing, and he was more fatigued than he cared to admit. Some time after Hector's departure, a second gunshot rang out. Perhaps Hector had found the hunter and asked him to signal that everything was all right. He composed himself on the seat and waited for his grandson's return. Finally he heard the sound of an engine. Surely now Hector was on his way back. He climbed stiffly out of the truck.

Hector did not come. José carefully negotiated the gully and walked slowly up the road. An afternoon breeze blew out of the valley, chilling him slightly as he looked down on the meadow, searching for a sign of his grandson. The wind whisked his hair into his eyes. He caught the distant sound of the engine again. It seemed to be coming from the direction of the horse trail. The two large pine trees that José remembered from his boyhood still stood majestically at the edge of the meadow where the trail began. He could not remember seeing the grass so lush and thick. With the sheep gone for so many years, the land had come back richly.

Hector was nowhere to be seen. José decided he must walk a little farther and investigate before returning to the truck. Something wasn't right.

3

Clouds filled the sky and ran like waves heading for a distant shore. Kerney watched them in the predawn light, waiting for rain that didn't come. For once, the ranchers wouldn't mind the absence of moisture. The high country was lush with abundant grass and wildflowers that told of a wet year and plenty of water. Some of the locals were predicting it would be the best rainy season in fifty years.

Kerney broke camp feeling rested and unruffled. The afternoon on the trail with a good horse under him and the night alone on the mountain away from civilization had been a wonderful break in his normal routine.

He got to the job site at first light as the last of the thick clouds created a searing red sunrise. To the west a cloudless sky began to deepen into turquoise blue. He found Amador Ortiz tucked into a sleeping bag. Seeing him brought back Kerney's instinctive dislike for the man. He unsaddled the horse, tied it to the string line, and turned back toward Amador, who was sitting up rubbing sleep from his eyes.

"You're here early," Amador said grouchily, between yawns.

Kerney nodded in agreement and looked around. The posts were set, the wire strung, and the water line buried, and a flatbed truck was parked next to the temporary equipment pen. It carried a large modular outdoor privy. Hitched to the bumper of the truck was a trailer with a forklift. He watched Amador get out of the bag, fire up a camp stove, and put water on for coffee.

"I'm ready to start," Kerney said.

Ortiz looked at him, yawned again, and shrugged. "Suit your-self. I need footers dug for each picnic table," he said sullenly.

"Location?" Kerney asked.

Amador tilted his head in the direction on his truck. "The plans are on the seat. Three tables go on each side of the water spigot, under the trees, this side of the fence. You can read plans, can't you?" Sarcasm laced the question.

Kerney nodded briefly in response and turned away to water the chestnut. He didn't want to start the day in a pissing contest with Ortiz. The chestnut drank deeply before moving off. Surefooted and quick to respond, the horse had pleased him on yesterday's ride.

The softer soil made for faster digging than the day before. By the time Ortiz's crew showed up, Kerney had finished trenches for two tables and sweated away his irritation with Amador, who kept his distance. The crew started cutting steel rebar, sledgehammer-ing the short pieces into the trenches and tying off long sections hor-izontally, in preparation for the concrete pour.

Kerney finished at midmorning. He watched the crew mix and pour concrete into the first trench, trowel it smooth, and set the an-chor bolts.

"Anything else you need me for?" he asked Ortiz, who had watched the work proceed from the comfort of his truck.

Amador shook his head. "You're finished. We'll post the trail signs, take down the equipment pen, and be out of here today."

Kerney washed up and saddled the chestnut, looking forward to another afternoon in the mountains. He would ride the trail that looped around Mangas Mountain and eased down the foothills to a place called Upper Cat Springs. As he tightened the cinch, he heard the sound of a vehicle coming fast down the dirt road. A state Game and Fish truck pulling a horse trailer stopped next to the equipment pen. A tall young man jumped out, spotted Kerney, and walked to him.

"Mr. Kerney," he said, smiling, extending his hand. "Bet you don't remember me."

Kerney shook the man's hand. He had a friendly smile and a strong grip. Kerney guessed him to be in his late twenties. "Refresh my memory."

He chuckled. "I'm Jim Stiles. I took an advanced course in in-vestigation from you a while back, when you were still with the Santa Fe Police Department. Up at the law enforcement academy in Santa Fe."

"You do look familiar," Kerney allowed. "Did you learn any-thing from me?"

"Good course, good teacher," Stiles replied. Almost as tall as

Kerney, with long arms and legs, he had white, even teeth below a neatly clipped red mustache that matched his hair. His eyes were light green and friendly. His nose, slightly broad, had a small line of freckles across the ridge.

"Thanks for the compliment," Kerney said. "What can I do for you?"

Stiles didn't get a chance to answer. Amador walked up and poked him in the ribs with a finger. "What are you doing here?" he asked cordially in Spanish.

"Be polite," Stiles chided back in Spanish. "Don't make the man feel bad because he can't speak the language." He nodded in Kerney's direction. "I need him to ride along with me."

Kerney said nothing. From what he'd heard so far, he spoke Spanish as well as Stiles.

Amador shrugged his shoulders and switched to English. "What's up?"

Stiles looked at both men and tilted his head toward the high country. "We've got a mountain lion down somewhere east of Elderman Meadows. A male three-year-old we translocated two months ago from the San Andres Mountains. Since it's on federal land, Mr. Kerney gets to help me find it." Stiles switched his attention to Kerney. "Carol Cassidy said to come and take you along. It should help you get oriented to your new patrol route. And you'll see some pretty country to boot."

"How do you know it's down?" Kerney asked.

"Radio collar," Stiles explained. "If the animal doesn't move for six hours, the radio sends out a rapid mortality beep. Our wildlife biologist did a flyover yesterday around dusk. It shouldn't be that difficult to find. I have a pretty good fix on the animal."

"Maybe he lost the collar," Amador suggested.

Stiles shook his head. "No way, Amador. Those collars don't come loose. You got to cut them off." Stiles looked at Kerney's horse. "I'll be ready to ride in a few minutes."

"I hope you know where you're going, because I sure the hell don't," Kerney said.

Stiles laughed, an easy, careless chuckle. "If I get us lost, my granddaddy will turn over in his grave. His name was Elderman. The meadow is named after him."

THEY WERE TWO MILES OFF the access road to the fire lookout tower on Mangas Mountain, moving down a switchback trail, when Jim Stiles turned sideways in the saddle and looked back at Kerney.

"You don't ride a horse too bad for a city boy," Stiles said.

"I wasn't always a city boy," Kerney answered.

"I can tell you've ridden some," Stiles responded. "Where do you hail from?"

"A ranch west of Engle," Kerney replied. "The place doesn't exist any more."

"The Jornada. I heard a story about you down there. It had something to do with a Game and Fish employee by the name of Eppi Gutierrez, now deceased."

"We ran into each other."

"Did that silly son of a bitch really try to kill you?"

"Damn near succeeded."

"I don't believe it. I worked with Eppi for a spell down at White Sands before I transferred back home. He was a wimp."

"Wimps can be dangerous," Kerney replied.

Stiles shook his head. "I guess. Did Gutierrez really find a stash of old Indian treasure?"

"Plunder from raids against the pony soldiers," Kerney said. "Worth millions. He was trying to smuggle it out of the country. The Army shipped it to West Point."

"I'll be damned." Stiles stopped and waited for Kerney to come alongside. "So, tell me something. What the hell are you doing with the Forest Service? Aren't you retired?"

"Sort of. Working keeps me out of trouble," Kerney answered, reining in the chestnut next to Stiles. The switchback ended a few yards ahead. A thicket of wild grape in front of a stand of sycamore trees seemed to block the way. Beyond the sycamores rose enormous crowns of ponderosas from the canyon floor.

"Think you'll get a permanent job at the Luna station?" Stiles asked.

Soft mare's tails, thin ribbons of clouds, flowed across the sky and steamed out of sight. Kerney shook his head. "That isn't going to happen," he said.

"So what's next?" Stiles asked, dismounting and throwing the reins over the head of his horse.

"Hell, I don't know," Kerney said, following suit. "I'll think of something."

"We walk a little," Stiles announced. "The trail gets rough for the next mile. Horses don't like it much."

The barranca dropped quickly past a series of volcanic flows that jutted against the deep cliff. The live stream at the bottom of the canyon undercut the vertical flows, creating an uneven line of columns suspended above the water. Stiles and Kerney waded around slippery rocks and plodded through the soft sand of the streambed under a canopy of evergreens. Cottonwood and willows took over at the narrowest stretch of the canyon, crowding the bank, making progress slow through the low branches. The remnant of a stone wall in the cliff face ten feet above the stream caught Kerney's eye. Behind the wall was a natural cave, the mouth blackened from the soot of numerous campfires. Small steps leading to the cave were chiseled out of soft rock under the opening.

Suddenly, the barranca opened on a piñon forest that spurted and stopped in the rangeland of a high valley. They were off the mountain, Mangas Peak hidden from view by the foothills. Stiles remounted.

"Hold up," Kerney called to him.

Stiles turned in his saddle, and Kerney gave him the reins to his horse. He walked back into the barranca, crossed the stream, climbed the stairs to the cave, and ducked inside.

The cave was deeper than Kerney expected. He sank to his knees under the low ceiling, waiting for his vision to adjust to the darkness, and listened for a sound. It came as shallow breathing.

"Who's there?" Kerney asked.

The breathing stopped.

Kerney raised his voice and asked the question again. He could hear Stiles climbing up to join him.

"Do not hurt me," a shaky voice answered in Spanish. It came from a small room at the back of the cave.

Kerney crawled toward the voice on his hands and knees, answering in Spanish. "I am a policeman," he said. "No one will hurt you." He could see the shape of a man pressed against the rock wall, his body shaking. *"Policia,"* he said again.

"Policia," the man repeated, unbelieving.

"Yes," Kerney replied softly. Eyesight adjusted to the dim light, he could see the man more clearly. Old and thin the way some men get as the body wears out, he was curled up with his knees to his chest. Kerney reached for his hand. It was wet and trembling. The man's clothing was soaked. "Who are you?" he asked.

"I do not know," the old man moaned, his voice breaking. "I cannot remember."

"What have you got?" Stiles called from outside the cave.

Kerney told him, and Jim crawled in to see for himself. Together they carried the man out of the cave and across the stream into the sunlight. The old man's lips were blue, his pulse rapid and uneven, and shaking racked his body. He was losing core heat. They stripped off his clothes, and Kerney dried him with a towel from his saddle-bags while Stiles fetched a blanket. Wrapped in the blanket, the old man still shivered. Kerney started a small fire, and after warming his hands over the flames, rubbed them on the man's clammy skin. He kept repeating the process while Stiles checked the soaked clothing for identification.

"Anything?" Kerney asked.

"Nope," Stiles answered. "But these aren't any cheap threads. We got designer labels here. How did you know he was in the cave?"

"The steps were wet," Kerney explained. "It took a minute for it to register. The cave is too high above the stream for any water to reach it. He must have scrambled in when he heard us coming."

"I didn't notice," Stiles said. He keyed the hand-held radio to call for help, then took his finger off the button. "You don't see too many people hiking in the mountains wearing expensive city clothes. What's this old man been up to?"

Kerney shrugged as he kept rubbing the man with his hands.

Stiles leaned over and spoke in the old man's ear. "Who are you?"

The old man looked at Stiles, his eyes blinking rapidly.

"Ask him in Spanish," Kerney counseled.

Stiles tried again, this time in Spanish.

"I do not know," the old man answered haltingly.

"Where did you come from?" Stiles inquired.

"Mexican Hat," the man answered, his teeth chattering.

"Where were you yesterday? Last night?" Stiles prodded.

"Mexican Hat," the man repeated.

"Damn," Stiles said, looking at Kerney and shaking his head in disbelief. "What the hell is an old man from someplace called Mexican Hat doing lost in a place where people aren't supposed to be?"

"Beats me," Kerney replied. "Call it in. Let's get this old guy to a hospital."

Stiles switched to the state police frequency, keyed the unit, and made contact. He asked for a chopper from Silver City and paramedics.

"The only place called Mexican Hat I know of is in southern Utah," Stiles said, when he was finished talking on the radio. "A small town near the Arizona border."

Kerney shook his head. "I don't think that's where he came from."

"How in the hell did he get here?"

"Your guess is as good as mine," Kerney answered. "Let's get him warmed up."

Stiles put away the radio and joined Kerney. Together they massaged the old man until his trembling started to subside.

"He's going to make it," Stiles predicted.

Kerney wasn't so sure; there was a nasty bruise on the man's temple, and his eyes were unfocused.

The rescue helicopter made good time, and Stiles used the

radio to guide it in. It landed as close to the mouth of the canyon as it could. Two men carrying backpacks and a stretcher hiked quickly up the hillside. The old man's breathing had improved, and a bit of color was back. The paramedics took over, wrapped him in more blankets, got an IV started, and carted him on the stretcher to the waiting chopper.

"Where are you taking him?" Kerney asked, as he walked alongside the stretcher. The old man wouldn't let go of Kerney's hand.

"Gila Regional in Silver City," one of the paramedics answered. "You guys did a good job."

"Take care of him."

"No problem. He looks like a tough old bird," the paramedic answered.

Kerney had to pry his hand free as the old man was lifted into the chopper. "You're going to be fine," he said, in Spanish.

"Carlotta," the old man whispered.

Kerney leaned closer. "Who is Carlotta? Your daughter? Your wife?" he asked.

The man looked confused. "My wife," he said. "You should know that, little one. She is your grandmother."

"Where is Grandmother?"

"Dead."

"Was she with you last night?" Kerney insisted.

The man shook his head sadly. "I'm not sure. You are a good boy, Hector. Take care of my father's sheep."

The chopper pilot waved Kerney away before he could question the old man further. He walked back to Stiles.

"Did the old man say anything?" Jim asked.

"He rambled on a bit in Spanish."

"Could you make anything out?"

"He called me Hector and said Carlotta was dead."

"So he speaks English," Jim ventured.

"No."

"Did he use the word *muerto* for dead?"

"That's what I heard," Kerney answered.

"Carlotta, who could that be?"

"His *esposa*, he said."

"*Esposa*, that means wife. Damn! I should have gone with you. My Spanish is pretty good. Maybe I could have gotten more out of him."

"Maybe," Kerney allowed. "But while we're looking for that mountain lion, I think we'd better keep an eye out for at least one or two lost people."

"Lost or dead," Stiles replied. He wadded up the old man's clothes and expensive oxford shoes and stuffed them into the saddlebags.

The helicopter, a speck in the sky, followed the gravel road that cut across the high valley of the mountains, on a fast track to Silver City through the passes.

Kerney turned, looked up at the mountain and back at Jim Stiles. "That old man didn't travel through the canyon we rode in on. We would have seen his sign."

Stiles nodded in agreement. "My bet is that he came in on the Mangas road or walked down from Elderman Meadows."

"Any way in by vehicle?" Kerney asked.

"An abandoned road goes to the meadows. Hardly anybody knows about it. It's not marked on any of the maps." Jim Stiles pointed at the lowest range of foothills that curved below them, running in a broken wave. "Mangas used to be a village around that

bend. The road takes off behind the school and climbs to the meadows. Maybe he tried to drive in and got himself stuck. It happens.
Last winter an old couple from someplace back east decided to take
a side trip on a ranch road. Storm came up, and two weeks later they
found the man dead in a snowbank and his wife frozen solid in the
car. You ready to look for that mountain lion?"

"Think that's all we're going to find?" Kerney replied, putting
out the small fire.

A grin broke across Jim's face. "This is getting more interesting all the time, isn't it?" He mounted and nodded at the closest
foothill. "We'll drop below that hill and pick up the trailhead.
Shouldn't be long before we know what the rest of the day will
bring."

At the trailhead, it took only a few minutes for Jim to find the
radio collar under a juniper tree.

"Cut," he said, picking it up with a stick. "Somebody killed the
cat." He wrapped the collar in plastic and tied it to the saddle pom-
mel. "We need to find the carcass." His expression turned sour. "If
there is one to find."

Kerney walked parallel to the trail, leading his horse, studying
the ground.

"What's up?" Jim asked.

"ATV tracks. And some shoe prints. Give me the old man's ox-
fords."

Stiles dug a shoe out of his saddlebag and tossed it to Kerney.
The prints matched perfectly.

"Looks like we found his trail," Kerney said. "But which came
first? The old man or the ATV? The tire tracks match the ones I saw
at a black bear kill."

"You're sure?"

"Same wear on the rear tires. Same tread pattern." Kerney looked up the trail. It disappeared into a shadowy climax forest of ponderosa pines, bare of undergrowth, entrenched in the rich soil. The land rolled up and up, lofty trees masking deep ravines. He looked back to find Stiles leaning out of the saddle studying the ATV tracks.

"You're not the only one who has seen these," Jim said. "I took plaster casts of the same treads at a bighorn sheep kill up in the Tularosas."

"You're positive?"

"Yep. I had the state crime lab analyze the casts. Two different brands of tires, front and back, with the same wear on the rear wheels. Looks like we got ourselves a serious poacher here."

Jim pulled a camera out of his saddlebag and gave it to Kerney. He shot some pictures while Stiles rode his horse slowly up the trail. He finished and climbed into the saddle just as Stiles called back at him.

"Come on. I want to show you Grandfather Elderman's meadow. It's a damn pretty sight. And who knows what else might turn up?"

Kerney got on his horse and followed Stiles toward the climax forest. "You like this stuff, don't you?" he called out.

Stiles turned and nodded his head vigorously. "Hell yes, I like it," he called back. "Who doesn't like a good mystery?"

THE MEADOW looked like an outstretched hand with elongated fingers cutting into the forest at the base of the mountain. On the peak, the Mangas fire lookout station surveyed hundreds of square miles of national forest. Spring wildflowers, hot yellow and pale blue, scattered color throughout the native grass that fluttered in a mild breeze. ATV tire tracks flattened the grass in two lines, running straight toward the center of the meadow.

Jim reined in his horse at the edge of the meadow and waited for Kerney. "Bet you a dollar we don't find the carcass," he said when Kerney pulled up next to him.

"Why do you say that?"

"Every part of a cougar is valuable. The blood. The bones. The skin. If it's a male, even the testicles are worth significant money. It all gets ground up, cut up, boiled, or mixed with other ingredients and sold as medicine and folk remedies on the Asian market.

"Did you know poachers are killing all the tigers in China and India?" Stiles continued. "Most are about done in. It's at the point now that any big cat is at risk, the demand is so great."

"What about the black bear?" Kerney asked. "A lot of that animal was left behind."

"It's still the same MO. The poachers only take what's valuable. The gallbladder is worth its weight in gold. It's used to make an aphrodisiac. With bighorn sheep, they go after the horns. It gets ground into powder and used for a medicine to treat a dozen or more illnesses."

"So this is poaching for pure profit," Kerney replied.

"Big-time," Stiles agreed, moving ahead. "What we're gonna look for is evidence of the kill. That's the best we can hope to find."

In the middle of the field they found what Stiles expected, the remains of a partially eaten, hamstrung rabbit used to lure the cat, and a small patch of dried blood where the lion had fallen after the kill. Kerney took pictures and Stiles bagged all the evidence.

"That should do it," Stiles said as he finished. "We have enough blood samples for a DNA comparison." He stuck the evidence in a canvas tote bag and tied it to his saddle. "I'll get this up to the Santa Fe crime lab tomorrow."

"How much would a poacher stand to make on a kill like this?" Kerney asked, passing the camera back to Stiles.

Stiles stuffed the camera in the saddle bag. "Two or three thousand dollars, easy. But the profit is in retail sales. Whoever markets the product overseas stands to make four or five times that amount." He pointed behind Kerney. "The old wagon road I talked about comes out over there, at the side of that mountain. Want to take a look? Maybe we can find out how that old man got up here."

First, they found the body of a young man thirty yards from the kill site. A coyote had chewed away most of the face and feasted on the chest cavity. When they turned him over, they saw the exit wound from the bullet hole. Kerney took a wallet from the dead man's pants and scanned the contents.

"Who is he?"

"The man's name was Hector M. Padilla," Kerney said. "A Mexican citizen."

"Hector," Stiles repeated. "Well, I'll be damned. Isn't that what the old man called you? Let's see what other surprises we can find before we call the state police."

Then they found the truck.

ALL THAT COULD BE DONE to secure the crime scene and conduct a preliminary investigation was accomplished quickly. Kerney found himself frustrated by their lack of equipment but at the same time pleased with Jim Stiles. He worked efficiently, made few mistakes, and had good cop instincts. They had a confirmed identity of the dead man and a strong suspicion, from the registration papers found in the truck, that the old man in the cave was Dr. José Padilla.

Positioned on a small rise with a clear view of the body, Stiles had a rifle in hand just in case the coyotes came back for another meal. He could see three of them moving in the tall grass, fifty yards away. Kerney sat down next to him. As they waited for the state police to arrive, he started asking Stiles questions.

"What do we know, so far?"

Stiles grinned. "Are we debriefing?"

"Why not?" Kerney replied.

"That's great. I haven't had anybody to debrief with since I transferred to Reserve. It gets boring analyzing things by yourself."

Kerney laughed. "I know that feeling. Let's build a scenario of what may have happened."

"Okay," Stiles said. "Hector and Dr. Padilla, citizens of the Republic of Mexico, drive up to the meadows, for God knows what reason, and get the truck hung up in a gully. Hector Padilla decides to hike out and get help, leaving the old man to wait in the truck. Why he decides to walk to the meadow instead of heading back down the road is a mystery. It's a shorter route, but how would he know about it? He runs into the poacher and gets himself blown away. Probably the old man would have been murdered too, if the killer knew he was in the vicinity."

"That makes sense. What about the killer?"

"He's got to be one of the locals."

"Why do you say that?"

"Elderman Meadows is protected. Off limits. Has been for years. It's prime elk breeding ground."

"Okay," Kerney said. "Not much traffic. Known only to locals and off the beaten path. What about the lion? You said it was relocated. Would the killer know it was here?"

"The word is 'translocated.' It's a technical term we Game and Fish types love to use. You've got to use it if you want to be politically correct."

"Okay, translocated. Tell me how the killer knew about the lion."

"We don't publicize translocations. Just a few of the area ranchers are informed so they don't start shooting when they see a cougar."

"Who knew?" Kerney prodded.

"Phil Cox and his father. The Johnstons, over by Allegros Mountain. Al Medley. Vance Swingle. Ray Candelaria down in Bear Canyon. Law enforcement personnel. That's it."

"Did any of the ranchers protest?"

Stiles shook his head. "Not a one. I know these people. They'd be on the telephone yelling at me in a minute if there was even a remote possibility that a lion was taking their stock. Demanding permission to kill it."

"People talk," Kerney suggested.

"True enough. We can't keep a project like this completely secret. That would be impossible. But I don't think folks sit around in Cattleman's Café talking to tourists about wild mountain lions."

"So it's a local," Kerney agreed. "Are there any prime suspects in other cases we can check out?"

"Not really." Stiles tugged at his ear. "How did these guys find the road up the mountain? It hasn't been used in decades. You can barely see the ruts. In fact, you can't see a damn thing at all from the highway."

"The Forest Service map in the truck was folded open to Mangas Mountain."

"I missed that," Stiles admitted. "That could mean these guys wanted to come here. Why?"

"Beats me," Kerney replied.

"Let me ask you a question. Are you ready for the shit to hit the fan?"

"What does that mean?"

"Last unnatural death we had in the county was this Texan who bought a ranch over by Spur Lake. The guy goes out rabbit hunting last summer and kills himself with a shotgun. Almost the whole damn county turned out for that one."

"Were you there?" Kerney asked.

Stiles laughed. "Damn right. Wouldn't have missed it for the world." He looked up at the sky. "Give it a while and this meadow is going to look like an annual convention for the Forest Service, the local cops, every EMT, and every search-and-rescue volunteer in Catron County."

"What do you suggest we do with our guests?"

"I'll tell you what I'd *like* to do. Let the sons of bitches figure it out for themselves. None of them are worth spit as investigators."

"Not even Charlie Perry?"

Stiles groaned. "That prissy, uptight asshole? If he gets his hands on this case, we can kiss it goodbye. It will disappear into the woodwork. By the time the party's over, you'll wish we had just kept our mouths shut and done the investigation on our own," Stiles predicted.

AN HOUR AFTER the arrival of an assorted cast of characters that included the county sheriff, three of his five deputies, a rookie state police officer who had never seen a dead body before, two Game and

Fish officers who were general nuisances, and the officious Charlie Perry, who arrived with Carol Cassidy and several others, Kerney admitted that Jim's prophecy had come true. Finally, when the search-and-rescue team arrived like a posse on horseback, hoping maybe somebody else might be lost and in need of their services, Kerney gave up, found Stiles, and broke him loose from his Game and Fish buddies. There were tight pockets of people scattered across the meadow holding earnest conversations about who was going to do what.

"This is a disaster," he bitched, pointing to the three helicopter pilots standing next to their aircraft, scanning the meadow with binoculars.

"I told you so," Stiles reminded him. "Think about it. What else is there to do in Catron County for recreation? Drink? Watch videos? Go to church? Poach game? That gets boring after a while. It can't be sex. The birth rate keeps steadily dropping. This is much more fun. In fact, it doesn't happen often enough to suit most people."

"How can you stand it?" Kerney asked. He watched the state cop line up the search-and-rescue team and send them across the meadow in a field sweep, looking for evidence.

"These are my friends and neighbors," Stiles said solemnly. "Good people, one and all. Look. Fred Langford just walked right over the poacher's nest without blinking an eye."

"Thank God we took pictures," Kerney said, grimacing. "Who's the medical examiner?"

Stiles answered with a straight face. "Petra Gonzales. She was a dental assistant in the Navy. She's almost finished with her training."

Kerney stifled a snicker.

"This is just round one," Stiles commented. "Wait until they start fighting over who gets to be in charge. I bet they divvy it up. The state police will give it to an investigator out of Socorro, the sheriff will make local inquiries which will lead absolutely nowhere, Charlie Perry will assign it to himself, and we'll get to write a report on the poaching incident that everybody will want for their files. End of story."

"And who's interviewing Dr. Padilla at the hospital in Silver City?" Kerney asked.

"Nobody, yet," Jim answered. "They'll get around to it as soon as Petra announces Hector's death was a murder."

"Can we trust her to do it?"

"The exit wound in Hector's back is pretty hard to miss," Stiles reassured him. "If you want more, we'll have to do our own investigation."

"We?" Kerney queried.

Stiles grinned. "Why not? You got something to lose?"

"Not really."

Stiles slapped him on the back. "Neither do I. Besides, my uncle is the chairman of the state Game and Fish Commission. How's that for job security?"

"That should keep you on the payroll." Kerney looked at the sky. Maybe four hours of sunlight left, he figured. Enough time to get back to the Mangas campsite before dark. "What are we waiting for?" He started for the horses.

"You got a plan?"

"First we talk to the lookout at the fire tower, then we visit everybody who lives on the road to Mangas. How many cars travel that road in a day?"

"I'd say no more than ten," Stiles answered, quickening his

pace to keep up with Kerney. "The highway department says it's one of the lightest-traveled roads in the state. They want to make the Forest Service maintain it. Only five families live on that road."

"Maybe somebody saw something."

"Is this real police work, Kerney?" Stiles was grinning from ear to ear.

"Yeah, but don't get your hopes up."

Carol Cassidy stopped them before they could leave the meadow. She greeted Jim Stiles and turned her attention to Kerney. "Are you taking off?"

Stiles answered before Kerney had a chance. "Yep. We'll leave it in the hands of the experts."

Carol laughed, an amused, throaty chuckle. "It is like a zoo out there," she agreed. "If I knew what to do, I'd put it right," she added, looking directly at Kerney, waiting for him to volunteer.

"Ma'am?" Kerney said, as innocently as possible.

Carol laughed again. "I can see that you two will make quite a team." Her expression became thoughtful. "What would you have done, Kevin, if this crime had happened in Santa Fe when you were chief of detectives?"

"I'd kick everybody who doesn't belong off the meadow, assign my best people, and give it top priority," Kerney answered.

Carol nodded as Kerney spoke. "I've been thinking the same thing."

"Let me guess," Stiles interjected sarcastically. "You're going to ask Charlie Perry to handle the case."

Carol didn't laugh. "Don't do that to me, Jim," she snapped. "I am not going to get sucked into sniping at a colleague."

Stiles clamped his mouth shut, swallowed hard, and nodded. "You're right. Sorry. I was out of line."

"No damage done," Carol replied, turning her attention back to Kerney. "Kevin, I want you full-time on this investigation until further notice. Tell me what you need and I'll try and get it for you. Use your discretion on how you want to proceed and keep me informed. But remember, your police powers are limited."

"I understand. I'd like Jim to work with me, if that's possible."

Carol's eyes widened in mock disbelief. "I said use discretion, Kevin, not poor judgment."

Stiles groaned and clutched his chest. "That hurts. I am truly mortified, Mrs. Cassidy."

"Good," Carol responded with a chuckle. "I'll call your boss, Jim. He's sat at my dinner table too many times to turn me down if I ask for a favor. It won't be a problem."

"Good deal," Jim said, his eyes dancing with pleasure. "Thanks."

Carol nodded. "Get going," she ordered the men.

After Carol left, the two men mounted and started down the trail. Jim Stiles looked over his shoulder, brushed his mustache with a finger to force down a smile, and said, "Hot damn! Real police work."

Kerney shook his head and rolled his eyes in response. From the meadow behind them the sound of Carol's voice, magnified by a bullhorn, floated down the trail. She ordered the area cleared of nonessential personnel. One of the helicopters fired up and soon flew over the men as they pushed the horses through the canopy of the forest.

AMADOR ORTIZ watched his crew through the windshield of the truck, one foot propped against the frame of the open door. He reached down and changed the frequency on his radio so he could listen in on the sheriff's traffic from Elderman Meadows. Nothing but static. He switched back to the state police channel. The state cop was asking for an ETA on the forensic team. He saw a shadow move across the windshield and looked up. Kevin Kerney was standing by the open truck door.

"Keeping up with the local news?" Kerney asked.

Amador nodded. "Who's the guy that got killed?"

"A Mexican national."

"How long has he been dead?"

"It's hard to say. Maybe twenty-four hours. Did anything unusual happen while you were camped here last night?"

"Nothing." Ortiz watched Jim Stiles put the horses in the trailers.

"Did you have any visitors?"

"No." Amador scratched his armpit. "Why all the questions?"

"Was there any traffic on the road?"

"Just a few campers and trucks pulling boats down from the lake."

"You saw nothing? Heard nothing?"

"That's what I said. Stop playing cop with me. If the guy has been dead for twenty-four hours, do you think whoever shot him would still be hanging around?"

"Sometimes it happens."

Amador snorted. "Not likely."

"Did you leave the campsite at any time last night?"

"No."

"Thanks, Amador." Ortiz's crew had knocked down the fence to the temporary equipment pen and were finished loading stuff onto the flatbed truck. "I'll see you around."

"Maybe," Ortiz answered. He pulled the truck door closed,

cranked the engine, and waved at his crew, who were waiting for him. The men piled into the flatbed cab and followed Ortiz as he drove away.

Kerney found Jim bent over the trailer hitch to his truck. Jim unfastened the safety chain, pulled the pin to the hitch, and lowered the tongue to the ground.

"No need to pull the horse trailer up to the lookout station," he said as he stood up. "I'll leave it here."

"I take it you're planning to interview the man at the fire tower," Kerney remarked. "Is there something you'd like me to do?"

Jim blushed. "Sorry. I didn't mean to sound pushy."

"I'll let you know if you get too obnoxious. Go ahead. Meet me at the Luna office when you're done. You can introduce me to the good folks who live along the Mangas Valley road."

Stiles smiled in relief. "You got it."

4

The blare of the alarm brought Karen out of a deep sleep. With one eye she squinted at the clock radio. God, it was only six in the morning. She reached out, hit the off button, rolled onto her stomach, put the pillow over her head, and tried to go back to sleep. Then she remembered: she had agreed to meet Phil for breakfast in Reserve. She groaned, kicked the blanket off, got up, and walked into the living room.

Elizabeth and Cody were bundled in sleeping bags on the floor, fast asleep. They had been such dears during the move back to the ranch. As a reward to celebrate the final day of unpacking, she had rented their favorite movies, made popcorn to munch on, and let them stay up late. It had been great fun.

She tiptoed around her children, went to the small bathroom adjacent to the kitchen, and ran a tubful of water. There was time for a long soak before she needed to dress and leave. She wondered what Phil wanted to talk about. He was so insistent that they meet alone and away from the family as soon as possible.

Karen took off her panties, stepped into the deep cast-iron tub, and sank into the water. It felt wonderful. Coming back home had been the right thing to do, she decided. It had been a happy place for her as a child, as it would be for Cody and Elizabeth.

IT WAS SUNDAY MORNING, and Cattleman's Café on the main highway through Reserve, the premier drinking, dining, and recreation center in town, opened early, serving up good food along with local news, politics, and gossip. With no newspaper or radio station in the community, Cattleman's was the de facto communication center for the county.

Kerney and Jim Stiles sat in the back dining room drinking coffee while they waited for breakfast to arrive. Dog-tired, Kerney was more than willing to let Jim do the talking. They had both been up all night, but Kerney thought Jim looked good for another nonstop twenty-four hours, while he felt like one of the living dead.

Two young cowboys were at the pool table in the front barroom. One of them, his cowboy hat pushed back at a jaunty tilt, looked no more than sixteen. He bent low over the table, studied the angle of the cue ball, and made an excellent bank shot into a side pocket. His companion, a slightly older kid with a broad, open face, grimaced as the ball dropped. Both boys wore holstered pistols in plain view, and the two older men sitting at the bar were also packing weapons on their hips. As far as Kerney knew, the state law prohibiting firearms in drinking establishments had not been repealed.

Stiles stopped talking, and Kerney nodded, not sure what he was agreeing with. "Isn't there a law against weapons in bars?" he asked.

Jim responded with a laugh. "Of course there is. But the county commission passed a proclamation last year urging all citizens to arm themselves to protect home, family, grazing rights, and timber sales. Most people around here believe in home rule, so as far as they're concerned the proclamation supersedes state law. Besides, it's damn inconvenient to have to shed your weapon every time you want to play a game of pool or have a drink, and the sheriff isn't going to enforce a law that everybody violates. That would be political suicide, especially in an election year."

"Do you agree with the sheriff?"

"Hell no, I don't. But there isn't a damn thing you or I can do about it, unless you want to start a gunfight."

"I'll pass," Kerney replied. He had been in one too many gunfights already. The knee that had been shattered in a shoot-out hurt bad. It felt as if the steel pins that held it together were grinding against bone.

While Stiles slugged down the rest of his coffee and waved his cup at the waitress to signal for a refill, Kerney mentally reviewed the events of the night. They had found the Padillas' abandoned trailer, and then waited four hours for a search warrant. Omar Gatewood, the county sheriff who showed up with the warrant, refused to let Kerney and Stiles conduct the search and did it himself. About the time Gatewood finished, Charlie Perry arrived and demanded to be briefed. With dawn breaking, Kerney and Stiles decided not to get involved in a jurisdictional tug-of-war with either man, so they left.

"Why were the Padillas at Elderman Meadows?" Kerney asked.

Stiles waited for the approaching waitress to pour his refill and leave before answering. "Don't know."

"Speculate," Kerney urged.

"Padilla is an old family name from around these parts. There's even a Padilla Canyon north of Mangas Mountain."

"Do you think the old man is from around here?" Kerney queried.

"It's possible. But all of the original Padillas are long gone, as far as I know. My granddaddy bought Elderman Meadows when it was sold at auction for taxes back in the Depression, but I don't know anything more about it."

The waitress brought breakfast, and Jim stopped talking. Kerney picked at his food. With part of his stomach gone, from a bullet taken in the same gun battle that had busted his knee and forced him into retirement, he ate lightly and carefully.

"When we found Padilla, he said he'd come from a place called Mexican Hat. Are there any landforms in the area that resemble a hat?" he asked, watching Jim pack away his breakfast.

Jim sighed. "I've been trying to figure that one out myself. There are none that I know of, unless he meant Hat Mountain down by Lake Valley. But that's a good long ways south, on the other side of the Black Range. Maybe the old man was just babbling," Stiles added.

"Maybe," Kerney replied, unconvinced.

Cattleman's got busy with breakfast traffic. Several customers joined the two men at the bar and ordered up a whiskey breakfast. A sign taped over the mirror behind the bar read:

CONSERVE WOOD AND PAPER PRODUCTS.
WIPE YOUR ASS WITH AN ENVIRONMENTALIST.

Additional firepower came in with the new customers. The scruffy pine tables covered with plastic tablecloths in the dining area filled with people, mostly ranchers wearing pistols, and the sound of conversation grew. The sight of so many civilians with weapons made Kerney uneasy. He positioned his chair so he had a clear view of the room.

"We need to look at the documents Gatewood took from the trailer," he said, as Jim finished wiping the last of the egg yolk off his plate with a piece of toast. "If they were important enough for Padilla to bring along, they must have some meaning."

Stiles nodded and spoke between bites. "Can do. The sheriff will let me see them. Omar's okay. Not smart, but okay."

" 'Not smart' is an understatement. Do you know anybody who might remember the Padillas?" Kerney asked.

"Just about any of the old-timers should, I imagine. But in this county that's sixty percent of the population." Stiles rubbed a napkin across his mustache and mouth, crumpled it up, and dropped it on the empty plate.

"That's not what I wanted to hear."

"I know it, but maybe we don't need to ask everybody over the age of seventy about the old man. José Padilla can tell us. We are going to talk to him, aren't we?"

"We aren't. I am."

"You'll need an interpreter."

"*Yo cero que lo puedo hacer,*" Kerney replied.

Jim screwed up his face. "*Estas lleno de sorpresas. Yo no sabia que pudieva hablar español.*"

"You didn't ask," Kerney replied. "Anyway, you seemed determined to give me a Spanish lesson yesterday. I didn't want to spoil your fun."

"Thanks a lot," Jim grumbled. "When do you plan to see Padilla?"

"After I get some sleep."

PHIL WAS WAITING for Karen in his truck outside of Cattleman's. There was no place for Karen to park in front of the fake old-west storefront that hid the metal skin of the building, so she left her car across the street. Phil saw her coming and opened the passenger door as she approached.

"It's been a long time, cousin," Phil said as Karen got in the truck. She was wearing jeans, boots, and a brown sweater vest over a crewneck top.

"Yes, it has. How have you been, Phil?"

"Holding my own, I guess. Ranching doesn't get any easier." He shifted his position so that his back rested against the door. "I've got to ask—what in hell are you doing back in Catron County?"

"It was time to come home," Karen answered. "For a lot of reasons."

"Are you planning to take over the Triple H?"

"That's part of it."

"Think you can handle it?"

Karen smiled sweetly at Phil. "Do you think it's too much for a woman to take on?"

"I didn't say that."

"But you thought it, didn't you?"

"I was hoping your daddy would sell out to me when the time came."

"I don't think my father started that ranch from scratch to see it wind up in the hands of his brother's son. Is that why you've been such an attentive nephew over the years? So you can get the Triple H at a family discount?"

"You're still as sarcastic as ever."

"Maybe if you fed me breakfast like you promised, I wouldn't be so testy. My stomach is demanding some food."

"Best to wait until the crowd thins out," Phil said. "Looks like everybody from town is inside, talking about the Elderman Meadows murder."

"What murder?"

"Some Mexican was killed. The police think a poacher was responsible."

"Any suspects?"

"Not that I know of."

"So, I might get to start my new job with a murder case," Karen said. "That would be interesting. Why did you want to see me, Phil? Surely you can't want to talk over old times."

"I don't. Your daddy paid my daddy a visit yesterday morning."

Karen searched Phil's face with disbelieving eyes. "That's not likely."

"It's true," Phil confirmed.

"Were you there?"

"No. By the time I saw Edgar's truck and left my house, he was driving away like a bat out of hell. Pop wouldn't talk to me about it, of course. He didn't say a word."

"Such a sweet old man," Karen said.

"Don't start, Karen. Pop's hard to deal with, I'll grant you that, but he is my father."

"Horseshit," Karen replied. "He never was a father to you. The day your mother left him, he just got meaner. He's a nasty old man. If you hadn't held it all together and busted your ass for the last twenty years the ranch would have gone to hell."

"I don't need you ragging on my daddy," Phil shot back. "And I don't need a family history lesson."

"Maybe you do."

"Let's stay on the subject. Until yesterday, our fathers haven't spoken to each other in sixty years. What changed that?"

Karen took a long minute before replying. "I'm not sure."

"Has anything unusual happened recently?"

"Daddy got a letter yesterday. A man dropped it off at the house while he was in Silver City with Mom. Dad read it and then left for town. When I asked him about it, he said it was nothing to worry about, but he seemed upset."

"Who was the letter from?"

"I don't know. But the man who delivered it said he was Hector Padilla."

Phil looked surprised. "Hector Padilla is the name of the man that was killed at Elderman Meadows."

Karen smiled vaguely at an older couple as they left Cattleman's, then frowned. "That's a little more than strange. There was an old man with Hector Padilla. Daddy's age, a little older perhaps, but the same generation. He stayed in the truck. Do you know what happened to him?"

"Jim Stiles and a temporary ranger named Kerney found him near the foothills of Mangas Mountain. In shock, from what I've heard. He's hospitalized in Silver City."

"This fellow Kerney gets around. He stopped at the house yesterday to ask Dad about a black bear poaching."

"Yeah, that's how I met him, too. PJ and I found the bear."

Karen faced her cousin squarely. "Didn't the family know some people named Padilla back in the thirties?"

"Padilla is a pretty common name in these parts. At least, it used to be."

"Maybe the old man knew Daddy and Uncle Eugene."

"Isn't that stretching it a bit?" Phil rebutted.

"No," Karen replied. "It doesn't seem like a stretch at all. Dad gets a letter, goes to see his brother he hasn't talked to in sixty years, and the man who delivers the letter turns up murdered."

"I don't think what happened sixty years ago has anything to do with the murder of some Mexican national."

"Do you know what happened sixty years ago? I sure don't. I'd love to know what it was."

"Ask your father," Phil snapped.

"Is that what you did?"

Phil shrugged.

"Of course you didn't. You wouldn't dare."

Phil threw back his head and laughed.

"What's so funny, Phil?"

"You are, cousin. You don't know me half as well as you think you do."

Karen closed her eyes, and sighed. "We're bickering, Phil. Just like old times. Let's give it a rest, okay?"

She opened her eyes, looked at Phil, and forced a smile. Jim

Stiles and Kevin Kerney were standing next to Phil's truck. Both men looked dragged-out. They had day-old beards and weary eyes and wore dusty, wrinkled uniforms. "Hi, Jim," she said.

"Karen. Phil," Jim said, greeting both with a nod of his head. "If you folks came to town for breakfast, the waitress is just now cleaning off our table."

"Thanks," Karen said.

"Do you two know Kevin Kerney?" Jim asked.

"Sure do," Phil said.

Karen nodded in agreement.

Kerney nodded back. "Mr. Cox," he said, his voice heavy with exhaustion, "I'd like to stop by and see you this evening. Would that be convenient?"

"Sure, drop by," Phil replied. "We'll set out an extra plate, you look like you could use a home-cooked meal."

"Good enough."

"What about me?" Stiles asked jokingly. "Don't I get an invite?"

"Come along," Phil replied. "I guess we can feed you, too."

"Just kidding," Jim responded. "Besides, I don't see the fun in spending time with two old duffers like you and Kerney."

"Watch what you say there, youngster," Phil shot back with a smile.

"Yes, sir, Mr. Cox, sir," Stiles said solemnly. He slapped his hand on the truck hood. "Gotta go. See you, guys."

Karen leaned across Phil to the window and smiled sweetly. "Wrong gender, Jimmy. Are you still confused about sex, girls, and the birds and bees?"

"I'm slowly working it out."

"God help her, whoever she is." She switched her gaze quickly to Kerney. "It nice to see you again, Mr. Kerney."

Her directness caught Kerney off guard. He'd been staring at her without realizing it. She was a damn fine-looking woman.

He smiled self-consciously. "My pleasure."

As the two men walked away, Karen studied Kerney for a minute, a vague memory tugging at her consciousness. It faded without expression. She returned her attention to Phil, told him to get off his butt, take out his wallet, and buy her breakfast.

"You won't pick another fight?" Phil inquired.

"It's a deal. No more fights. You can fill me in on Doris and the kids."

"WHAT'S THE STORY on the woman?" Kerney inquired. He and Stiles were at their trucks. The overflow from Cattleman's Café had spilled across the street to Griffin's Bar, a long building done up with a slat-board facade, a porch with a railing covered by a sloping roof, and a wooden walkway, designed to give it a frontier appearance.

Stiles waited until a logging truck rumbled by before answering. "Real good-looking for an older babe, isn't she?"

"She doesn't look like an older babe to me."

"I knew you were going to say that. Her name is Karen Cox. Phil's cousin. She used to be my baby-sitter. Left years ago for college up in Albuquerque. Dropped out. Stayed in the city. Got married, went back to college, and taught school for a while. Then she got herself a law degree, and a divorce, and took back her maiden name. She's our new ADA. Starts tomorrow, as a matter of fact. I thought you'd met her."

"I did, but not officially," Kerney answered.

"Wait until you meet old Gene Cox, Phil's daddy."

"Tell me about him."

"He's a tough old son of a bitch. Got himself crippled up in a shooting accident when he was a boy. He's been almost completely paralyzed from the waist down ever since. It didn't slow him down much when he was younger. He even got married and sired two sons.

"Until Phil took over the ranch, Gene worked it with a truck and a golf cart that were fixed up with special controls. For a long time he kept riding—he even trained a horse to respond to hand and rein signals. He installed a winch and hoist on the truck so he could cut and haul wood. Used a walker to pull himself around when he was working outside."

"He does sound tough."

"And then some. What's next?" Jim asked.

"I need some rack time," Kerney replied. "Meet me at my trailer in six hours. You can go with me to see José Padilla."

"Yes, sir," Stiles said, giving Kerney an offhand salute.

Kerney got to his trailer, gathered up every bath towel he could find, and soaked them in hot water. He stripped out of his uniform and wrapped the hot towels, one at a time, around his bad knee. One full and one partial ligament held the leg together. He sat in the living-room chair and let the heat work on the pain. Through the open door of the trailer he could see the forested mountains east of Reserve that squeezed against the open fields and forced the San Francisco River into a confined, fast-running channel at the end of the valley. At the high school, children from a nearby subdivision were playing a softball game on the athletic field.

Under the floor of the trailer the mice were busy. There were fresh rodent droppings on the carpet by a window. The threat of hantavirus registered in Kerney's mind. It was a pulmonary illness, spread by deer mice, that killed people. He tried to remember the precautions, but he was too damn sluggish to think straight. He would let his landlord deal with the problem.

Kerney put the soggy towels in the kitchen sink, took four aspirin, closed the front door, set the alarm clock, and fell on the bed, asleep almost immediately.

KAREN SAID GOODBYE to Phil at Cattleman's and walked down the street to the county courthouse, an ugly two-story red brick building with aluminum-clad windows. The front office of the sheriff's department, a single-story annex, was manned by a radio dispatcher who sat at a console behind a long counter. Karen asked to see Sheriff Gatewood.

Gatewood came out of a rear suite of offices. A burly man in his late fifties with a slight potbelly, he wore an off-white straw cowboy hat and civilian clothes. His badge of office was clipped to his belt next to the high-rise holster that contained a four-inch .357 revolver.

"Miss Cox," Gatewood said. His voice was raspy and his face looked haggard.

"Why are you being so formal, Omar?" Karen said, shaking Gatewood's hand.

"Well, you aren't just Edgar Cox's little girl anymore, are you?" he said with a smile. "I sure don't want to get off on the wrong foot with the new assistant district attorney." He gestured to the open door behind him. "Come on in. I was just about to call you anyway. Figured you might want a rundown on the Padilla homicide."

"I do," Karen answered.

It took half an hour for Gatewood to finish his briefing. He sat behind his oak desk, made by inmates at the state penitentiary, and answered Karen's questions.

"No leads on any suspects?" she inquired. Gatewood's office was a small cubicle with one window that looked out on an empty lot.

"Not a one. Until Dr. Padilla recovers enough to be interviewed, we don't even know if we have a witness."

"What's his condition?"

Gatewood shrugged and rubbed the corner of his eye with a finger. "Don't know. The state police aren't releasing any information to us. That's typical. They know I don't have anybody on staff who's worth a damn as an investigator. We'll do whatever grunt work they decide to throw at us," he added unhappily.

"From what you told me, it was Kevin Kerney and Jim Stiles who found Padilla, discovered the murder victim, secured the crime scene, and located the camper trailer."

"That's true."

"Happenstance?"

"You could chalk it up to that," Gatewood responded, "but I wouldn't."

"Why not?"

"Until he got shot and had to retire, Kevin Kerney had a reputation as one of the best criminal investigators in the state. He was chief of detectives up in Santa Fe. There was even some talk that he was going to be the next police chief."

"When did he get shot?"

"Three or four years ago."

"Tell me about Jim Stiles."

Gatewood sighed. "I'd hire Jim in a flash, if I had the money and could pry him away from Game and Fish. He's smart and well trained. Carol Cassidy over at the Luna station has put Kerney on the poaching case full-time and arranged with Game and Fish for Stiles to work with him. Don't know how much good they can do with limited police powers."

Karen considered the information. "Can you arrange to have them meet us early tomorrow morning?"

"That shouldn't be a problem. What do you have in mind?"

"If we can get some free talent, why not use it? Running a murder investigation out of Socorro, a hundred and thirty miles away, isn't going to get the job done, no matter what the state police say. I'll appoint Kerney a special investigator and you deputize Jim Stiles."

The frame squeaked as Omar Gatewood leaned back in his chair. He had come up through the ranks before getting elected and needed one more term in office to qualify for a full pension. His opponent in the June primary was a former sheriff with a lot of support who wanted his old job back. Gatewood didn't give a damn about the dead Mexican, but if he could show the good people of Catron County that he was using every possible means to solve the case, it might make a big difference come election day.

He looked at Karen Cox with a new appreciation. "Now that's an idea that warms my heart."

EDGAR COX found Margaret in the kitchen with Elizabeth and Cody, busily preparing Sunday breakfast. The Silver City paper was folded neatly on his place mat along with a steaming cup of coffee. A vase of fresh-cut flowers formed a centerpiece. From the aroma in the room, he knew Margaret had cooked up apple pancakes, one of her specialties.

"What are we celebrating?" he asked, smiling at his wife and grandchildren.

"A beautiful morning," Margaret replied, wiping her hands on the seat of her jeans, the way she always did when she was cooking. She walked to her husband, gave him a warm kiss, and stroked his cheek with her hand.

Edgar studied her face. She wasn't hiding anything from him as far as he could tell, and she looked fine. He loved the tiny overbite to her mouth. And her long, elegant neck was as flawless as it had been forty years ago. Margaret wore her hair in a bun the way he liked it, which was usually reserved for very special occasions.

He asked the gnawing question anyway, his worry a tight feeling in the pit of his stomach. "How are you feeling?"

Margaret's expression changed to mild reproof. "The question is, how do I look?" she asked, her head held high.

Margaret at sixty-five amazed Edgar. With soft brown eyes that didn't miss a trick, full lips above a strong chin, high cheekbones, and pale skin, Margaret Atwood Cox was still a beauty.

"Gorgeous," he admitted.

"That's the right answer," she said, patting him on the cheek. "Now, go sit down, read your paper, and drink your coffee. Breakfast will be ready in a few minutes."

"Where's Karen?"

"Meeting Phil for breakfast in Reserve."

"Any particular reason?" he asked cautiously.

"No," Margaret said, turning back to the stove. "Just to visit and catch up, I imagine."

With Cody and Elizabeth to distract him, Edgar didn't get to read the Sunday paper until breakfast was over and the dishes were washed and put away. When Margaret went to dress for church, he sat in his favorite chair in the living room and unfolded the paper. The front page blazoned the story of a murder on Elderman Meadows. Edgar read it with interest. His curiosity quickly changed to apprehension. He didn't know the victim, Hector Padilla, but he sure as hell knew José Padilla.

He got up from his chair and walked rapidly to the bedroom. Margaret stood in front of the full-length mirror, fastening her brassiere. He prayed she wouldn't need a mastectomy and that the lump was benign. And he hoped to God José Padilla was dead in the Silver City hospital.

Margaret saw her husband's face reflected in the mirror and turned. A small twitch at the corner of one eye telegraphed Edgar's anxiety. "What is it?"

"I have to go to Silver City."

"Why?"

"Business."

Margaret slipped into her blouse, her eyes locked on her husband. "What does that mean?"

"Just what I said," he replied. "Take yourself to church. Karen should be back before you need to leave."

"Edgar?"

"Yes?"

"What kind of business?" she demanded.

"Old family business."

Margaret took a deep breath. Edgar's phrase was the euphemism he used to talk about Eugene. "I'll go with you."

"I don't want you involved."

Margaret tucked her blouse into her skirt and walked to her husband. "It's forty years too late for that. Now, tell me what's wrong."

Edgar told her, and when he finished, Margaret wrote a note to Karen and left it on the kitchen table, so her daughter would know the clan was off for an impromptu Sunday drive and lunch in Silver City.

CHURCH BELLS TOLLED for late Sunday services as Kerney got up and dressed. He had time before Stiles was due to arrive. He walked the quarter mile to his landlord's house, and asked if it would be possible for the mice to be removed from in and under the trailer. Doyle Fletcher, a man who looked about Kerney's age, with a suspicious, stingy face, stood in the partially open doorway, grunted in agreement, and said it would take him a day or two to get around to it. Kerney thanked him, went home, and waited for Jim, wondering why Doyle Fletcher seemed so put out.

He shrugged it off and passed the time listening to a Haydn concerto, trying not to think too much about Karen Cox. He'd gone back to his solitary lifestyle after Sara Brannon, the Army officer who had worked with him on the White Sands case, left for her new duty station in Korea. That was more than a while back, and he found himself missing her.

After Stiles showed up, they drove to Silver City hospital and learned that José Padilla was still in the Intensive Care Unit. A hospital security guard at the ICU door asked Kerney and Stiles who they wanted to see. Kerney gave him José Padilla's name and showed his badge. The guard shook his head and said the state police had forbidden any visitors. Kerney asked to speak to the nursing supervisor.

Erlinda Perez came to the door and inspected Kerney's badge. "What does the Forest Service have to do with this?" she asked.

Nurse Perez, a thin, middle-aged woman with a long, narrow nose, had coal-black eyes and a rather stern demeanor. She crossed her arms and waited for an answer.

"We found the gentleman," Stiles said in Spanish, before Kerney could speak, giving the nurse his most winning smile. "We're interested in how he's doing."

Erlinda relaxed a bit. She answered in English for the other man's benefit. "Mr. Padilla will be with us for a while. He had a stroke a few hours after he was admitted."

"Is he oriented?" Kerney inquired.

"Not to time, place, or person," Erlinda responded. "We have him stabilized, but it will be some time tomorrow before the doctor can determine the extent of the cerebral damage."

"What's your prognosis?" Kerney queried.

"I'm not a doctor," Erlinda replied.

"That's why I asked."

Erlinda smiled. "I'd say fair, but you never can tell. He has some physical impairment. The right side of his body is paralyzed. He may recover from that, to a degree. With any trauma to the brain it's impossible to predict how much function can be restored. Especially at his age."

"Has he talked about anything at all?" Stiles wanted to know. "Names? Places? Events?"

"He calls me Carlotta. That's it."

"His wife's name," Kerney said. "He told me she was dead. Has the family been notified?"

"Yes. His daughter should be here shortly. She's flying in from Mexico City. It was her son who was murdered."

"Any other visitors?" Stiles asked.

"Just the two of you and some reporters. People may have called or asked about him at the front desk. You can check there. I've got to get back."

"Thanks for your time," Kerney said.

At the reception desk Kerney asked the volunteer lady if anyone had called or stopped by to inquire about José Padilla.

"Yes. An older couple," the woman responded. "They came in this morning."

"Did you get their names?"

"No, but I remember seeing them on Friday. I usually only volunteer on Sundays, but one of our girls was out sick, so I filled in for her that day. The woman came in with her husband for an outpatient test."

"What kind of test?"

"A mammogram. She asked me where she needed to go."

"Did she give you a name?" Kerney asked.

"No. But the admitting office is open. They might be able to help."

The clerk in the admitting office resisted releasing the names of the mammogram outpatients until Kerney convinced her he wasn't interested in medical information, just names. She checked with the administrator on duty, got approval to give out the information, and wrote the names on a piece of paper.

Kerney took it, read it quickly, and passed it to Jim. "Who is Margaret A. Cox?" he asked.

"I'll be damned," Stiles said. "The only Margaret Cox I know is Karen's mother."

"Do any other names look familiar?"

"Not a one."

"Let's pay Mr. Cox and his wife a visit."

"I THOUGHT he might be somebody I knew," Edgar said. He sat back in his reclining chair, his long legs dangling over the foot-rest, looking at Kerney with an expressionless gaze. Margaret was across from Edgar on the overstuffed couch, sitting next to Jim Stiles. Kerney sat in an easy chair at the narrow end of a squat maple coffee table.

The room felt snug and lived-in. There was a television in a floor-to-ceiling bookcase that held a small but nice collection of Indian pots and framed family photographs. The furniture was ranch-style, all in good taste, with a few antique pieces mixed in.

"You thought you knew José Padilla," Kerney repeated back to Edgar Cox.

"I went to grammar school in Mangas with a boy by the same name. It was a one-room schoolhouse with about sixteen students. José was one of the older boys at school that I liked. I'd say he would be in his early eighties by now."

"And you got the information about Padilla from the Sunday paper," Kerney added.

On the wall behind Edgar Cox was a glass display box containing military memorabilia. It held four rows of service ribbons, the silver oak leaves of a lieutenant colonel, a Combat Infantry Badge, a World War II unit insignia, and an impressive array of medals, including the Purple Heart.

"That's what I said," Edgar replied.

"So, you wanted to renew an old acquaintance?" Kerney probed.

"Look, my wife and I took our grandchildren out to Sunday brunch. The medical center was nearby. It was a spur-of-the-moment kind of thing."

"You were just checking to see if it was the same José Padilla you knew as a boy."

"This is getting old real fast, Mr. Kerney," Edgar replied.

Margaret Cox, her arms folded, legs crossed at the ankles, looked only at her husband. Everything about her posture was tense and secretive. Kerney's smile in her direction had no impact.

Kerney pushed on. "Was there something specific you wanted to say to Mr. Padilla?"

"Am I under suspicion for something because I asked about the welfare of a patient at the hospital?" Edgar retorted.

"Not at all," Kerney answered. "It's just that we know very little about Dr. Padilla. The more we can learn about him, the better our chances to find out why his grandson was murdered."

"I can't help you. I never got to see him. I'm not even sure if he's the José Padilla I knew or not."

Kerney fell silent and watched Edgar Cox. A minute passed without conversation. Cox's hands were gripping the armrests of the recliner when Kerney broke the silence.

"Assuming Señor Padilla is your old friend, can you think of any reason he would come back to Catron County?"

"When you get to be my age, Mr. Kerney, there's a tendency to want to reacquaint yourself with the past. If José Padilla is my old school chum, I will enjoy seeing him, and offer him a helping hand, if he needs one."

"That makes sense," Kerney agreed, standing up. "Thanks for taking the time to talk to us. It was very kind of you."

Edgar Cox rose from his chair and said nothing in reply.

Kerney and Jim said goodbye to a distant and worried Mrs. Cox at the door. Her husband stood as though his feet were glued to the floor.

"What do you think?" Jim asked, as they climbed into the truck.

"He's holding something back," Kerney replied, "and his wife knows it."

KAREN HEARD A VEHICLE leaving as she left her house to round up Mom and Dad. Finally, everything was clean and organized. Even the books were arranged on the shelves that covered most of the walls in the small living room. Cody and Elizabeth were freshly scrubbed and neatly dressed—an achievement for Cody—and Karen looked forward to serving her parents the meal she had prepared to celebrate her homecoming. She found Edgar alone in the living room, looking wistfully at the family pictures on a bookcase.

"Did you have visitors?" she asked.

Edgar turned his head in Karen's direction and nodded. "Jim Stiles and a ranger. That Kerney fellow you met. They wanted to ask some questions about the black bear that was shot on the mesa. I wasn't much help. How was your visit with Phil?"

"We started out arguing, as usual."

"I wish the two of you could get along."

"That's hard to do when we're on opposite sides of a lifelong feud between two brothers, and neither of us knows what the conflict is about."

Edgar winced at Karen's criticism. "I'm sorry it strains your relationship with Phil."

"It might help both Phil and me, if we knew why you and Uncle Eugene hate each other so."

"It would do no good to talk about it. Nothing would change."

"Phil told me you went to see Uncle Eugene yesterday."

"I sort of figured he would."

"What was it about, Daddy?"

"It was a business matter," Edgar replied shortly.

"You'll have to do better than that," Karen snapped, sticking her chin out.

"It doesn't concern you."

"If your meeting with Eugene has anything to do with the murder of Hector Padilla, it damn well concerns me."

"Are you accusing me of wrongdoing?" Edgar could hear the annoyance in his voice.

"No, and I didn't say that. But if there is a connection between Hector Padilla's delivery of a letter to you and his murder, in my official capacity I need to know about it. The case falls under my jurisdiction."

Edgar waved off his daughter's demand. "There is no connection."

"What did the letter say?"

There was a long silence before Edgar answered. "The letter was for Eugene, requesting payment on a shipment of Mexican cattle."

"The letter was addressed to you, and Hector Padilla asked for you by name, not Uncle Eugene," Karen countered.

"He made a mistake."

"Why didn't you drop the letter in the mail?"

"Because I figured there was some urgency to the situation. Are you finished giving me the third degree?"

Karen bit her lip. It all sounded reasonable, expect for a feeling she had that her father was lying. The visit to his brother was an unheard-of event in the family. "We'll leave it at that for now," she said, studying her father's face intently. "Tell Mom dinner is ready. That's if you're still planning to eat with us."

Edgar looked away, then looked back and forced a smile. "Of course we are."

Karen could not recall a time before when her father had lied to her. Demoralized by the thought, she tried unsuccessfully to dismiss it.

WITH JIM OFF ON HIS OWN to interview the area ranchers who knew about the mountain lion translocation project, Kerney headed for the Slash Z. The homestead looked much the way he remembered it. His only visit had been years ago as a teenager when he had competed in the state high school rodeo championships. He and his best friend, Dale Jennings, made the trip in an old truck and camped out at the rodeo grounds to save money. Unable to get away, both Dale's and his parents were back at the Jennings ranch, where Kerney's father worked as the foreman.

Cory Cox, Phil's older brother, who was also competing in the championship, had invited Kerney and Dale out for dinner, which had turned into a rather gloomy event. Eugene Cox had not been a gracious or pleasant host.

The old man on the porch in the wheelchair grunted at him as he walked up the ramp.

"Who the hell are you?" Eugene Cox demanded.

"Kevin Kerney."

Eugene squinted at him. "I know that name. Did I ever meet you before?" He looked exactly like his brother except for sunken cheeks that gave his face an unhealthy cast and a mouth fixed in a perpetual scowl.

"A long time ago, Mr. Cox. When I was in high school."

Eugene stared at him for a long time. "Damn if you aren't right. You're that kid from Engle who beat Cory in the finals of the high school rodeo championship, the year they held it in Reserve. Cory should have won that buckle."

Kerney smiled. "That's what you told me then."

"I still mean it. What do you want?"

"How is Cory?"

"Dead. Vietnam."

"Sorry to hear it."

"Don't be," Eugene said flatly.

Kerney sat on the porch rail and looked at the view. The Slash Z was close to the Mangas Mountains. The sun was low in the sky, about to drop below the crest. A red-and-gold sheen frosted the forest canopy. Kerney could imagine himself running a spread like the Slash Z. He couldn't think of a happier thing to do with his life. But it would take a mountain of cash to buy anything equal to the Slash Z these days; it was a multimillion-dollar ranch.

The thought of the ranch his parents had lost to the Army still made Kerney's gut ache when he dwelled on it too much. He shook it off. "Pretty country," he finally said.

"It'll do." Eugene pushed his chair closer to Kerney. "Did you drive out here to look at the view?"

Kerney chuckled. "No. Phil asked me to stop by and visit."

Eugene pointed at the house at the other side of the horse pasture. "He's home."

"I see his truck," Kerney said. "What do you think about the murder at the meadows?"

"I'll tell you what I think. Last ten years or so there's been a hell of a lot of Mexicans coming up here trying to buy every ranch that comes on the market. I think somebody got sick and tired of it. I know I am."

"The victim was a medical student," Kerney noted.

"I know that," Eugene growled. "It doesn't change my feeling. It's a damn shame that our government lets foreigners buy American property. There ought to be a law against it."

"There was an older man with him by the name of José Padilla, who may have lived here at one time. Does that ring a bell with you?"

"José Padilla, you say? No. There were a lot of people by the name of Padilla living in Mangas back in the twenties and early thirties. I went to school with some of them, but I don't remember anybody by that name. Doesn't mean he wasn't living in the valley. But I don't recall him. I didn't socialize all that much with those folks. Still don't."

"Your brother said he might know him."

"Did he, now? That doesn't surprise me. He always took to Mexicans a lot more readily than I did."

Kerney smiled, tipped his hat, and took his leave.

Phil's wife, Doris, was setting the supper table when Kerney was ushered into the house by PJ, who introduced him to his mother. A tiny woman, Doris wore no makeup, and her brown hair was cut short. She had straight eyebrows that almost ran together. After a shy greeting, her brown eyes darted away as she returned her concentration to arranging place mats and setting out the knives and forks.

"Phil's cleaning up," she said. "He'll be with you in a minute. PJ, take Mr. Kerney into the living room and make him comfortable."

In the living room Kerney met PJ's younger brother and sister. Bobby, about the same age as Karen's son, had a chunky frame and a sober baby-fat face. Looking bored, he wandered off after a few minutes to the television set in the family room. Jennifer, who was two years younger than PJ, looked a lot like her mother, with the same coloring, thin frame, and shy smile. Kerney tried some small talk with her and PJ, which fell flat. Both children seemed shut down, with nothing much to say. He was rescued by Phil Cox and a call to the dinner table by Doris.

Over dinner, a meat-and-potatoes meal, Phil dominated the conversation. The children stayed quiet, and Doris kept her contributions to automatic slight nods of her head whenever Phil looked her way. She busied herself serving food and correcting the children's table manners, with an occasional glance and small smile in Kerney's direction. It reminded Kerney of his long-ago meal with Eugene Cox.

Kerney asked Phil a lot of questions and found that he had nothing of value to add to the investigation, but the food was decent, and Phil seemed to enjoy the company.

After dinner, with the children excused and Doris in the kitchen, Kerney was about to take his leave when Phil was called to the phone.

He returned shaking his head and chuckling. "That was my father," he said, as he pulled out his chair and sat down. "I told him you had stayed for supper, and he didn't like it one bit. Said I shouldn't be letting the man who stole Cory's championship eat at my table. Why the hell didn't you tell me who you were?"

"That happened a long time ago."

"Yeah, it did, but I should have remembered. I'll tell you one thing: Cory never saw it the way Dad did. He said you won that buckle fair and square."

"That's good to hear."

Phil stood up. "Let me get PJ in here. He'd love to hear about how you and his Uncle Cory went head to head in the state finals." He stopped at the kitchen door. "Doris, bring us in some coffee," he ordered.

Before leaving, Kerney spent a pleasant hour talking with Phil and PJ about horses, rodeo, and Cory. He got the impression PJ was Phil's favorite. Jennifer and Bobby never reappeared.

A deputy sheriff was parked at the trailer when he got home. The deputy asked Kerney to stop by and see the sheriff in the morning. Kerney asked why, but the deputy didn't know. He was just the messenger boy.

Kerney told the deputy he'd be there.

5

Stretched out on his back, fast asleep, Edgar Cox snored. After one final ripping snort, his breathing slowed and became tranquil. Margaret waited for a few minutes, got out of bed, gathered up her robe and slippers, and went softly into the living room. Outside, false dawn had faded into morning and the first robin of the day sang. Bubba, the children's puppy, met her halfway to Karen's house. He sniffed Margaret's slippers, wagged his tail, and barked a greeting. She reached down and scratched his ears. Karen sat on the top porch step of the old ranch house dressed only in a tank top, shorts, and sandals. Margaret wrapped the robe tightly around her waist and wondered how Karen could be so warm in the morning chill.

Karen smiled, scooted to one side, and patted the porch step in an invitation for her mother to join her. They sat in silence for a moment watching the robin until it flew away.

"How do you like being back home?" Margaret asked.

"I love it," Karen replied.

"No regrets about leaving the city?"

"I don't miss Albuquerque at all."

"There was a time when I thought you'd never come back to the ranch."

Karen laughed. "Neither did I."

"Are you absolutely sure you want to live here?"

"I am," Karen answered with an emphatic nod of her head.

"No regrets about Stan?" Margaret asked.

"God no. It wasn't a marriage. He wanted to own me. I think I knew I would eventually divorce him. It was just a question of when it would happen."

"I could never understand what made Stan believe he could hold on to you. In a conventional sense, I'm not sure any man can."

Karen's eyes danced in amusement. "You've always known that about me, haven't you?"

"Has it changed?"

"No. I don't think marriage suits me. I'm sorry things were so tense at dinner last night."

"Edgar said you had a rather heated conversation with him. You and your father are two of a kind. That can make the sparks fly."

"I see no reason why he can't talk to me about Uncle Eugene."

"He doesn't talk to anybody about it."

Karen shook her head, rejecting the statement. "That's not completely true. He talks to you about it. He must."

Margaret rubbed her daughter's arm affectionately. Karen's skin was warm to the touch. "That's different."

"This time the situation is different. If it's a legitimate inquiry into a homicide investigation, I may have to force him to talk about it."

"I'd rather you wouldn't push it. Your father has enough on his mind right now."

"Are there problems?"

Margaret remained silent. She had hoped Karen would ask the question.

"Is something wrong?" Karen prodded.

"Oh, he thinks I'm going to die. He can't stand the thought that he might outlive me."

Karen's hand covered her mother's. "Die? What's wrong?"

"I had a mammogram last Friday. The doctor's fairly certain I have cancer. I was going to wait to tell you until the biopsy results came back."

"When will you know?"

"Tomorrow." Margaret could see tears in the corners of Karen's eyes. She wiped them away with a fingertip. "Don't cry."

"Why not? It makes me so damn sad and angry."

Margaret laughed gently. "I'm going to beat it, sweetie. I plan to be around for a while. Long enough to become a very old, crotchety great-grandmother."

Karen sniffled. "How can you be so sure?"

"Call it woman's intuition. I just feel it. I'll survive." Margaret got to her feet. "Edgar will be up soon, wanting his breakfast. He loves you very much."

"I know."

Margaret bent down and kissed Karen on the forehead. "And so do I."

Karen stood and hugged her mother tightly.

"Send the children down to the house when you're ready to leave for work," Margaret said.

"I can't have you watch them for me. Not now."

"Don't be silly." She kissed her daughter again. "I'm looking forward to it. I need to spoil them a bit more."

Margaret returned home. Edgar was out of bed and in the bathroom shaving. She made fresh coffee, feeling somewhat guilty about her talk with Karen. Everything she'd said was true, but her motives were sneaky. If disclosing her illness deflected Karen from pursuing Edgar's secret, it was worth the effort.

IN THE PARKING LOT at the county courthouse, Jim Stiles lounged against the front of his truck, one foot on the bumper. He was wearing jeans, a straw cowboy hat, a white shirt, and a pair of snakeskin boots.

Kerney limped toward him. The hitch in his right leg seemed a little more pronounced. Kerney's getup pretty much matched Jim's, except for a big rodeo buckle Kerney wore on the belt around his waist.

He stood with Jim facing the entrance to the sheriff's department, a forlorn annex to the courthouse, plastered adobe brown.

Stiles stared at Kerney's belt buckle. "Is that the real McCoy?"

"Sure is. Somebody reminded me I won it, so I dug it out and decided to wear it."

Jim squinted to make out the date it was awarded. "It's a damn antique."

"Watch what you say, youngster," Kerney cautioned lightly.

"Just kidding." Jim's green eyes crinkled with humor. "I'm impressed. Hell, I'm jealous. I didn't know you were a rodeo cowboy."

"That's stretching it," Kerney replied. "I was a ranch kid who liked to rodeo."

"Do your parents still ranch?"

"They're dead," Kerney replied. "The Army took our ranch when White Sands Missile Range expanded. My father got a job as a foreman at a nearby outfit."

"That sucks."

"It's old news."

"I don't think I could be so cool about it if it happened to my parents."

Kerney's laugh was tinged with bitterness. "I only sound indifferent. It's not the way I feel." He started walking toward the sheriff's office. "Got any idea why Omar Gatewood wants to see us?"

"None whatever," Jim admitted, as he walked alongside.

"How did your interviews go?"

"Chalk up a big fat goose egg. Not one of those good folks has had any problems with cougars killing their stock. They don't know where in the hell Mexican Hat is and never heard of José or Hector Padilla, and the closest thing to an ATV I saw was one of those sit-down John Deere lawn tractors. How did you do with Phil Cox?"

"About the same," Kerney replied, holding open the door to the office.

Sheriff Gatewood had a guest with him, Karen Cox. At the front of Gatewood's desk were two straight-backed chairs. Karen sat in a padded vinyl armchair at the side of the desk. Kerney took the empty chair closest to Karen. In a dark blue business suit, a linen blouse, hose, and pumps, she looked elegant and professional. The office, a small space with cheap wood paneling, felt oppressive. On one wall hung Gatewood's framed commission as sheriff and a dozen training certificates from various law enforcement seminars, all of them listing slightly off-center.

Karen nodded a greeting at Jim and Kerney. Her skirt stopped at mid-thigh and revealed her slender, well-formed legs.

"Thanks for coming in, boys," Gatewood said, leaning back in his squeaky chair.

"What's up?" Jim asked.

Gatewood gave Jim his most winning smile. "Miss Cox and I have a proposition for you."

As Gatewood explained the purpose of the meeting—commissions for Kerney and Stiles with primary responsibility to conduct the Padilla murder investigation on behalf of the department—Kerney kept his attention on Karen, who seemed to deliberately avoid making eye contact with him. Finally she looked at him, and a small smile crossed her lips.

Gatewood finished his pitch, and Jim chuckled. "Is this another one of your schemes to get me to go to work for you, Omar?"

"I'd like that, but I can't afford you," Omar replied with a grin. "Nope. This murder case needs to get the attention it deserves. Unless we do something it will go on some state police investigator's back burner within a week, and that doesn't sit right with me. Now, I don't have the manpower or the specialists to solve the damn case, so Miss Cox here had an idea: we borrow the two of you and put you to work on it." He turned to Kerney for a reaction. "What do you think?"

Kerney looked at Stiles, who was nodding his head vigorously. "The idea has merit."

Gatewood smiled and rested his hands on his stomach. "I figured you boys would like the idea."

"Who would we report to?" Kerney asked.

"To me, of course," Gatewood replied.

"What you're proposing, Sheriff, is a special operation. That calls for as much independence as possible. If you want this scheme to have more than a snowball's chance in hell to succeed, turn the case completely over to us."

"I won't do that, Kerney," Gatewood retorted, scowling.

Kerney stood up, caught Jim's eye, nodded at the door, and smiled at Karen, who had been watching Kerney intently. "I'm sorry you've wasted your time," he said to her.

Karen rose and held Kerney back from leaving. "One minute, Mr. Kerney. Suppose we give you the autonomy you want, with the understanding that you are to operate strictly under the color of the law, and consult with me on all legal questions. Would that satisfy you?"

"Almost."

"What else do you want?"

"A thousand dollars to buy information."

"What kind of information?" Karen demanded.

"Padilla's murder was not premeditated. He was in the wrong place at the wrong time. Why kill a complete stranger over a crime that, at the most, would cost a fine and six months in jail? According to Jim, money is probably the motive. There has been a pattern of organized big game and exotic animal kills that may be tied to a smuggling operation that exports rare animal parts to Asia. Information about a scam like that isn't going to fall into our laps."

Sheriff Gatewood cocked his head back and snorted. "Charlie Perry has been working poaching cases for a couple of years now, and I've never heard him talk about any smuggling."

"It's an angle we need to pursue," Kerney replied.

"Do you assume the killer is from the area?" Karen asked.

Stiles got to his feet. "Absolutely. Only a few people in the area even knew cougars had been translocated to Elderman Meadows."

"The poaching was done for sport, if you ask me," Gatewood said, as he pulled himself out of his chair, feeling like the odd man out. "This smuggling notion is way off base. I think whoever shot that Padilla fella did it to cover his tracks."

Kerney concentrated his attention on Karen. "We'll chase down any theory that holds water, but I think we need to look at them all."

Karen mulled it over before answering. "I'll put up the money you need from the DA's account. You'll carry a commission through my office." She switched her attention to Gatewood. "Sheriff, I'd like your cooperation on this. If it will make you feel more comfortable, you can commission Jim and assign him to work under me."

Gatewood grunted, thought about it for a moment, and smiled shrewdly. Karen's offer would allow him to lay off any blame on her if things went wrong and the shit hit the fan. "I'll go along with that."

"Then it's agreed." Karen glanced from Kerney to Stiles to Gatewood and back to Kerney. "Is that satisfactory?"

"Good enough," Kerney replied. "I'll keep you fully informed."

"See that you do," Karen replied.

A politician's smile spread over Gatewood's face. "I'm glad we got this ironed out. I already gave the Silver City paper a statement on your appointments."

Kerney looked at Gatewood in amazement. "That was a stupid thing to do."

"Now wait a minute, Kerney . . ." Gatewood blustered.

"I'll try to get the story killed," Karen cut in, freezing Gatewood with an abrupt look.

"Good," Kerney replied.

Kerney and Stiles signed the necessary paperwork, got sworn in, and left. Kerney had a draft for a thousand dollars from the local bank tucked in his wallet. In the parking lot, Jim shook his head in disbelief. "You played hardball in there," he said.

"I don't want Gatewood calling the shots," Kerney answered. "Besides not being very bright, he's a politician. We're going to have to improvise if we hope to solve this case, and Gatewood would keep us on a short leash. Fill me in a bit more on Karen Cox. Where does she get her influence?"

Jim laughed. "Her daddy served two terms on the county commission, helped Gatewood get hired as a deputy, and supported him for sheriff when he ran for office. Edgar carries a lot of political weight. The last thing Omar wants to do is piss off Edgar or his daughter. Especially in an election year."

"Is everybody in this county in bed with each other?"

Jim grinned. "Not me. My girlfriend lives in Silver City."

"Exception noted. Are you bragging or complaining?"

"Both. So what's next, boss?"

"You get to review every piece of paper that was found in José Padilla's travel trailer. I want a full report when I get back."

Jim groaned in dismay.

"You wanted to do real police work, remember?"

Stiles groaned again. "Why did I ever say that? And where in the hell are you going?"

"South," Kerney replied.

EARLIER IN THE DAY Karen had rearranged the office so she could sit at her desk and look out the window. The seventh judicial district operated on a circuit court schedule in Catron County, and she had a week to prepare for her first court appearance. A stack of active files filled her briefcase. She was pretty much up to speed on the contents.

She sat down, pushed her shoes off, and wiggled her toes. She hated to wear panty hose. As far as she was concerned it was the major drawback to the job.

When Kerney had stood up, ready to walk out on the deal because of Gatewood's stubbornness, Karen had momentarily lost her train of thought. The belt buckle he wore sparked a forgotten memory. At the age of twelve, she had accompanied her parents to the state high school rodeo championships in Reserve to watch her cousin Cory compete. Afterward, she and her girlfriends giggled and fantasized for weeks about the tall, good-looking high school senior from Engle with the square shoulders and the pretty blue eyes who had beaten out Cory for the best all-around cowboy title. Kevin Kerney. She smiled at the girlhood silliness of it all.

Kerney had aged well, she decided. He was a little taller now and slightly fuller in the chest, with a flat stomach and baby-fine brown hair that was just barely receding. All in all, a good-looking man. It was Kerney's intense blue eyes that drew Karen in, and during the meeting she had worked hard to keep from looking at him. He had caught her sneaking a glance only once.

She smiled at the thought that Kerney seemed much more interested in her now than he had when she was twelve. The smile faded as Karen thought about her mother. She stopped herself from reaching for the telephone. There was no sense in disturbing Mom with her overabundant concern. Let her enjoy her time with Elizabeth and Cody, Karen thought, as long as she is able. But how long would that be? It frightened Karen to think about it. Her mother had always been an anchor point in her life.

She pushed back the emotion and found herself thinking about her father. He was a strong-willed man who didn't bend easily. The prospect of pressuring him to reveal the contents of the Padilla letter was distasteful, although she was still mad as hell at him for lying about it. For now, the issue could remain dormant. Karen hoped it would stay outside the scope of Kerney's investigation. But what if it didn't? How could she protect her father without violating her professional ethics? If necessary, she would have to rein Kerney in. Somehow, she didn't think Kerney was the type of man who would take that easily.

She put in a call to the Silver City paper and got through to the editor, who told her it was too late to kill the story. She hung up wondering if Omar Gatewood even realized how badly he had blundered by letting the cat out of the bag to the media. She seriously doubted it.

KERNEY CASHED THE CHECK, drove to his trailer, and swapped the Forest Service truck for his own vehicle, a late-model GMC pickup. Making a quick stop at the hospital in Silver City, he found the same guard at the door of the ICU and asked to speak to Erlinda Perez.

She arrived quickly, stepped halfway into the hall, and held the door open with a hand. "I'm very busy, Mr. Kerney."

"I won't take much of your time. Did Dr. Padilla's daughter show up?"

"She's here now."

He gave Erlinda a business card and switched to Spanish. "Please give her my condolences, find out if she will tell me where she's staying, and ask if I may speak with her this afternoon. Tell her I wish to be of assistance in finding the person who killed her son."

Erlinda nodded, told him to wait, and returned after a few minutes. She told Kerney where the woman was staying.

"She'll be at her motel in the afternoon," she added. "She would like to meet with you."

"That's great. What's her name?" Kerney asked.

"Cornelia Marquez."

"Have the police talked to her?"

"I don't know," Erlinda said.

"How is Señor Padilla?"

Erlinda shrugged. "The same. He fades in and out. Not very responsive. He remembers almost nothing."

"Is he talking?"

"Not really. A word here and there. The doctor thinks the damage may be permanent."

"Thanks."

"Por nada." Erlinda watched him leave. Generally, she was not impressed with cops. But this gringo didn't run a macho game or act like a tough guy. Also, he didn't wear a wedding ring. She wondered if he was married.

KERNEY BURNED UP THE ROAD getting to El Paso. In Juarez he drove through the sleazy tourist district that never seemed to change, except to smell worse and look more appalling. He fought his way around crazed motorists until he was off the strip and heading for the suburbs.

Francisco Posada's home, a modern two-story affair with arched windows, a red tile roof, Grecian columns under a domed entrance, and meticulously landscaped grounds, qualified as a mansion. It harmonized nicely with the rest of the Juarez neighborhood. The entire district could easily be part of any wealthy Southern California enclave.

Señor Posada's houseboy answered the door, recognized Kerney, and blocked his entrance.

"I don't think it is wise for you to be here," Juan said.

"I need to see him now," Kerney replied. "Don't make me walk over you to do it."

Juan considered the threat, his soft black eyes flickering over Kerney's face, and decided not to resist.

"Very well," Juan said. "Follow me."

Escorted into the spacious living room and left alone, Kerney sat in front of the Diego Rivera portrait of a beautiful Mexican woman that had captured his admiration during his first meeting with Posada, when he'd been tracking down Eppi Gutierrez's smuggling contacts. Hung above the fireplace, it was a remarkable painting, filled with an odd mixture of passion and piety, and Kerney was delighted to see it again.

Glass walls on either side of the fireplace climbed to a vaulted ceiling, bringing the outdoors virtually inside. The yard had as a centerpiece a large swimming pool and cabana ringed with palm trees and potted tropical plants. In the living room were three separate seating areas of matching, richly upholstered chairs and couches that blended nicely with the off-white carpet and walls.

Guided by Juan, Francisco Posada entered from the adjoining library. Kerney stood up. The old man shuffled slowly to him. The arthritis that so grotesquely crippled his hands had obviously wors-

ened. Deep circles beneath his small eyes stopped at his cheekbones. The loose skin around his neck looked almost detached.
Pain was etched in his expression.

"Please sit," Posada said, in his elegant Spanish. He joined
Kerney on the couch, Juan helping to lower him down. "I did not
expect to see you again, Señor Kerney."

Juan, slight, dark, and as slender as a girl, stood at the side of
his employer, eyes fixed on Posada, his expression guarded. During
Kerney's past visit, Juan had seemed much more attentive to Posada.
He wondered what was up between them.

"Nor I you, Don Francisco," Kerney replied, in Spanish.

Posada smiled. "I assume you did not come to present your
apologies for deceiving me."

On his past visit, Kerney had hoodwinked Posada into selling
him valuable information that had led to a major break in shutting
down a smuggling operation and solving the murder of Kerney's
godson.

"Circumstances prevented me from telling you the truth," Kerney replied.

"I am not interested in that. I am interested in the money you
owe me."

As an inducement to do business with him, Kerney had agreed
to pay Posada a percentage of the gross profits from the sale of the
stolen historical artifacts.

"The percentage you were promised was based on the delivery
of certain items. The delivery was never made."

"It was never intended to be made."

"You did not consider that possibility," Kerney countered.

Posada laughed nastily.

"Have I amused you?"

"I do not like the notion that I was so easily duped."

"Can we do business?"

"It depends. What is it you require?"

"I need the names of people who smuggle endangered animals to the Asian trade. Specifically for compounds used in medicines sold by folk healers and herbalists."

"Is this a police matter?"

"Yes."

"Does your investigation extend into Mexico?"

"No."

"Can you pay my fee?" Posada asked.

Posada charged a minimum of five thousand dollars for information. "Not all of it up front," Kerney admitted. "But I'm willing to trade. I'll give you a thousand dollars cash and provide advance warning when we plan to shut down the pipeline. If you move quickly, you should be able to corner the market and turn a tidy profit from the last shipments that cross the border."

Posada's eyes narrowed. "You know my fee is not negotiable. I see no reason to put my trust in you, given your past performance. It gives me great pleasure to refuse you, Señor Kerney. Please do not come back here again. Juan, would you show Señor Kerney out?"

Kerney got to his feet and bowed in Posada's direction. "Good-bye, señor," he said gravely. "I am sorry we were unable to do business."

"Old enmities die hard," Posada replied flatly.

Juan walked Kerney through the grand vestibule to the front door. "Señor Posada will not live much longer," he said.

"What will happen to you when he dies?"

"I hope to continue in the trade," Juan answered. "But the señor has severely cut back on his workload, and does not seem inclined to turn over the business to me. He has a niece who will inherit."

"I would welcome the opportunity to do business with you," Kerney proposed.

Juan made an empty gesture with his hands. "A thousand-dollar fee does not suffice, Mr. Kerney. Unlike the señor, I do not have the resources to act on the information you proposed as a trade."

"The expenses of starting out can be considerable," Kerney noted. "Is there something else that might satisfy you?"

"I would welcome the opportunity to have a permanent American visa. I would like to offer my services in the North American market without fear of legal entanglements."

"I believe that can be arranged. I know a customs agent who could be very helpful." Kerney held out the thousand dollars. The money disappeared into Juan's shirt pocket.

"Call me in two hours," Juan said, giving Kerney a phone number. "Señor Posada will be resting. We can exchange information then."

Kerney's contact in the El Paso U.S. Customs office was very interested in Juan as a potential long-term informant. After advising Juan on how to get in touch with the agent, Kerney wrote down Juan's information and hung up. He had a short list of three smugglers: two in El Paso and one in Deming, New Mexico, a small city thirty miles from the Mexican border. According to Juan, the market was highly specialized and controlled by only a few people operating in the States.

THE MOTELS IN SILVER CITY, mostly mom-and-pop businesses mixed in with a few budget franchise operations, were concentrated along the state highway that ran north from Deming. Cornelia Marquez was registered at a motel on the main drag fairly close to downtown. The establishment boasted a restaurant that looked out on the highway and featured a daily radio talk show aired by a local station.

Kerney stopped in for a light meal. His stomach was grumpy—the norm rather than the exception with half of his gut shot away—and he had to eat judiciously in order to keep it functioning properly.

The talk-show host, at a table with a microphone and two telephones, sat by the large plate-glass window taking calls about a small group of environmentalists who had used the courts to stop timber sales in the Gila. Loudspeakers let the customers listen in on the conversations. One caller phoned in to say that the members of the group had better stay the hell out of Catron County, since they were nothing but a gang of radicals who didn't know a damn thing about the west or its people. The customers, mostly working men in for a coffee break, applauded in agreement.

Kerney finished his meal as the subject of repealing the Endangered Species Act was introduced by the host. The first caller to respond wondered why the government thought spotted owls were more valuable than people. It kicked off a diatribe against Washington politicians.

Cornelia Marquez opened the motel-room door immediately after Kerney knocked. A matron in her fifties, of average height with a thickening body, she wore a plain tan dress and a pair of sensible flats. Her eyes were puffy and red and her mouth was drawn in a tight, sad line.

Kerney identified himself and showed the lady his badge.

"Nurse Perez said that you found my father," Cornelia said, sniffling. She stepped aside to let Kerney enter. "I am most grateful."

"It was nothing," Kerney replied. Something about her made him take a formal tone. "Would you rather I came to see you some other time?"

"No." Cornelia's smile was thin-lipped. "I would welcome some distraction. My husband cannot join me until this evening. He was in Argentina on business and is flying in from Buenos Aires."

She sat at the small table in front of the window and asked Kerney to join her. The room was a standard motel box with a queen-size bed, television, and dresser. A mirror and several silk-screen prints of desert flowers were securely fastened to the walls.

"Have you found who killed my son?" she asked.

"Not yet. If I knew why your son and father came here it might be helpful."

"How would that would be helpful? The state police investigator who spoke to me at the hospital said that Hector was shot by a stranger. A poacher."

"That is probably true," Kerney allowed. "But other possibilities cannot be ignored. Yesterday, I spoke to an older gentleman who said that he might have known your father many years ago. His name is Edgar Cox."

"The name is not familiar to me."

"Is there some reason for him to believe he knows your father?"

"It's possible. My father was born here. In the Mangas Valley. His ancestors settled the area. But he has lived in Mexico most of his life. Ever since he was a young man in medical school."

"Dr. Padilla seemed to have had a specific destination in mind. Do you have any idea why he went to Elderman Meadows?"

"I never heard of Elderman Meadows until today."

"How about a place called Mexican Hat?"

Cornelia frowned. "I have heard him speak of such a place."

"In what context?" Kerney asked.

She toyed with the band of her diamond wedding ring and wet her lips before answering. "My father has an obsession. He believes his father was murdered at Mexican Hat."

"What gave him that idea?" Kerney inquired.

"When my aunt died last year, he was the executor of her estate. She had many of the old family papers. Among them he found official letters from the American government to his father questioning the legal title to the land."

"What suspicions did those letters raise?"

"I'm not sure. He was very secretive about it."

"Why?"

"Because it opened an old wound between my parents. Long before I was born, my grandfather died and my parents traveled to New Mexico to attend the funeral. An argument developed between them. My father wished to drop out of medical school and remain in Mangas. Mother threatened to leave him if he did. They were newly married. She was also a medical student, and they had planned to go into practice together. But she hated New Mexico. It was not her world. It was too isolated and unsophisticated. She was a city girl. She made my father promise never to take her there again."

"And he kept his word?"

"Yes. Until the day my mother died, three months ago. There was really nothing for him to go back to. His brothers and sisters had scattered. The ranch was lost. The village abandoned."

"Did she share his theory that Don Luis was murdered?"

"I don't think she cared, one way or the other."

"So he returned with your son to uncover a murderer," Kerney proposed.

"Real or imagined," Cornelia agreed testily, her voice rising. "My father is gravely ill. Possibly he will never get better. And do you know how I feel, Señor Kerney? Right now, I am angry with him. To the depths of my soul, I am angry. My son is dead because of an old man's obsession with the past. It is senseless."

"I am truly sorry for your loss, señora," Kerney said.

Cornelia Marquez did not hear him. She buried her head in her hands and sobbed.

Kerney stayed with her until she stopped crying. When he left he took with him Señora Marquez's written permission to visit Jose Padilla in the hospital.

THE HOUSE Jim Stiles lived in, a hundred-year-old adobe with a high-pitched tin roof and buttresses at the corners to hold the adobe walls in place, sat in the valley exactly halfway between Reserve and the old Spanish settlement known as Lower San Francisco Plaza.

With his feet propped on a chair, Jim lounged at the kitchen table with the back door open, reading the documents found in Padilla's travel trailer. Omar Gatewood had given him permission to sign out the evidence and take it home.

The day had turned hot, but the thick walls kept the house cool. A slight breeze pulsed through the doorway, bringing with it the sound of the river gurgling over the rocky streambed two hundred yards away.

Stiles finished a document and turned it upside down on the

stack he'd already read. The papers and letters were all written in Spanish, and while Stiles spoke the language pretty well, he was much less proficient at translating the written word. What he could make out was damn interesting stuff, although it didn't seem to have a bit of relevance to the murder of Hector Padilla.

Among the papers were the last will and testament of Don Luis Padilla and a plat of the village of Mangas that had been filed with the territorial government over a hundred years ago. There were a lot of personal letters to Don Luis from important New Mexicans of the day. Solomon Luna and Thomas B. Catron, two political heavyweights during the first years of statehood, had written to Don Luis about investing in something called the American Valley Company, whatever the hell that was.

Until Stiles could find someone to do an adequate translation of the material, all he'd be able to tell Kerney was that José and Hector Padilla were descendants of the same clan that had settled the Mangas Valley, and that the government had challenged Padilla's title to his landholdings back in the early thirties.

The phone rang just as Stiles started in on another letter. He grabbed the receiver from the wall-mounted telephone, hoping it was Kerney.

"Hombre," Amador Ortiz said. "I hear you've changed jobs."

"What are you talking about, Amador?"

"The Silver City newspaper, Jimmy. It says you and Kerney are working for the sheriff and the district attorney."

"Shit! That story was supposed to be killed."

Amador chuckled. "You know you can't keep a secret around here. So is it true?"

"It's a temporary thing. I'm still with Game and Fish. What's up?"

"I've been thinking about Kerney wanting to know if I saw anything suspicious around Mangas Mountain."

"What have you got?" Stiles tried to hold back the excitement from his voice.

"Maybe nothing. You know that old mine at the upper end of Padilla Canyon, north of the lookout tower? Last week I was with my crew barricading the road to the mine to keep hikers out of the canyon. I saw some tire tracks."

"What kind of tire tracks?"

"Looked like an ATV to me. This morning I got to thinking you can get to the meadows from the upper canyon, pretty easy. At least you could before we blocked the road. A game trail runs from the mine to the meadows. Elk use it a lot. I thought maybe you'd want to pass that on to Kerney."

"Hell yes. Thanks, *mano,*" Stiles said.

"*De nada, primo.* You owe me a beer at Cattleman's if you find something."

"You got it," Stiles responded.

He hung up the phone, went quickly into a small second bedroom that served as his study, and pawed through the quadrangle maps on the desk. If he remembered correctly, it was maybe a two-hour hike from the mouth of Padilla Canyon to the mine.

Stiles found the map and studied the contours. It was a no-sweat walk in the woods. With the map in his back pocket, he returned to the kitchen, gathered up Padilla's papers, and stuffed them into a manila envelope. He whistled to himself as he left the house and fired up the truck. He switched the radio frequency to the sheriff's department, and called in to report he was operational.

When the dispatcher responded, he gave his destination and ETA, and left a message for Kerney to meet him at Padilla Canyon.

He thought about waiting for Kerney or asking for backup, and dismissed the idea. It would only slow him down. Besides, if Amador was right, he might have the first break in the case. That would make Kerney sit up and take notice.

Damn! Nobody had thought to look north of the meadows in Padilla Canyon. The search had been concentrated south into the foothills and valley. He'd buy Amador a case of beer if the tip panned out.

Stiles reached down and hit the switch to the emergency lights. He'd run with lights flashing all the way to the mouth of Padilla Canyon. It would save him a good thirty minutes.

UNEXPECTEDLY SUMMONED to a meeting, Carol Cassidy sat in the small conference room at the Glenwood District Office with the forest supervisor from Silver City, the regional forester from Albuquerque, and Charlie Perry. Samuel Ellsworth Aldrich, the acting regional forester, a heavy-boned man with a double chin and thick lips, presided over the meeting. He had his suit jacket off, shirt sleeves rolled up, and tie loosened. He was smiling pleasantly at Carol.

Charlie and the regional forester were across the table. Perry whispered something to Aldrich, who nodded automatically back at Charlie. Jack Wyman, the forest supervisor and Carol's boss, a contemporary she had worked with for a number of years, avoided looking at her. It was not going to be a cordial meeting.

Aldrich concluded his opening remarks, which consisted of bitching about being unable to get out into the field as often as he would like. He spread his hands palms down on the table and gave Carol a patronizing smile.

"Thanks for coming down on such short notice, Carol," he said, nodding in Wyman's direction. "Jack and I have some concerns we'd like to discuss with you."

"I'd like to hear them, Sam," Carol replied, wondering what in the hell was brewing. Her annual operational review by the regional office was months away. There had to be a special reason Aldrich wanted to see her.

"I got a telephone call this morning from an Associated Press reporter," Aldrich went on. "She wanted to know if the Catron County sheriff and the ADA had usurped the state police investigation in the Elderman Meadows murder case. I told her I didn't have a clue what she was talking about. So she faxed me a copy of an article from the Silver City newspaper. She told me Gatewood gave the story to the newspaper. Have you seen it?"

"Yes."

"Is it accurate?"

"It is. Sheriff Gatewood called me after the fact to tell me about the appointments. I had no prior knowledge."

"I'll accept that." Aldrich stopped to clear his throat.

You damn well better, Carol thought to herself.

"To make a long story short, I called Jack for a briefing on the situation and he didn't know anything about it either. Charlie Perry filled me in. He was meeting with Jack when I called."

"You could have called me, Sam," Carol said, "instead of relying on secondhand information." She shot a hard look in Charlie's direction. "From a reporter," she added.

Aldrich smiled charmingly. "That's why you're here. And that's why I flew in from Albuquerque to meet with you. What, exactly, is going on?"

"To set the record straight, the investigation hasn't been usurped. I've assigned an experienced investigator who is working in tandem with a state Game and Fish officer on the poaching case only. Since the poaching and the murder may be tied together, it seemed the sensible thing to do."

Aldrich shook his head in disagreement. "That's not how the state police feel about it. I got a call from the chief. He isn't happy with Sheriff Gatewood, the ADA, or you. Thinks the story is bad press for his department and nothing more than small-town political posturing. I tend to agree. As hard as I tried to stop it, a follow-up article on our unusual involvement in the case is going to hit the Albuquerque paper this afternoon. And I've had calls from two television reporters while we were waiting for you to arrive. They're asking pointed questions. Has the Forest Service lost confidence in the state police? Why have a ranger and a Game and Fish officer been given authority by an assistant district attorney and the local sheriff to investigate a murder case? We've got a damage-control problem here, Carol. There is already too much resentment about the Forest Service in the community. It has to be solved quickly."

Carol saw the writing on the wall. "How do you want it solved?"

"The man you assigned to the investigation . . ." Aldrich thumbed through some papers. "Kevin Kerney. He's a temporary employee, correct?"

"That's right. Hired out of your office."

"Terminate him. I want you and the district out of this before it becomes an imbroglio. My staff has prepared a press release which should put the matter to rest. It will clearly state that we see a conflict of interest in having one of our employees reporting to another law enforcement agency, and that Mr. Kerney has been released from his job so that he can pursue the investigation for the district attorney."

"That's not fair to a man who has done excellent work for me," Carol said evenly.

"He may well be outstanding, but now he's a liability. If he's so damn good, the district attorney's office can put him on their payroll. I've got ranchers and environmentalists barking at my heels. I don't need to have the state police and others in the law enforcement community joining in the chorus. Terminate him."

Carol stood up. Jack Wyman's eyes were lowered. Charlie Perry was twiddling a pencil between his fingers, looking pleased.

She decided to test a growing realization. "I'll assign someone else to cover the poaching case."

"That won't be necessary," Aldrich replied. "Charlie will handle it."

"I see," Carol said, heading for the door. "It's good to see you again, Sam. Come visit more often."

Aldrich's charm returned. "I will, Carol."

Wyman gave her a weak smile and Charlie nodded a haughty goodbye as Carol closed the door behind her.

After getting over being steamed with Aldrich and his spineless bureaucratic meddling, Carol was back in her office when an idea came to her. In spite of Aldrich's order to fire Kerney, maybe she had some latitude. It was worth thinking about.

6

The road to the old mine in Padilla Canyon ended abruptly at a new rock barrier and fence that forced Jim Stiles to travel on foot. He checked his day pack to make sure he was adequately equipped. With a flashlight, water, freeze-dried rations, flares, matches, a first-aid kit, sweater, and a lightweight tarp, he could handle just about any situation. He added a hand-held radio and his holstered sidearm to the pack, slipped his arms through the shoulder straps, and started out at a brisk pace.

The new trail, built by Amador's crew, soon separated from the road and scaled the canyon wall. Jim stayed on the roadbed, searching for any indication of motorized travel. Halfway up, he found a pull tab to a beverage can in the fine sand of a small arroyo that cut across the road. He bagged it, made a search of the area, found nothing more, and moved on. Beyond him, the new trail dipped to a low ledge before twisting up the side of the canyon. He scrambled to the trail and scanned the old road in both directions. A glimmer of reflected light in a cluster of boulders caught his eye. He climbed down to investigate. It was an aluminum beer can. Using a twig to retrieve it, he bagged the container and put it in his pack.

The canyon, wide at the mouth, narrowed as it ran against Mangas Mountain. Tree cover thickened until the forest canopy cut off his view of the lookout tower on the peak. The canyon closed in sharply before it fanned out into a small clearing at the mine. All that remained at the site was the rubble of a stone cabin, a few rotted pilings that once held up a wooden sluice used to divert water from a small creek, and a ramp with tracks for ore carts that ran from the shaft to where the canyon floor met the creek.

The creek was still running. Jim splashed water on his face before shedding his pack and looking around. Maybe Amador had seen evidence of an ATV, but all Jim could find were elk tracks near the creek that trailed off in the direction of Little Springs, the last watering spot before the meadows. It wasn't surprising; wind and recent rain would have erased any tread signs.

Stiles turned his attention to the mine. Above the shaft entrance a horizontal row of logs braced by two vertical timbers held back the hillside. The entrance, trussed with a thick beam and joists, was square-cut and less than six feet high. He crawled in, flashlight in hand. The chamber plunged abruptly, the angled walls supported by heavy timbering above the ore-cart tracks. It looked decidedly unsafe. The beam of his flashlight was swallowed up by the darkness of the tunnel.

Disappointed, Jim sat back on his heels. There was no way he could climb down without a rope and someone to pull him up in case he ran into trouble. He crawled out, stood up, and felt something sticky on his knees. His jeans were stained with motor oil. He rubbed a finger on the smudges and sniffed it to make sure. There was no doubt.

Back in the mine he found an area saturated with oil. Smiling to himself, Jim worked on a scenario. Any poacher who knew his business would scout the meadow on foot until he was sure of the cougar's territory. An elusive animal rarely seen in the wild, a mountain lion could range up to fifty square miles in two days or less. It would take a lot of stealth and patience to bring the animal down, and driving an ATV deep into the cougar's range would spook it and defeat any possibility of a sighting. The old mine was a good place to stash the ATV while hunting the cat.

It plays out, Stiles thought. The killer had to know that the Padilla Canyon road was closed the day he took the mountain lion and shot Hector Padilla. So he followed the horse trail partway with the ATV, hiked in, baited his trap, and waited at the shooter's blind. He was probably in position long before the mountain lion appeared to take the bait. Only an experienced, patient hunter could pull it off.

He sopped up the oil with a handkerchief and put it into his shirt pocket, thinking a lab analysis might help identify the type of vehicle that had been hidden in the mine.

Outside, Jim nestled the flashlight under his armpit and bent over to brush the grime off his jeans. As he straightened up, he felt the bullet slam into his left side. The impact drove him against the cliff. A second round missed, splintered rock fragments into his face, and blinded him. It felt as if he had been gouged by dozens of flaming-hot barbs. He lay where he fell, unable to see, pain searing down his arm. He couldn't tell if the first shot had passed through his upper arm into his lung. The shots had come from above him on the canyon rim. The shooter would have to work his way down to confirm his kill.

He stayed motionless, opened his eyes, and saw nothing. He thought about trying to crawl to the day pack for his handgun and gave up on the idea. Even if he could make it to the pack, he couldn't see to shoot. He would play dead and hope his sight came back. He listened intently, trying to make out the crunch of footsteps, the whisper of movement through the trees, the sound of snapping twigs. He felt pretty stupid about coming up the canyon alone. Then he lost consciousness.

KERNEY ARRIVED at the Catron County Sheriff's Department expecting to find Jim Stiles stashed away in a cubbyhole studying José Padilla's papers. Instead, he encountered a lone dispatcher in the outer office who looked like a younger version of Omar Gatewood, with the same puffy cheeks and stocky frame.

Kerney introduced himself and asked for Stiles.

"Ain't here," the boy replied. "He's up in Padilla Canyon."

"Doing what?"

"Don't know. Said for you to meet him there. At the old mine."

"When did he leave?"

"About three hours ago."

Kerney pointed to the radio. "Call him up."

"Can't," the kid replied. "Transmitter won't reach into the canyon. It's a blind spot."

"Who can talk to him?"

"The forest lookout on Mangas can," the kid replied.

"Call," Kerney suggested. "See if they've had any contact with Stiles."

"Sure thing."

The kid made contact, and Kerney listened to the conversation. There had been no communication between Stiles and the lookout tower.

The kid looked up at Kerney. "Anything else?"

"Who's working in the tower?"

"Henry Lujan."

"Ask Henry the quickest way to get to Padilla Canyon."

"I can tell you that," the kid replied.

"Fine. Then ask Henry to get Stiles on the radio. Tell him to keep trying until he gets a response."

"Ten-four," the kid replied. He passed along the message and gave Kerney directions to Padilla Canyon.

"Put search and rescue on standby," Kerney said, as he headed for the door. "And tell your father."

The kid's eyes brightened. This might turn out to be as good as the Elderman Meadows murder. He was keying the microphone before the door slammed behind Kerney.

KERNEY FOUND JIM'S TRUCK and started up the trail at a fast pace, his anger with Stiles building as he ran. Going into the canyon alone was dumb, and failing to call in made it worse—raising the possibility that something had gone wrong.

He pushed himself to run faster, and his knee almost buckled in protest. He hated the damn thing for slowing him down. The pain that ran like a spike up his thigh he could handle, it was the permanent subpar performance the knee caused that really pissed him off.

Finally the knee locked up and he was forced into a slow trot. Pockets of white clouds, empty of any rain, blocked the late-afternoon sun and cooled him down, but he had lost a lot of body fluid and his mouth felt like dry cotton. He started sprinting again when he saw Stiles sprawled in front of the mine entrance. Breathing hard, he reached Jim and bent over his body. He was alive but unconscious. His face was a bloody mess, and his left eyelid was almost torn off. A bullet had cut through muscle in Jim's left arm and he was bleeding freely. On the ground were the shattered remains of a flashlight. Using his handkerchief as a tourniquet Kerney stemmed the flow of blood and checked Jim's pulse. It was fast and erratic, and his skin felt cool to the touch.

Jim's day pack yielded a first-aid kit. Working as quickly as possible, Kerney cut off the sleeve with a pocket knife, cleaned the wound with hydrogen peroxide, and bandaged it. When he saw the small dark stain on Jim's shirt pocket he flinched. Quickly he ripped the shirt open and found nothing but a deep bruise on the rib cage. If the flashlight casing and batteries hadn't stopped the bullet, Stiles would be dead.

He pulled a soggy handkerchief from Jim's shirt pocket and took a whiff. It smelled like motor oil.

Using the hand-held radio, Kerney called Henry Lujan at the lookout tower, gave his location, and reported an officer down. He picked Stiles up, carried him to the creek, stretched him on the ground, raised his feet, and covered him with a sweater and tarp from the day pack. He flushed Jim's face with water, cleaning off the blood and some of the rock fragments, working carefully around the eyes.

Then he gently put gauze over each eye and taped them for protection. Stiles moaned as Kerney finished up.

"You're going to live," Kerney said.

"Jesus, Kerney, is that you?"

"It's me."

"I can't see a fucking thing."

"Your eyes are patched."

"Am I blind?"

"I don't think so. Who shot you?"

"Didn't see him. It happened too fast. The son of a bitch probably followed me up the canyon."

"No. I saw only your tracks on the way in. Who knew you were coming?"

Stiles forced a small laugh. "Probably half the county. I used the police frequency to give my destination. Every citizen with a scanner could have been listening."

Kerney started stuffing some aspirin in Jim's mouth.

"What are you doing?" Stiles mumbled, his mouth half full of capsules, as Kerney put the canteen to Jim's mouth.

"Aspirin," he explained. "It will dull the pain a bit." Kerney watched Stiles drink deeply. When Jim finished, he treated himself to a swallow, and looked around for a chopper landing site. The canyon was too narrow for a helicopter to fly in, and there was no adequate clearing where it could set down. He looked back at Jim. Stiles needed to get to a hospital as quickly as possible.

"Can you walk?" Kerney asked.

"Help me up," Stiles replied weakly.

Kerney stuffed the gear back into the pack, slung it over his arm, got Stiles to his feet, and walked him a few yards down the canyon. Jim leaned heavily against him, wobbly and uncoordinated. Walking him out wasn't going to work; he would have to be carried. Kerney put the day pack on Stiles and slung the man on his back. When Jim protested that he could make it under his own steam, Kerney told him to shut up.

Each time Kerney stopped for a brief rest, Jim told him a bit more of what had happened. They heard the chopper long before it passed overhead, and soon the distant sound of sirens echoed through the mountains. Kerney picked up the pace. After a long stretch without stopping, Kerney stumbled and almost fell flat on his face. He put Stiles down and collapsed next to him.

"Almost there," he said, gasping, trying not to sound completely winded. His chest was heaving, and his knee felt as if someone had pounded it with a hammer.

"Let me try to walk."

"There's no need," Kerney replied. Four search-and-rescue team members came into view, trotting quickly up the canyon. "We're about to be rescued."

Stiles turned his head in the direction of Kerney's voice. "Did I remember to thank you?"

"You just did," Kerney answered, removing the day pack from Jim's back.

He turned Stiles over to a paramedic, who did a quick check of vital signs, started an IV, elevated Jim's feet, and wrapped him in a blanket. The patches over Jim's eyes were removed, the damage quickly assessed, and fresh dressings applied. Kerney's spirits sank as the paramedic pointed to his own left eye, shook his head, and made a face, before ordering his companions to put Jim on a stretcher.

Kerney followed the men to the landing zone. No time was

wasted getting Jim in the chopper and on his way to the hospital. At the barricade a half mile farther down the canyon, he found a gathering of men and vehicles, including Omar Gatewood, two deputy sheriffs, a Game and Fish officer, and one of Carol Cassidy's permanent rangers. For some unexplained reason, two sheriff's patrol cars had emergency lights flashing, the colors almost completely washed out in the bright aquamarine sky. It must be for crowd control, Kerney reckoned, eyeing the canyon, empty except for the small circle of men, thinking that he was starting to catch Jim's offbeat sense of humor.

Sheriff Gatewood pulled Kerney aside for a briefing. They stood next to Gatewood's patrol unit. The police radio cracked with traffic about the ambush.

"What in the hell happened up there?" Gatewood demanded.

Kerney filled Gatewood in with an absolute minimum of facts.

"Who would want to shoot him?" Gatewood asked, as though Kerney could supply the answer.

"The more important question is *why* was Jim shot," Kerney proposed.

"Hell if I know," Gatewood admitted, tugging an earlobe. "I'll send the boys up the road to see what they can find." He waved his hand in a come-here gesture at the officers. "Give your boss a call," he added. "She wants to see you."

"What's up?"

"Can't say," Omar said, bending down to brush dirt off his shiny boots with a handkerchief. He walked to meet the officers halfway, issued some orders, and caught up with Kerney at his truck. "I'm going to make sure Jim gets a special commendation out of this."

"That's a good idea," Kerney replied, trying to bite back the sarcasm. It didn't work. "After you do that, why don't you dispatch a deputy to patrol the Mangas road and get a reconnaissance chopper in the air, just on the off chance they may spot somebody coming out of the forest."

Gatewood's expression changed to a scowl. "You got a bad habit of telling me what to do, Kerney. You know that?"

"Wrong, Gatewood. I'm just suggesting that maybe you ought to get your priorities straight." He threw Jim's day pack in the cab, fired up the truck, and left Gatewood in a puff of road dust. In the rearview mirror he saw Omar bending down to brush off his boots with a handkerchief one more time.

The early-evening sky was a banner of pink-and-white clouds bordered by azure blue. Kerney checked his watch. Quitting time had come and gone. Carol was probably at home. He'd swing by and see her.

CHARLIE PERRY drove past as Kerney turned onto the road to the compound where Carol and her family lived. Kerney waved at Charlie to be polite and got a quick nod in exchange.

Carol's husband answered Kerney's knock, invited him inside, and had him wait in the front room. With a piano against one wall, a loom with an unfinished weaving next to a window, and the remaining space filled with homey overstuffed chairs and oak furniture, the room felt both cluttered and comfortable. Carol came out of the kitchen, drying her hands on a dish towel.

"I've been listening to the scanner," she said, before Kerney could greet her. "Is Jim going to be all right?"

"I think he'll make it."

"Thank goodness." She draped the dish towel on the arm of a chair and sat down. "Please," she said, motioning to another chair across from her.

Kerney joined her. "You wanted to see me?"

"Yes. There's no easy way to say this, so I'll just barge ahead. I've been ordered to fire you."

Kerney took it in. "Is that why Charlie Perry was here?"

"Peripherally. He's been given the mountain lion case."

"Any particular reason why?"

"Because the acting regional forester, who's something of a barracuda, decided my decision to use you on the investigation was illadvised. Charlie kissed up to him and got the assignment."

"Are you in trouble?" Kerney asked.

"No way. Charlie hasn't got that kind of juice. Neither does the regional forester."

"So what's this really about?" Kerney inquired.

Carol shrugged. "Public relations. Bad press. Inability to take the heat. You name it. Aldrich got bitched at by the state police chief and grilled by some reporters. Seems that Omar Gatewood's press release raised the attention of the media."

"That man is a real work of art."

Carol shook her head. "Tell me about it. I chewed him out for not including me in on the plan."

"I assumed you knew."

"Not until I read it in the newspaper."

Kerney gave Carol an apologetic look. "I should have told you what was happening. Are you sure you're not in hot water?"

"Not to worry. I already told you I wasn't." Carol stopped talking for a minute. "You seem more concerned about me than your-self."

Kerney laughed. "It hasn't sunk in yet. I've never been fired before."

"I haven't told anyone about your termination, although I'm sure Charlie Perry will get the word out, if he hasn't already. So, I'm giving you two weeks' notice, and placing you on administrative leave with pay. Technically, your commission will remain valid till then."

"Do you want me to work undercover?"

Carol's eyes flashed. "You bet I do. Especially after what happened to Jim Stiles. Now it's personal. I like that young man a hell of a lot. This shooting wasn't a random act of violence. It couldn't be. It has to be tied in with the murder at Elderman Meadows. Are you game?"

"More than game," Kerney replied.

"Catch the bastard, Kevin."

"It would give me great pleasure."

"Two weeks," Carol reminded him. "That's all the time I can squeeze out for you without being insubordinate."

"A lot can happen in two weeks," he replied.

HENRY LUJAN, the seasonal employee who manned the lookout tower on Mangas Mountain, gave Kerney a tour. The building, an elevated room on steel pillars with an outside deck that ran around the perimeter of the structure, was glassed on all sides. The amenities consisted of an outdoor privy situated under a tree at the base of the structure and a holding tank for drinking water, replenished by truck as needed.

Kerney walked the deck with Henry, a college student in his

third year as a summer worker. The views in every direction were incredible, especially to the west, where a blood-red sunset slashed across the horizon. Lujan pointed out some landmarks before taking Kerney inside: a mountain top in Arizona, the solitary Allegros Peak on the Continental Divide, and the barely visible plateau that marked the sacred Zuni Salt Lake.

"I can't believe what's been going on around here," Henry said. He hitched himself into a sitting position on a counter that held communication equipment, his feet dangling off the floor. He was about five feet five with a well-developed upper body. He had an easygoing style. "First the thing at Elderman Meadows, and now Jim Stiles getting shot." He shook his head in disbelief. "Too much, man."

"Jim talked to you about Elderman Meadows."

"Yeah. The same day it happened. There wasn't much I could tell him. I don't pay any attention to the meadows. Nobody goes in there except our people and Game and Fish."

"What were you doing at the time?"

Lujan nodded at the cot in the corner of the room. He had a young face for his age, bony and not yet fleshed-out. Under the cot was a set of barbells. A color television on a metal stand stood at the foot of the cot. "I was crashed. The radio traffic woke me up. Weekends, I work split shifts because we've got more people camping in the forest. Mornings and nights, that's when I work. When the man-made fire danger is the greatest. Campfires. Cigarettes. That kind of stuff."

"So you were asleep?"

"Yeah. I heard Stiles call in that you'd found that old man. I listened for a minute and went back to sleep."

"You didn't get up to take a look?"

Lujan laughed. "Look at what? I can't see anything through the forest canopy. I didn't start scanning the meadows until you reported finding a dead body. By then I was awake."

"Did you see anyone today in the vicinity of Padilla Canyon?"

Lujan pushed himself off the counter, got a pair of field glasses, gave them to Kerney, and pointed in the direction of Padilla Canyon. "That's almost impossible for me to do. Take a look for yourself. The canyon is hidden by timberland. You can't even tell it's there, except for a few small breaks in the cover. I can't see anything."

Kerney trained the glasses where Henry had pointed. The kid was right. All he could see in the fading light was a faint gash of the deep ravine obscured by forest. "Did you have any visitors?"

"Today? Just you."

"How often do you report in by radio?"

"Every hour I log onto the fire watch system. That's during working shifts. I keep the scanner going and the radio on all the time."

Kerney handed Lujan the field glasses. It should be easy to verify Henry's schedule. "Do you know a fast way to get from Mangas Campground to Padilla Canyon?"

"Maybe fly?" Lujan suggested with a grin and a shrug. "I haven't the foggiest. Hiking isn't something I'm into. Besides, some of the trails are new. Not even on the map yet."

"But you can see some trails from here," Kerney proposed.

"Sure. I'll do a visual sweep if someone's reported lost or overdue. Otherwise, I concentrate on general surveillance."

Next to the cot was a workbench with some tools and a partially disassembled portable shortwave radio—one of the old vacuum-tube models. "I hear you're going to college," Kerney said.

"Yeah. I just finished my second year at Western New Mexico in Silver City."

Kerney looked at the workbench. "What's your major? Electronics?"

"No, it's forestry. I bought the radio at a garage sale for ten bucks. It doesn't work. I'm just tinkering with it to see if I can fix it. It passes the time when there's nothing good on the tube."

"Sounds like fun. Play any sports?"

"What? Oh, you mean my weights. I wrestled in high school. Don't have the time for it now, so I work out just to stay in shape."

"Good idea." It was dark outside. The blackness of the forest was vast, interrupted by the dim lights of the few small hamlets that shimmered like frail earthbound stars in the valleys. It was time to get going. "How well do you know Amador Ortiz?" Kerney asked.

"He's my uncle," Henry replied. "He helped to get me this job when I graduated from high school."

"Did he talk to you about seeing tire tracks in Padilla Canyon?"

"If he did, I don't remember it."

"Do you keep any guns up here?"

"I don't, but there's a twenty-two rifle behind the door. It belongs to the Forest Service. You can look at it if you like."

Kerney knew it hadn't been a twenty-two that put the hole in Jim's arm. "That's not necessary. Thanks, Henry."

"Come back and visit anytime. And tell Jim I'm sorry about what happened. Tell him to hang in there."

"I'll do that."

Henry walked Kerney to the deck, watched him climb stiffly down the ladder and get in his truck. He waved as Kerney drove out of sight. Inside, he wrote down the time of Kerney's visit in his daily log, made a quick visual sweep with the field glasses, and started working on the shortwave radio.

DR. HARRISON WALKER, ophthalmologist, surgeon, and former Army medic with two Vietnam tours to his credit, walked into the lobby of the Gila Regional Medical Center. Visiting hours were over, and the lobby was empty except for one man, sprawled in a chair, fast asleep. A pile of papers had spilled from his chest onto the cushion. From personal experience, Harrison Walker knew what it meant to keep a vigil for a buddy. If he was hurt, you had to be there for him, period. End of story. It was a code Walker believed in and liked to see practiced by others. He picked up the papers and glanced at them. Some were official documents and others were handwritten letters, all in Spanish.

The fatigue etched on Kerney's face made Walker reluctant to wake him up. From what Walker knew about the incident in Padilla Canyon, Kerney had found Stiles, treated his wounds, and carried him out most of the way on a badly damaged leg.

Walker shook the man gently awake. "Mr. Kerney."

Kerney's eyes snapped open. "Doctor," he replied, sitting up.

"Mr. Stiles is in his room, and his parents have gone home. You can have a couple of minutes with him. Then I'm going to kick your ass out and order you to get some rest."

Kerney smiled in agreement. "How are his eyes?"

"The fragment cut a ligament and damaged the cornea in his left eye. It missed the optic nerve but partially detached the retina. I've repaired the damage. The right eye was a breeze—mostly fine grains of rock dust with one small perforation. He can use it, although things may be fuzzy for a day or two. He'll keep his vision."

"That's good news. Thanks, Doctor."

"Thank you for patching him up and helping to get him here quickly. It reduced the chances of further damage." Harrison stopped, studied Kerney's face, and shook his finger. "I'm serious about you needing some sleep. You look like shit."

"Is that a medical opinion?"

"It's an expert medical opinion," Harrison retorted. "You'd do well to act on it."

"I believe it."

Harrison held out the documents. "You may need these."

"Thanks, Doc," Kerney said, taking the papers.

Kerney found Stiles awake in his bed, his left eye covered with a dressing wrapped around his head. The surgical team had repaired the muscle damage in his arm. There were bouquets of flowers from the Fraternal Order of Police and the Game and Fish Department on the bedside table.

"You look like shit," Jim said, holding out his hand.

Kerney grabbed it and squeezed. "I thought you couldn't see anything."

Jim grinned. "I can see your ugly face. Dr. Walker said maybe all I'll need is physical therapy to strengthen the eye muscles."

"That's great." Kerney searched Jim's face. It was still a mess. At least two dozen shrapnel wounds had been repaired, some requiring stitches to close the lacerations. "And the arm?"

"The bullet missed the bone. It's my face I'm worried about. I look like I have permanent chicken pox."

"You're not going to be pretty for a while," Kerney agreed. "But then you never were."

"Thanks a lot."

Kerney sank into the chair next to the bed, grateful to be off his feet.

"You missed my parents. I wanted you to meet them."

"I just got here," he fibbed. "Some other time."

"Count on it. My dad said my department wants to give me a commendation. Omar Gatewood called and told him. Can you believe it? An award for getting ambushed."

"Let them do it."

"Are you serious?"

"You take a risk every time you put on a badge and gun. That counts."

"I suppose you're right." Jim's mouth was dry from the anesthesia. He took a sip of water. "Did you bring my day pack?"

"It's in my truck. Do you need it?"

"No, you do. I picked up an empty beer can on the road to the mine. It's in a plastic bag along with a pull tab. See if you can get any prints off them."

"That's a long shot."

"I know it. One more thing—when you pop open a cold one, do you pull off the tab before you take a drink?"

Kerney looked at him quizzically. "No. What's your point?"

Jim smiled. "I do. Sometimes my mustache gets caught on the tab. It hurts like hell when it happens. The beer can I found didn't have a tab."

"So I should look for a guy with a mustache who drinks beer?" Kerney ventured.

"Unless you know a woman with a really hairy upper lip," Stiles countered.

"You've narrowed the field down to one gender. Good thinking," Kerney replied in mock seriousness.

"It's a clue," Jim shot back. "I can't be expected to do everything for you."

"You can do something for me." Kerney dropped José Padilla's papers on the bed. He had read through the documents before falling asleep in the waiting room. "Use your contacts and find somebody to research the history of the Padilla ranch. I want to know everything about the American Valley Company. Incorporators. Stockholders. How it was organized. What happened to that part of it Don Luis Padilla owned. And I need a search of newspaper archives on the Padillas, especially anything having to do with the death of José's father."

"I know just the person to recruit," Stiles said with a grin.

"As long as he's trustworthy and can keep a tight lip," Kerney cautioned.

"*She's* absolutely trustworthy," Jim replied, with a smile.

"Good enough."

"Sorry I fucked up today. Thanks again for bailing me out."

"Learn from it," Kerney replied. "You don't have a job that allows for poor judgment."

Jim took the criticism like a slap in the face, and Kerney wished he could erase his words. He patted Jim's hand. "Forget I said that. I'm dead on my feet and you're all shot up. You don't need me ragging on you. I'm just glad you didn't get yourself killed."

Jim's smile came back. "Well, that's some consolation."

He left Stiles and stopped by the ICU. The state police had pulled security off the door. He rang the buzzer. The duty nurse, a man with an amiable expression, opened up. Kerney asked to see José Padilla.

The nurse sadly shook his head. "He died two hours ago."

"Thanks." Kerney turned on his heel and left, stewing over the information. It was the perfect end to a shitty day, he thought. He had been counting on the old man for some answers. He swallowed hard against the memory of his ill-timed scolding of Jim Stiles. It had been poor form and bad manners, coming as it had on the heels of Jim's expression of gratitude.

He drove to a motel, got a room, soaked his knee with a hot compress, and collapsed in a stupor on the bed.

7

It was early morning when Kerney turned the corner of the hospital corridor on his way to see Jim before leaving Silver City. He almost ran over Karen Cox. She wore black linen trousers and a vanilla-colored jacket over a silk shirt. It made her seem even more willowy.

"How's Jim doing?" he asked, glancing down the hallway to the hospital room where Stiles temporarily resided.

"He seems okay, thankfully. I expect a full briefing from you."

"Whenever you say."

"Not now. I'm running late. I understand you had a talk with my father," she said. "What was that about?"

"Didn't he tell you?"

"I'd like to hear your version."

"According to your father, he came to the hospital on Sunday to find out if José Padilla was someone he once knew."

Karen blinked. Kerney waited for more of a reaction.

"And?" she demanded.

"He's not sure," Kerney replied. "But if it turns out that Padilla is an old acquaintance, your father may be a source of information."

Faced with confirmation that her father had lied to her about his meeting with Kerney, Karen struggled to keep her composure. "What did you learn about José Padilla?" she asked.

Kerney read the distress in Karen's eyes. "He was born here. He was attending medical school in Mexico City when his father died. He came back because he believed his father, Don Luis, was murdered sixty years ago."

Karen's tone became guarded. "I thought the working hypothesis was that Hector Padilla was shot to protect the poacher's identity."

"That's one motive," Kerney said. "Another is that the killer simply panicked when Hector came on the scene. A third motive is that the killing might be tied to José and Hector Padilla's arrival in Catron County to look into the death of Don Luis."

"When can I talk to José Padilla?"

"You can't. He died last night. What I've learned was supplied by his daughter, who came up from Mexico City."

"I want to talk to her."

Kerney told Karen where Cornelia Marquez was staying.

She nodded, broke eye contact, looked at her wristwatch, and glanced at him impatiently. "Anything else?"

"What can you tell me?" Kerney leaned forward to test Karen's reaction. She inched back from him. Something had her uptight.

"I have no new information."

"Do you think your father is holding something back?"

"Why would he do that?"

"I don't know." He held out the special investigator commission card. "Here. Take it. I'm afraid you can't borrow my services any longer."

Karen looked from the card to Kerney's face, her expression vexed. "What's this all about?"

Kerney shrugged. "Politics. I got fired. Read the morning paper."

"What will you do?"

"I'll think of something," he said, placing the card in Karen's hand.

She reached out and touched Kerney on the arm. "I'm sorry."

"Me too. I was looking forward to working with you."

She reacted with a flush of agreement in her voice. "I still need you to fill me in on what happened."

"I will." He left her standing in the hallway and paid a quick visit to Jim.

"You just missed Karen," Jim said. He was propped up in bed with two pillows stuffed behind his head.

Kerney nodded. "How are you doing?"

"The food sucks and I want to go home."

Full vision was back in Jim's right eye, but the doctor wanted to keep him under observation for another day. His arm was sore as hell. They talked a bit about José Padilla's death, and Jim promised he'd redouble his research efforts now that the only potential eyewitness was gone.

Kerney groaned at the pun and waved goodbye. Jim belly-laughed as Kerney left the room.

As Kerney crossed the lobby he saw Karen in the gift shop buying the morning paper. For someone who was running late, he wondered why she was still at the hospital. He dismissed the thought as he walked outside. Carol Cassidy's decision to give him two extra weeks to solve the case was a nice gesture, but Kerney had already decided before the offer was made to nail the perpetrator, no matter how long it took. He hated leaving a job unfinished, and Jim Stiles deserved to have the asshole who shot him caught.

KAREN BOUGHT THE PAPER and looked at the wall clock in the gift shop. Her parents were due to arrive soon for Mom's appointment with the doctor, and Karen had made arrangements to go to work late so she could be with them when they received the results of the biopsy. Mom had made sure Daddy knew that Karen had been told about the cancer. Both had welcomed her demand to be included in on the meeting with the doctor.

She was angry at her father—much more so than before. He had lied to her twice. She wanted to believe that his lies were inconsequential, motivated by his desire to protect her from his personal conflict with Eugene. But now it seemed more damaging. Raising the issue with him today was out of the question. She wondered if bringing it up with him at all was the right way to go. Maybe she needed to do some digging on her own before broaching the subject again.

She folded the newspaper under her arm and walked to the hospital cafeteria. It had just opened for business, and no one was in the serving line. She poured a cup of coffee, paid for it at the cashier's station, and carried it to an empty table in the corner of the dining room, away from the only other occupants, a surgical team dressed in green scrubs and plastic booties, sitting in an area reserved for hospital staff.

She took a sip, and opened the paper to the front page. The headline read:

FIRED RANGER RESCUES
WOUNDED GAME AND FISH OFFICER

Kevin Kerney, a ranger fired yesterday from his job with the Forest Service, rescued Game and Fish Officer James Stiles, who had been shot by an unknown assailant while investigating the murder of Hector Padilla, a Mexican national. According to the Catron County sheriff, Omar Gatewood, Kerney found Stiles, administered first aid and carried him out of a remote canyon in the Mangas Mountains north of Reserve to a waiting helicopter. Stiles, who was wounded in the arm, face and left eye, was airlifted to the Gila Regional Medical Center, where he is listed in satisfactory condition.

According to Dr. Harrison Walker, attending physician, Officer Stiles will make a complete recovery from his wounds. Walker credits Kerney for responding in a "timely and appropriate manner," and for "possibly saving Officer Stiles' life."

Kerney, who was released from his position with the Forest Service because of his appointment as a special investigator with the district attorney's office, served as the chief of detectives for the Santa Fe Police Department until a gun battle left him seriously wounded and forced him into retirement.

Kerney was fired from the Forest Service after having been enlisted by Assistant District Attorney Karen Cox to assist in the inquiry into the murder of Hector Padilla. Acting Regional Forester Samuel Aldrich released a press statement from his Albuquerque office saying "the investigation of a murder is not an appropriate function for Forest Service personnel. We regret having to terminate Mr. Kerney's temporary employment sooner than planned, but are pleased that he's now free to pursue his investigation for the district attorney's office without distraction."

Sheriff Gatewood, who commissioned Stiles to help his department investigate the Padilla murder, has announced that Stiles will receive special commendations for bravery from his office and the state Game and Fish Department. Stiles, Gatewood said, will continue to hold a commission with the sheriff's department until the murder of Padilla is solved. There are no suspects or new developments in the case, but police believe that the murder of Padilla and the wounding of Officer Stiles may be linked.

Last year, Kerney was praised by Dona Ana County Sheriff Andy Baca for solving the case of a murdered soldier at White Sands Missile Range and recovering historical artifacts stolen from the military installation. Kerney was serving as a lieutenant in the department at the time.

Carol Cassidy, supervisor of the Luna District Office, said that Kerney's performance on the job had been "exemplary." Assistant District Attorney Cox, who was recently appointed to her position, has not yet issued a statement. Attempts to reach Kevin Kerney for comment have been unsuccessful.

Coffee forgotten, she quickly scanned the related articles. Kerney deserved a hell of a lot better treatment than he was getting, she thought soberly. He had no choice but to turn in the commission card. The state law was very clear: without a full-time salaried law-enforcement job, Kerney could not legally serve as a special investigator. He was now simply a civilian with no police powers.

EDGAR COX walked between his wife and daughter into the bright midmorning sun, his mind racing. The lump in his wife's breast was cancerous, of that the doctor was certain. The fact had stunned Edgar into silence. Margaret and Karen had asked all the questions during the consultation, while Edgar looked on blankly. He had listened to the discussion with a feeling of unreality as the doctor recommended a mastectomy. Margaret had put on her reading glasses, and with handwritten notes taken from her purse, had begun asking questions: good, solid inquiries about alternative treatments and less intrusive procedures. Edgar had been amazed by her rock-solid performance. She was tough as nails. The meeting had ended with Margaret agreeing to the operation as soon as possible.

Margaret stopped and looked up at him. "You've been very quiet."

"I know. Sorry."

"Tell me what you're thinking," Margaret prodded.

"You're one tough cookie," Edgar replied, placing his arm around his wife's waist.

Margaret laughed and leaned against him. "Are you just finding that out?"

"No, I knew it the day I met you."

"How do you feel about the operation?"

"Scared," Edgar answered. "I don't want you to have to go through this."

"I'll be fine."

"Promise?"

Margaret nodded solemnly. "Promise."

"That's good enough for me," Edgar said, hugging Margaret. He looked at Karen. "How about you, Peanut? Think all this is going to work out?"

Karen forced a smile, trying to dispel the worry in her father's eyes. "I think Mom's going to be with us for a very long time."

He reached for his daughter and pulled her close. He felt her stiffen and looked down at her. Karen's expression was one of frank appraisal as she scanned his face. He had never seen that look from her before.

"God, I hope so," Edgar said.

AMADOR POKED A FINGER under his T-shirt and scratched his belly button. "I feel bad about what happened to Jimmy. Almost like it was my fault."

"Somebody was waiting for him at the mine," Kerney countered. "Did you tell anyone else about the ATV tracks in the canyon?"

Using the same finger, Amador scratched under his lower lip and used his chin to point in the direction of his crew. The four men were at the back of the maintenance building, restocking construction materials and cleaning tools.

"We all saw the tracks," Amador replied. "It wasn't a big deal or anything like that. A lot of people use off-road vehicles to get into the mountains. I didn't even think about it until after the murder up on the meadows. Then, when I remembered it, I thought it might be important."

Kerney restated: "Did you tell anybody about your suspicions, before or after you talked to Jim?"

"No. I was off yesterday. I just stayed at home working around the house. Didn't see anybody to talk to, except the family. Why are you asking me these questions? Shouldn't you be out looking for a job?"

"Do my questions bother you?" Kerney countered.

"It's no skin off my nose, but you're wasting your time. You got no job, no authority. So why push it? It ain't gonna make you any friends, not that you have any I know of."

Kerney shrugged. "You're Henry Lujan's uncle. Tell me about him. Is he having any kind of problems at college? Money worries, perhaps?"

Amador got red in the face. *"Madre de Dios,* are you out in left field. If you think Henry's got anything to do with this, you're crazy."

"Everything's okay with Henry? Is that what you're saying?"

"I'm not saying anything," Amador corrected. He pointed at a small man with a receding hairline who was restacking plywood. "That's Steve Lujan. Henry's father. Maybe he'll talk to you, maybe he won't. But don't do it on my time, while he's working."

"What's the problem, Amador?"

"I don't have a problem, you do," he snorted, looking up at the gringo. "Poking around in other people's business isn't healthy. You get my meaning?"

"It's been fun working with you, Amador. Thanks for all the help."

"Screw you," Amador replied.

Kerney walked out into the sunlight, thinking that it must have taken Steve Lujan a good long time to grow the Zapata mustache that drooped majestically over his upper lip. It also occurred to him that Amador was right: he hadn't made very many friends in Catron County.

CAROL MADE a final check mark on the inventory control sheet and raised her head. She pushed the box filled with Kerney's uniforms, equipment, weapon, and shield to one side of her desk. "That does it," she said, as Kerney dropped the keys to the ranger vehicle in her hand. "I'll get you a ride back to Reserve."

"Thanks," Kerney replied.

"Anything happening you'd like to tell me about?"

Kerney tilted his head toward the open office door.

Carol got up and closed it. "What is it?"

"What do you know about Henry and Steve Lujan?" Kerney asked. "I need some background information, and Amador wasn't inclined to cooperate."

"That doesn't surprise me," Carol said, returning to her chair behind the desk. "He keeps family matters to himself. Both Henry and Steve are temporary employees who work every summer for me. Henry's a college student, and his father sells firewood, flagstone, and landscape rock to the folks in Silver City during the off-season."

"What do you know about Henry?"

"Not much. Amador recommended him to me. He's been reliable. Uses the money he makes for his college living expenses. He went to school up in Albuquerque his first year. Didn't like being so far away from home, so he transferred to Western New Mexico University in Silver City. Is he a suspect?"

"No, but he's one of two people who were in the area when Padilla was murdered."

"That's stretching it," Carol replied. "He was on duty at the lookout tower. I checked the radio log. He couldn't possibly get to and from Elderman Meadows in an hour. Impossible. Who's the other person?"

"Amador," Kerney replied. "He camped out at the construction site the night before we found José Padilla and his grandson's body."

"I didn't know that," Carol said, wrinkling her nose. "Although he's done it before. It's not out of character."

"That's good to know. And Steve Lujan?"

"He got laid off at the copper mine down by Silver City. Three years ago, I think it was. Worked there for ten or fifteen years. Commuted home on the weekends. It must have hit him hard, financially. He's got three kids in college. Henry's the youngest."

"Are all the kids still in school?"

"The oldest, Leonard, is working on a master's degree in El Paso. Henry and his sister are still going to Western as far as I know."

"What about Henry's mother?"

"Yolanda works down at the Glenwood District Office as a secretary. Charlie Perry hired her right after he came to the district. About two years ago. I'm sure you've met her."

"I have. Does anybody in the family have a criminal record?"

Carol raised an eyebrow. "That's a tall order. The Lujan. and Ortiz families are rather large. How deeply do you want to delve?"

"Just the principals we've been talking about."

"Amador served eighteen months for a residential burglary when he was younger. Twenty years or so ago. He got a governor's pardon right before he started working for the Forest Service."

"Do you know the reason for the pardon?" Kerney inquired.

"I think Edgar Cox arranged it for him. Edgar was chairman of the county commission at the time."

"So Henry and Steve have a clean slate?"

"As far as I know. Henry, certainly. With Steve I'd only be guessing, but Catron County is too small for me not to have heard something."

"Any womanizing?"

"Steve?" Carol asked incredulously. "Yolanda would hand him

his *huevos* on a platter if he tried. And if she didn't do it, Amador would." She spread her hands out in a gesture of helplessness. "Sorry I can't give you more. As far as I know, Steve, Henry, and Amador are solid citizens. I don't see them as bad guys."

"That helps."

"Speaking of bad guys, Charlie Perry came back this morning. He wanted to know if you had filed a final report."

Kerney held out the papers.

"Thanks," Carol said. "I think I'll mail it to him. Another reply came in to your inquiry right after Charlie left. A BLM officer down in Deming would like you to call him. He just got back from a trip to Washington and read your fax message." Carol pushed a piece of paper across her desk.

Kerney picked it up. "You aren't going to give this to Charlie?"

Carol smiled sweetly. "Of course I am. I'll mail it to him with your report. He should receive it in three or four days."

"That should do nicely."

"I thought you'd appreciate it." Carol's leaned forward, her expression earnest. "You did one hell of a job saving Jim. I think you deserve recognition for it."

"You're not going to get all mushy on me, are you?" Kerney chided.

Carol giggled. "Absolutely not. But you do deserve something better than a pink slip for your efforts."

"I'll take that ride to Reserve," Kerney proposed.

LEANING AGAINST the corral fence, Edgar watched Cody practice roping his pony. A dark sorrel mare with a bald face, standing barely fourteen hands high, Babe was a gentle horse. Cody made another throw, the noose of the lariat fell short, and Babe loped to the far side of the corral, a good hundred feet away from the boy.

"I still can't do it, Grandpa," Cody moaned, slapping the rope against his leg.

"Yes you can," Edgar replied, as he stepped over to the boy. "Watch me one more time." Edgar uncoiled his lasso and started a slow spin with the noose. "You need to twirl a circle," he said. "Don't let your noose flatten out. Don't try to spin it too fast. Let your wrist do the work for you. Swing the loop up above your head. Listen to the sound it makes. Don't throw the rope at the horse. Let it float out to where you want it to go."

Edgar walked toward Babe with long, fluid strides, Cody at his heels. Swinging the noose slowly above his head, letting it gradually pick up speed, he flicked his wrist and the loop settled over Babe's neck. He walked to the mare and retrieved the lasso. Babe snorted at him and walked away.

"What kind of sound did you hear?" Edgar asked.

"Kind of a whisper. A hissing whisper," Cody answered.

"That's the sound."

"I'll never get it right," Cody complained in frustration.

Edgar rubbed Cody's head. "Yes, you will." He took Cody's lasso and shortened the loop. Babe had moved to the gate by the horse barn, where Carl Sloan, one of two hired hands, was cleaning out stalls. Edgar caught the mare by the halter and brought her back to the center of the corral.

"Let's try it with you sitting on my shoulders," Edgar said, as he lifted the boy up and moved ten feet back from the mare.

Babe gave them a snort and a curious look. Cody spun the lasso and Edgar waited until the sound it made cutting through the air was just about right. "Let it go."

The noose fell neatly over Babe's neck.

"I did it!" Cody shouted.

"You sure did." He set Cody down, walked to the corral fence, and dropped his rope over a post. "Now try it again."

As Edgar watched Cody, his thoughts wandered. It was hard for him to pretend it was just another ordinary day. Margaret was in the kitchen with Elizabeth, working up meals for the freezer that would carry Edgar through her surgery and hospitalization. She acted as though she were preparing for nothing more than one of her periodic visits to her sister. On top of that worry, he was damn unhappy with himself for lying to Karen. While she hadn't said a word about it, he knew she didn't believe him. He could see it in her eyes.

Engrossed in his thoughts, Edgar didn't hear Kerney drop over the corral fence.

"Mr. Cox," Kerney said politely.

Surprised, Edgar turned his head. "Mr. Kerney." He looked back at Cody, who was moving in on Babe for another try. He didn't want to think about Eugene, José Padilla, or any of it. Not now.

Kerney remained silent.

Edgar got tired of waiting. "What can I do for you?" he asked, his blue eyes searching Kerney's face.

"I thought you'd like to know about José Padilla. Seems he is from around these parts."

"Did he tell you that?"

"No, his daughter did. Padilla died last night."

"I'm sorry to hear it."

"She also told me why Padilla came back. He thought his father was murdered."

"That's pretty unlikely."

"Why do you say that?"

Edgar paused, rubbed his palm along the smooth corral railing, and tried to stay calm. Cody's throw snaked out and the noose snapped against Babe's neck. The horse whinnied and skipped back from the boy.

"Let the noose open up before you throw it," Edgar called. "Remember the circle. Don't let the noose flatten out."

Cody nodded glumly and walked toward the mare, coiling his lariat for another throw.

"Why do you say Don Luis wasn't murdered?" Kerney asked.

"Because he died in a fall with his horse."

"You're sure?"

"I'm sure. Don Luis was an old man who went into the mountains alone once too often. He got caught in a blinding spring snowstorm and tried to find his way home. His horse plunged off a ridge. Dropped a good sixty, seventy feet. Took Don Luis with him."

"Where did this happen?"

"Near Elderman Meadows. They didn't find his body for two weeks."

"What was he doing up there?"

"His sheepherder quit on him to take a WPA job building roads for the county. He hired a replacement, but the man didn't show. When the storm blew in, he went to check on the herd. He needed those sheep. He planned to sell them at the end of the season to pay a bank note and taxes. He was trying to hold on and get through the Depression, just like everybody else."

"What happened to the sheep?"

"Stolen. Most folks figured the sheep had been rustled before Don Luis left the hacienda."

"Was the crime ever solved?"

"No."

"Ever hear of a place called Mexican Hat?" Kerney asked.

"Can't say I have," Edgar answered. "I hear you've been released from your position."

"That's true."

"Will you be staying on in Catron County?"

"Probably not."

Edgar watched Cody. He was all tensed up again and twirling much too hard. "I didn't think so. Not many jobs hereabouts."

Cody let fly, and the lariat whipped out and snapped Babe in the eye. The horse bawled, pitched back on her hind legs, forelegs flailing, and headed straight for Cody, who stood frozen in position. Before Edgar could react, Kerney grabbed the lasso from the fence post and ran toward the mare, measuring the distance to the horse, spinning the lariat in a tight loop at his knee parallel to the ground. He let it go and the noose caught the mare by the forelegs. He yanked it tight and the horse went down hard on her side less than a foot in front of Cody.

Babe was on her back kicking in the air when Edgar scooped up Cody.

Kerney released the mare. She got up, shook herself off, snorted, and trotted away.

"Where did you learn that trick?" Edgar asked, holding Cody tightly in his arms.

"A fellow by the name of Blas Montoya taught it to me when I was a boy."

"Well, I thank both you and Mr. Montoya. That's some damn fine roping."

"You're welcome."

He stroked Cody's head. "Are you all right, cowboy?"

Cody's eyes were wet, but he wasn't crying. "Yeah. That was scary."

"It scared me, too," Edgar said. "Is there anything else we need to talk about, Mr. Kerney?"

"I don't think so," Kerney replied.

Edgar stuck out his hand. "Well then, good luck to you, and thanks again."

Kerney shook his hand and left, wondering what it would take to shake out Edgar's secret. He was damn sure there was one. Maybe Edgar had all the family skeletons locked in a closet that required a special key.

IN DEMING, Kerney went looking for a smuggler. South of town, along the state highway, in view of the Tres Hermanas Mountains twenty miles distant, he found a mailbox with the right numbers at a roadside business that had gone under. The old farmhouse, bordered by cotton fields on three sides, had a front yard filled with rows of sagging wooden bins that once contained rocks for sale to the tourist trade. Signs at either end of the yard, the painted letters faded by the desert sun, welcomed rock hounds to the defunct establishment. There was a Keep Out sign posted on the front door of the house. Kerney parked and looked in the windows as he walked around the building. The rooms were empty except for some litter and a thick carpet of sand on the plank floors. Nobody had been inside for a good long time.

The wire strands to the back fence were filled with fluffs of raw cotton from the last harvest. In front of the fence was a level spot of sand and gravel near a utility pole with an electric meter attached to it. A dented propane tank sat on the other side of the site. It was clear that a house trailer had been recently moved off the property. The tracks of the truck that had hauled it away were barely filled in with drifting sand.

Kerney kicked at the sand with the toe of a boot, pissed off at himself for taking too long to follow up on Juan's lead. It was another dead end, and he was getting tired of running into walls. He looked down the road. About half a mile away, at the intersection of the highway and a county road, was a farm equipment and supply business. Beyond that, cotton fields gave way to desert that ran up against the dark groundmass of the Tres Hermanas.

At the dealership, a metal-skin building with a large plate-glass window that bounced the sun into his eyes, he stood next to a hundred-thousand-dollar tractor and talked with the owner. Clancy Payne was in his sixties. He had a cheerful smile and a trace of a west Texas twang. He shook his head and said he didn't know much about the man up the road. Kerney learned that his target, Leon Spence, had sold the house trailer and moved to Tucson. Other than that, and a belief that Spence was a traveling salesman of some sort, Mr. Payne knew nothing more.

"When did Spence move out?" Kerney asked.

"I don't know when he left, but they hauled the trailer away over the weekend," Clancy replied.

"Were you open for business on Saturday?"

"I sure was, but I didn't see Spence, if that's what you're wondering."

"What kind of car does Spence drive?"

"He's got two vehicles. One of them is a Toyota four-by-four sport utility and the other is a four-door Chevy. A Caprice, I think it is. The Toyota is a dark blue and the Chevy is white."

"New Mexico plates?"

"Yeah, but don't ask me for the license numbers. I can't even remember my own."

LAID OUT ON A GRID, Deming ran parallel to the interstate until it petered out at both ends of the main street. On a smooth desert plain, broken only by low sand mounds and shallow arroyos, the locals fought the starkness of the land and lost the battle. There would never be enough greenness, no matter how many trees were planted or lawns were sodded, to combat the sparseness, dryness, dust, and wind that constantly wore at the town.

With all of that going against it, Deming had been discovered by working-class retirees on limited pensions, and new, inexpensive subdivisions were pushing back the cotton fields, as the city touted its resurgence with billboards and bumper stickers.

On the outer limits of Deming's main street, in the air-conditioned comfort of a restaurant that gave customers a great view of the interstate highway and the railroad tracks, Kerney called the BLM officer, who agreed to meet him for a cup of coffee. While he waited he borrowed the phone book and called the electric and phone companies, hoping that Spence had left a forwarding address. No such luck. He called mobile home movers. None had hauled Spence's trailer. The BLM cop arrived, and Kerney sat with him in a window booth, the sun's glare cut by a thick plastic shade that made the outside world look dark brown.

"You did the ibex investigation in the Florida Mountains," Kerney said, after the small talk concluded.

Mike Anderson, a man with a blocky face and fat earlobes, took his sunglasses off and wiped some dust out of the corners of his eyes. "That's right. Couldn't get anything definite on it. I called a state police buddy of mine to help out, but we couldn't get a damn bit of hard evidence other than the tire tracks. That didn't pan out either. The impressions didn't take. Not enough tread depth."

"So, what have you got?"

"Two days before I found the kill site, I stopped a kid on a four-wheel ATV. He was on state land outside of my jurisdiction, but I gave him a butt-chewing anyway. Said he was camped at Rock Hound State Park with his family."

"Did you ID the kid?"

"Got a name," Anderson said, pulling a small notebook from his shirt pocket. "The kid was maybe twelve, thirteen years old." Anderson thumbed through his notes. "Here it is. Ramón Ulibarri. Said he was from Reserve. I called up there after I found the trophy kills, just to check it out. There was only one Ulibarri listed in the phone book and the telephone had been disconnected. So I called the Catron County sheriff."

"And?" Kerney prodded.

"I talked to the sheriff. He didn't know any kid by that name, and nobody matched the description I gave him. I figured in a town that small, the sheriff would know."

"You talked to Gatewood?"

"Sure did."

"Describe the boy to me," Kerney asked.

Anderson gave him a rundown. Four-six or -seven, slender build, wearing floppy jeans and a baseball cap with the bill turned backward. He closed the notebook and put it away. "The kid told me that he was camping with his family at the state park, but later when I talked to the manager he said there was nobody registered from Reserve during that time."

"So the kid lied to you."

"Appears that way."

"Do you know a man named Leon Spence?" Kerney asked. "Used to live on the highway to Columbus."

Anderson suddenly got busy stirring his coffee. "Doesn't register."

Kerney pushed a bit. "He had a trailer behind a vacant house that used to be a rock-hound shop. You must have seen it."

"I've seen it," Anderson allowed. "Didn't know who lived there."

Kerney picked up the check for the coffee. "Thanks for your time."

"Hope I didn't waste yours," Anderson replied. He put some change on the table for a tip, shook Kerney's hand, and wished him good luck before putting his sunglasses back on and pushing his way out the door into the simmering desert furnace of the day.

As he paid the bill, Kerney pondered Anderson's behavior. The man had gone from one extreme to another. He'd been more than willing to talk about poachers, but went into a complete shutdown when Leon Spence had been mentioned. That was damn interesting.

Anderson hadn't left much of a tip for the waitress. Kerney went back and put more money on the table.

"READING WITH ONE EYE isn't easy," Jim said. "And I don't do it very well."

"Maybe you shouldn't try," Kerney replied.

Jim sat in the chair next to his hospital bed, a pile of papers in his hand. The dressing covering his eye had been replaced with a patch and his left arm was in a sling.

The bed was occupied by a very pretty, blue-jean-clad, blond-headed young woman with a dimple in the center of her chin, who sat cross-legged with a laptop computer balanced on her knees.

"That's Molly Hamilton," Jim explained. "My research associate. When she gets desperate, I'm allowed to date her."

"Shut up, Jim," Molly said sweetly, looking at Kerney. "Hi."

"Hello."

Molly held out a modem cord to Kerney. "Plug this in the phone jack, please. State archives is sending me some confirming information."

Kerney did as he was told. "Where did you find such good help?" he asked Stiles.

"Molly's the chief research librarian at the university," Jim explained. "I can't get her to quit her job, marry me, and have my babies."

"Shut up, Jim," Molly, said, her fingers busy at the keyboard. "Don't listen to him, Mr. Kerney. Want to hear what we've got so far?"

"I'd love to."

Molly punched a few more keys and put the laptop on the pillow behind her. "Okay. Before statehood, Thomas Catron owned most of the land west of Magdalena to the Arizona border. What he didn't own, Solomon Luna controlled, along with the Padilla family. Don Luis was kind of a junior partner. They pooled their resources and formed a limited partnership called the American Valley Company. There were a few more partners, but Catron bought them out except for Luna and Padilla. The venture never made a profit. Catron was overextended financially and couldn't raise the money for development. In his day, he was just about the biggest landowner in the country. He held title to, or controlled, millions of acres in New Mexico. When beef prices plummeted in the 1890s and the drought hit, it was all he could do to hold on to the land."

"That's interesting," Kerney said, "but it doesn't get us very far."

"What's interesting, Mr. Kerney," Molly said, arching her back in a stretch, "is what Catron did. He recruited a new partner with working capital: William Elderman."

"My granddaddy," Jim added proudly. "A real scoundrel."

"True enough," Molly replied. "After the American Valley Company dissolved, Catron and Luna walked away from the venture, leaving Elderman and Padilla the biggest landowners in the county, but with a binding agreement that gave each of them first option for a buyout."

"So did Elderman exercise his option for the land with Padilla?" Kerney asked.

"Padilla wouldn't sell, even though Elderman hounded him for years. It took the Great Depression to bankrupt Padilla."

"Did Elderman get the land for back taxes?"

"Don't jump the gun," Molly said, waving a censuring finger. "The only entity buying land in the valley during the Depression was the federal government. The feds wanted to expand the Datil National Forest. That's what it was called back then. And the land they wanted was owned by Padilla. Elderman knew it. Padilla didn't. It was pure discrimination. The feds didn't want to deal with the Hispanics."

"Is this speculation or fact?" Kerney inquired.

Molly tilted her head in Jim's direction. "Fact. Most of what we know comes from an unpublished autobiography written by Woodrow

Stringhorn, the first park superintendent. His family donated the papers to the university after his death. Stringhorn consummated the deal with Elderman to buy the land for the national forest. He wrote in his autobiography that he was ordered by Washington to have no dealings with Padilla, and to wait until the land came under Elderman's control.

"There's even a letter from Elderman to Stringhorn, in which he writes that Padilla probably wouldn't be able to meet his obligations to the bank when his note came due. Seems that old William had an inside source on Padilla's finances."

"Who owned the bank?" Kerney queried.

"Another scoundrel," Jim replied. "Calvin Cox. Karen's granddaddy. Is this a good story, or what?"

"A very good story," Kerney agreed. "So Elderman got control of Padilla's land through Calvin Cox, turned around, and sold a chunk of it to the feds."

"Right," Molly agreed. "Elderman Meadows. There was no tax auction. We think Calvin Cox covered the tax liability until the proceeds from the land sale came through. Elderman probably paid through the nose for the service, but he walked away a rich man after selling out to the government." She glanced at Jim. "Are you rich?"

Stiles grinned. "No, but my grandparents were, and my parents are well off. I guess that makes me part of the landed gentry."

"Dirty money," Molly said, wrinkling her nose.

Stiles nodded his head enthusiastically. "It's how the west was won."

Molly wrinkled her nose again, in disgust at the idea.

"I don't like it any more than you do, really," Jim said.

Molly's smile returned. "You'd better not." She turned her attention back to Kerney. "That's about it. What I asked for from state archives should fill in some of the blanks."

"Did you find any reference to a place called Mexican Hat?" Kerney asked.

"Nothing," Molly answered. "It could be one of those local place-names that never got recorded."

"How about the Cox family? I've haven't heard one word spoken about Eugene's wife."

"Be patient, Mr. Kerney," Molly replied. "Research takes time." She uncrossed her legs, slid off the bed, and kissed Jim on the lips. "Gotta go. I'll pick up my laptop when I stop by to see you tonight."

"See ya," Jim said. "And thanks."

"It's going to cost you."

"I certainly hope so."

"Shut up, Jim," Molly said sweetly as she waved and left.

Jim smiled, his eye fixed on the empty doorway.

"Nice-looking younger babe," Kerney noted.

"I knew you were going to say that," Jim replied with a laugh. "Doesn't she do good work?"

"Is that what you like about her?"

"No comment."

Kerney and Stiles spent the next ten minutes going over what they knew.

"Old José Padilla may have been right about his father's death," Jim said. "It's too bad he didn't make it."

"He may have left us enough to work with. Let's see what Molly digs up."

Jim nodded enthusiastically. "She's something, isn't she?"

"A gem," Kerney agreed. It was clear Jim was in love.

The car that had been with him since he left Deming followed at a discreet distance as Kerney pulled out of the hospital parking lot.

8

The campus of Western New Mexico University, a tidy complex of buildings situated on a hill near downtown Silver City, was quiet and nearly deserted. At the administration building, Kerney learned that no information about students could be released without written parental permission. In the business office, he had better luck. After a little cajoling, a billing clerk agreed to pull up financial information on a computer screen and let Kerney read it. None of the Lujan kids, including the oldest one who had graduated, had received student loans, and all payments for tuition, housing, and fees had been made in full and on time by checks written against the account of Steve and Yolanda Lujan. Kerney found that pretty amazing for a couple who lived on the income of a secretary and a seasonal worker with the forest service. Lujan must sell a hell of a lot of flagstone, landscape rock, and firewood during the off-season in order to pay the freight for three kids in college.

The car following Kerney in Silver City was nowhere to be seen on the drive back to Reserve. He pulled to the shoulder of the road near the town limits and waited for it to reappear. It never showed up. Whoever was following him had either switched cars or dropped the surveillance.

The Lujans lived in a settlement south of Reserve called Lower San Francisco Plaza, where the river squeezed into a confined channel and rushed through the mountains toward Glenwood before veering west to Arizona. A bridge crossed the river below the settlement, and a paved road twisted through the high country up to Snow Lake. The plaza, a collection of a half-dozen widely scattered houses and double-wide mobile homes, was one of the last remaining Hispanic enclaves in the county that hadn't passed into Anglo hands.

Kerney drove from house to house until he found the Lujan residence, a sprawling, unstuccoed adobe dwelling hidden by stacks of seasoned and fresh-cut firewood, piles of flagstone, and mounds of landscape rock on wooden pallets. From the look of it, Lujan had quite an inventory built up, which certainly wasn't putting cash into his pocket.

The property was enclosed by a chain-link fence and steel panel gate. Inside the fence sat a one-ton truck outfitted with a winch, hydraulic tailgate, and dual rear tires. A load of green pine had been dumped next to a commercial log-splitter. Two vehicles, a late-model Pontiac Grand Am in cherry condition and a beat-up full-size Ford Bronco, were parked facing the front porch. A chained German shepherd sprawled between them. The dog barked angrily as Kerney stepped through the open gate.

Steve Lujan waited on the porch and watched Kerney approach. "What the hell do you want?" he asked.

"What's your dog's name?" Kerney countered as he walked to the animal. It stopped barking and sniffed Kerney's hand.

"Loco," Lujan answered. Small-boned and lean, Lujan stood in a defiant pose with his legs spread and his arms crossed. His bushy mustache completely covered his upper lip.

"Does he bite?" Kerney asked cordially.

"Only when I tell him to," Steve replied. "What are you doing here?"

"Would you mind answering a few questions?"

Steve considered the request. "I don't have to tell you nothing."

"I know that."

"I've got nothing to hide," he said gruffly. "Come inside."

Steve led him through the front room, past a big-screen television set, expensive-looking reclining chaise rockers, sofa, oak-veneer end tables with ceramic lamps, and a gun cabinet filled with hunting rifles, and into the kitchen. Yolanda was at the sink. She turned and nodded abruptly at Kerney. A dumpy woman, dressed in leggings and a loose top that covered a thick waist, she had a testy expression.

"Hello, Yolanda," Kerney said.

She cleared her throat and shot a glance at her husband before responding. "Hello."

Steve settled into a chair at the kitchen table, crossed his legs, and reached for a pack of cigarettes. "Sit down."

"No thanks. I'll only stay a minute."

Lujan tapped a smoke on the table, lit up, and glanced at Yolanda. "What do you want to ask me?" He pulled back his head to look up at Kerney.

Yolanda took the cue, turned back to the sink, and began rinsing off the dinner dishes.

"Where were you when Jim Stiles got shot?"

Steve blew smoke in Kerney's direction and uncrossed his legs. "Day off. I was cutting wood on a mesa. I always cut wood or haul rock on my free time. I've got a bunch of regular customers down in Silver City. I sell about fifty cords every fall and winter."

"What's the going rate for a cord?" Kerney asked.

"It depends on the weather," Lujan replied. "Between a hundred and a hundred and twenty. You need some wood? I'll cut the price by twenty dollars a cord if you load and haul it yourself."

"I'll pass, but thanks for the offer." Kerney did a rough calculation in his head. Lujan would be lucky if he cleared three thousand dollars on the wood after expenses. "Did anybody go with you yesterday?"

"No, I went alone." Lujan took another puff on his cigarette.

"Did you run into anybody?"

Steve stubbed out the cigarette, tilted his chair, and tipped his head so he could look Kerney in the eye. "No. Do I need an alibi?"

"Are you a hunter?"

Tired of craning his neck, Steve let the chair drop down on all four legs and stood up. Kerney still towered over him. He reached for another cigarette and lit it. "I take a deer every season. That's all I have time for."

"Nothing else?" Kerney queried.

"Elk, when I can get a permit. I'm not a poacher."

Kerney switched gears. "You have a boy in graduate school and two kids at Western New Mexico, don't you?"

"Yeah. So what?"

"It must be expensive to put three kids through college at the same time."

Lujan laughed bitterly. "Don't you mean how can a peon like me come up with that kind of money?"

"I didn't say that," Kerney replied calmly.

Lujan thrust his face forward. "You don't have to *say* it to *mean* it. I had an industrial accident at the copper mine a few years before I got laid off. Hurt my back. The union helped me settle with the company. I got a cash payment. The money went into savings for the kids' education. We don't use it for anything else."

Lujan turned to the sideboard behind him, opened a drawer, pulled out a bank passbook, and flipped it onto the table. "Check it out for yourself. Every dollar pays for tuition, books, dormitory costs, and expenses."

Kerney looked. From the amount of the initial deposit it was apparent the Lujans certainly could cover the cost of three children in college. It had been spent down systematically over a period of years.

"Satisfied?" Lujan asked. He had forgotten his cigarette. It was in an ashtray on the table burning down to the filter.

"Where were you the day Hector Padilla was murdered?" Kerney asked, holding out the passbook.

Steve took it and returned it to the drawer. "That's a stupid question. You know where I was. I was at the campsite with

Amador and the rest of the crew." He pulled another smoke out of the pack.

"Did you leave the job at any time?"

"No."

Kerney glanced at Yolanda. She stood with one hand on her hip, her eyes darting from him to her husband. Her expression was one of masked resentment.

"That about does it," he said. "Thanks for your time."

Steve grunted, lit up, and blew smoke in Kerney's direction. "Let yourself out."

Loco, the German shepherd, wagged his tail when Kerney stepped off the porch. He rubbed the dog's snout and let him sniff his hand again before moving on to his truck. It seemed that Steve and Yolanda had been expecting his visit. Probably Amador had told Steve that Kerney might come around asking questions. But that didn't explain why Lujan had been so forthcoming with someone he thought no longer had any legal authority to question him. And why was he so nervous?

IT WAS EVENING when Kerney got home and found Karen Cox standing next to her station wagon waiting for him. She wore jeans, cowboy boots, and a ribbed scoop-neck shirt. He parked, got out of the truck, and stretched his knee to ease some of the stiffness. He had spent too many hours driving with the leg locked in one position.

"You don't have a telephone," she said as he reached her.

"The phone company is supposed to put in a line, but now I guess I won't need it. Are you here to ask me about Padilla Canyon?"

"Not really. Jim Stiles filled me in. To him you're quite a hero."

"Hardly. I did what was necessary. What can I do for you?"

"Can we talk inside?"

In the trailer, he turned on the ceiling light and offered her the choice of the chair or the couch. She sat on the couch and waited while he opened windows to let out the heat of the day. The metal skin of the trailer absorbed heat like a sponge, and the room was stifling hot.

Except for two Navajo saddle blankets that hung on the walls, the living area held no personal touches. From the weave and the pattern she guessed both were late-nineteenth-century trade blankets, worth a considerable amount of money. The room, a combination kitchen, dining nook, and sitting area, was tidy but bleak in the harsh glow of the overhead light.

Kerney turned on a table fan, sat in the overstuffed chair, and stretched out his legs. It felt good to let the knee rest.

"What's on your mind?" he asked.

Karen smiled apologetically. "I came to thank you for rescuing Cody. My father told me what you did. I appreciate it."

"No thanks are necessary. I think your father could have handled it without me."

"That's not the way he saw it. Why did you go to see him?"

"Are you wearing your ADA hat now?"

Karen shifted her weight on the lumpy cushion. "You could say that."

Kerney nodded. "Fair enough. I'll trade with you."

"Trade what?"

"Information."

"I don't have to do that."

"What's holding you back?"

"From what I've learned from Jim Stiles, you're still directing the course of his investigation. I can't allow that."

Kerney smiled in amusement. "That's quite a stretch you're making, Counselor. I've provided nothing more than friendly advice to Jim."

"That doesn't relieve you of the responsibility to tell me what you've learned."

"I've already done that."

"Not completely. You said you had information to trade."

"It's more like a suspicion."

"Of what?" Karen demanded.

"Something happened a long time ago that brought José Padilla back to Catron County. It has put your father between a rock and a hard place. Maybe it ties into the deaths of Hector and José Padilla, and maybe it doesn't. But until there is a solid lead on the killer and the motive, it can't be discounted."

"Now you're the one making a stretch."

"I don't mean to put you in an uncomfortable position."

"I didn't say that."

"You got uptight as soon as I mentioned your father in the same breath with José Padilla. You did the same thing this morning when we talked about it at the hospital."

Karen looked at her hands, clasped tightly in her lap, and forced herself to relax. "Why are you pushing this?"

Kerney leaned forward in his chair, his blue eyes filled with anger. "Because whoever shot Jim Stiles was worried about something. But the question is, what? The poaching case? Hector Padilla's murder? The death of a man your father knew sixty years ago? All of the above?

"I like Jim. He's good people, and he deserves to have the son of a bitch who shot him caught. Besides, Jim was my partner, and the cop in me won't let it go until I catch the bastard. And that's what I plan to do."

Karen nodded vaguely, thinking he'd been straight with her and deserved the same treatment in return. Maybe it was time to trust him. "The day Hector Padilla was murdered he left a letter with me to give to my father. He said it was from José Padilla."

"Any idea what was in it?"

"None at all. What I do know is that my father hasn't spoken to his brother in his entire adult life. Whatever was in Padilla's letter broke that silence. My father paid a visit to Eugene the day he got the letter."

"Something had him worried," Kerney ventured.

"This afternoon I started doing some digging of my own. I got a copy of my grandfather's will from the probate court. He changed it the same month that Uncle Eugene was shot in a hunting accident and my father ran away to join the Army. Grandfather Cox left everything to Eugene. My father was completely cut out of a considerable inheritance."

"Calvin Cox left nothing to his wife?"

Karen shook her head. "My grandmother died of influenza when the twins were twelve years old."

"So why do you think he did it?"

"I don't know. But cutting a son completely out of an inheritance is the act of a very angry parent."

"I agree. What happened to Phil and Cory's mother? She could be a source of information."

"She left Eugene when Phil was six and Cory was twelve, and just disappeared. It caused quite a scandal. Eugene packed Phil and Cory off to military school in Roswell as soon as they were old enough. After college, Phil came back to run the ranch. Cory never came back from Vietnam."

Karen waited for a response. "Well?" she finally asked.

He stood up. "Are you going to dig into this any deeper?"

"I'd like my father to come to me on his own."

"I hope he does."

"So do I." Karen got up from the couch. "Will you keep what I told you confidential?"

"As long as I can."

"Fair enough. You don't remember me, do you?"

"Phil jogged my memory when I had dinner with him," Kerney said. "I remember three young girls who followed me around the rodeo grounds when I was here for the high school state finals. One of them had black hair and beautiful blue eyes, and made Cousin Cory introduce me to her every chance she got."

Karen laughed and extended her hand. "That was me. In my age of innocence."

"Innocence doesn't last very long, does it?" Kerney replied, taking her hand in his.

"No, it doesn't. You'll keep me informed of what you do?"

"Of course I will."

Kerney saw Karen to the door, said good night, changed into his sweats, and did a two-mile run. He mulled over his meeting with Karen and came to the conclusion that the woman had some fire and steel to her—appealing qualities that increased her attractiveness. The knee felt better when he got back to the trailer. Jim's girlfriend, Molly, was sitting on the step.

"Hi, Mr. Kerney. The wounded hero has me running a messenger service."

"Come in," he said.

She sat in the overstuffed chair with an attaché case on her lap. Kerney took a seat on the couch.

Molly glanced around the room and made a face. "This place is a pit."

"You don't find it homey?"

"You have mice."

"The landlord has promised full eradication."

"Good." She cocked her head sideways and studied him. "You don't talk like a cop."

"Thanks, I think. What have you uncovered?"

Molly quickly turned to business, opening the case and shuffling through some papers. "You wanted information on the Cox clan." She paused and fixed her gaze directly on his face. "Do you still want it?"

"You bet I do."

"Haven't you been fired?"

"I'm unemployed," Kerney confirmed.

"Then what good will all this do? Jim's so angry about you getting canned he's spitting bullets. He didn't know about it until he turned on the evening news."

"Tell him to chill out. I'm going to stay with it."

Molly's gave him a delighted smile. "That's great." She dropped her attention to the papers in her attaché case and arranged them in order. "Okay, here it is. Calvin Cox owned the local bank that carried the mortgage on the Padilla ranch. Before the property went on the auction block for back taxes, Cox bought it and immediately resold it to Elderman at an inflated price. Elderman passed the price increase on to the Forest Service. Both men made a chunk of money on the deal."

"What have you learned about Eugene's hunting accident?"

"He was out alone when he got shot. When he didn't come home, Edgar went searching for him and brought him down the mountain."

Molly flipped over a paper and studied her notes. "When Eugene recovered enough to be questioned, he said he never saw who shot him. The state police speculated that whoever rustled Padilla's sheep shot Eugene."

"Eugene wasn't a suspect in the rustling?"

"Nope. He was back home with a bullet in his spine the day before Don Luis left the hacienda for the meadows."

"According to whom?"

"Calvin Cox, Edgar, and the doctor who treated Eugene."

"What about Eugene's wife? Any leads?"

Molly shook her head. "Vanished without a trace, but Jim's looking." She put her notes away and got up. "That's all I've got. Can I tell Jim my research assignment is over, please? I need to get back to my real job."

"Only if you tell me something."

"What is it?"

"Are you going to marry him?"

"Probably, but don't you dare tell him. I want to soften him up a bit more."

Kerney grinned. "I promise I won't."

Molly stepped over to Kerney and kissed him on the cheek. "Thanks for saving him for me, Mr. Kerney."

Kerney blushed and patted her on the shoulder. "No thanks are necessary. Call me Kerney. Most of my friends do."

Molly tossed her hair out of her face and smiled. "Okay, Kerney, you've got a deal. Jim gets to go home tomorrow morning. Actually he's staying with me, so I can nurse him back to health." She wrote her address on a piece of paper and handed it over. "You'd better stop by to see him. He likes you a lot. So do I."

"The feeling is mutual on both counts," Kerney replied. "Give Jim my best."

"I'll do it."

WHEN KAREN RETURNED from her meeting with Kerney, Edgar carried Cody and Elizabeth up to the old house—Cody sitting on Grandfather's shoulders—to tuck them into bed. Margaret and Karen waited for him to return. When he didn't come back they looked for him out the living room window. The light was on in the horse barn, and they saw his shadow through the open door as he moved around inside.

"He'll be fine," Margaret predicted. "He always putters when he's worried."

"I'm worried too," Karen admitted.

"It will all be over soon." The surgery was scheduled for eight o'clock in the morning. "I plan to breeze right through it," Margaret said, patting her daughter's cheek.

"See that you do."

When Karen left, Margaret turned out the living-room lights and waited for Edgar to come back inside. Ten minutes passed before the kitchen door squeaked and Edgar walked quietly into the living room. She turned on the reading lamp next to the couch, and Edgar looked at her in surprise.

"Didn't the doctor tell you to get a good night's sleep?" he asked.

"He did. I will. Sit down, Edgar, I need to talk to you."

Edgar's expression grew grim.

"It's not about the surgery," Margaret reassured him.

He walked to his chair and eased his long frame down, his face still gloomy. "What is it?"

"I want you to promise me something," she said.

"Anything you want."

Margaret held back a smile. "I want you to tell Karen what happened on Elderman Meadows."

"I can't do that."

"Yes, you can. It's time, Edgar. I've kept your secret for over forty years, and I've seen it eat at you from the day we were married. Tell Karen and let her help you. A promise is a promise, and you've always been a man who kept his word."

Edgar, stunned by the request, knew he was trapped by a woman who wouldn't let him off the hook. He tried anyway. "It's a hard thing you're asking me to do."

"But you will do it."

"When?"

"Soon. Very soon."

"You know what it may mean," he countered.

"Yes. A burden will be lifted and we can get on with our lives."

Edgar took a deep breath and let it out slowly. Margaret, still waiting for his answer, would keep him rooted in his chair until she got what she wanted. Maybe she was right and the time had come.

"I'll tell her," he said. "Before you come back home."

Margaret went to him, sank down on his lap, and pulled his arms around her. Her wet eyes smiled. "Thank you, Edgar."

He held her tightly, and neither spoke for a very long time.

KERNEY SPENT A HOT, long day in El Paso checking out the last two smugglers on Juan's list. Both seemed to operate legitimate businesses, which made Kerney's snooping by necessity discreet. After posing as a customer in each establishment, he staked-out the buildings until it became clear that he would need a surveillance team to help him and a lot of luck to catch any kind of a break. Frustrated, he gave it up late in the afternoon, wondering how far he could get going it alone with limited resources.

The only bright spot to the day was leaving El Paso. Big cities made no sense to Kerney at all. After the clutter of the strip malls, gas stations, and fast-food restaurants on the main drag out of town, he reached the desert that spread out like a vast ocean of glistening sandy breaks rising to steep-walled mountains on the western horizon. He cranked the air-conditioning up a notch, flipped down the visor, and headed west toward the enormous pale pink sun hovering at the horizon. It was a two-hour haul from El Paso to Silver City. If he made good time, he might arrive early enough in the evening to pay a social call on the convalescing Jim Stiles and his lovely nurse.

Kerney's unknown traveling companion was back, and had been with him all day. Whoever was driving used a different car each time and tailed him like a pro. Kerney checked the rearview mirror and shrugged it off. Up ahead, the sun had vanished before it could set. A shroud of yellow dust came straight at him, pushed along by crosswise gusts that buffeted the truck. He turned on the headlights and reduced his speed. The cars coming at him were nothing more than floating beams of dull lights as the dust cloud boiled over the highway.

The storm blew through quickly, leaving a clear evening sky in the west and a huge sand cloud billowing to the east behind him.

Drivers parked on the shoulder of the road, heading in Kerney's direction, pulled back into traffic. He watched for the car tailing him to emerge from the storm that still swallowed up the asphalt ribbon of highway in his rearview mirror. Nothing. Smiling, he increased his speed, fairly certain he had shaken the tail with the help of Mother Nature.

IN KERNEY'S MIND, Silver City had two redeeming characteristics: the foothills where the town sat, and the historic district, slowly coming back to life after years of neglect. The old hospital on the main drag, abandoned after the new medical center opened, looked like a relic from a World War II bombing raid. And the growth along the strip was a checkerboard of vacant land alternating with commercial enterprises surrounded by parking lots that appeared large enough to accommodate the cars of the entire city population at one time.

But downtown Silver City appealed to Kerney, with its long row of brick and stone storefronts with rounded second-story windows and elegant parapets, substantial old warehouses in back alleys still showing the faded letters of failed enterprises, the Big Ditch Park where Main Street once stood until a flood early in the century washed it away, and Victorian houses that climbed the hills on narrow streets.

Molly Hamilton lived in one of the Victorian cottages on a hill. A steep set of steps rose to a covered porch and an oak door with a leaded glass window. A brick chimney jutted at one end of the pitched roof.

Molly's brown eyes filled with censure when she opened the door. "Where have you been?" she demanded.

She shook her blond hair in mock dismay and pulled him by

the hand into the living room, where Jim scowled at him from the comfort of an easy chair, his feet propped on an ottoman. He still wore an eye patch, and the cuts on his face had turned into bright scarlet splotches.

"Why the hell didn't you tell me you'd been fired?" he snapped at Kerney. "I had to find out about it on the TV news."

"I didn't want to induce a relapse." Kerney's attempt at humor felt flat; Jim kept scowling. "It's no big deal," he added lamely.

"It sucks, big-time," Stiles retorted.

"Stop bitching at him, Jim," Molly ordered, turning to look up at Kerney. "He's been moaning and groaning all day that you probably packed up and left without even coming to see him."

"I wouldn't do that," Kerney replied.

"That's what I told him."

Jim's expression softened, and his boyish grin reappeared. "What I was really worried about was having to solve the damn case by myself with one eye, my arm in a sling, and a face like Boris Karloff."

"You might be able to frighten the truth out of people," Kerney acknowledged.

"Good!" Molly proclaimed, clapping her hands. "You've kissed and made up. I love this male-bonding crap. Sorry to leave you boys, but kitchen duty calls." She pranced out of the room, looking lovely in her tunic top and cutoff jeans that showed her legs to advantage.

The room was the nicest Kerney had been in for some time. It had a high ceiling, a fireplace bordered by a cast-iron surround, oak wainscotting, and two wooden casement windows that faced the street. The modern, comfortable furniture, slightly undersized and placed at angles to the walls, gave the room a feeling of space.

Kerney settled into the chair next to Jim, thinking of the time when he'd been living with Laura, a bright-eyed, feisty woman who seemed to have every desirable attribute he was looking for in a lover. They had rented a small adobe home on a hill above Palace Avenue near downtown Santa Fe. It was a gem of a house that looked down at a cluster of mud-plastered homes and a dirt lane bordered by ancient cottonwoods. But it wasn't a happy place to live as Laura became more and more disenchanted with the demands of Kerney's job as a detective. He came home one night to find Laura and a stranger packing her belongings into her car. The stranger turned out to be Laura's new boyfriend, the man she was moving in with.

"Do you want to tell me what you've been doing?" Jim asked.

Kerney nodded and started talking, leaving out very little. He chose not to mention the tail—which hadn't reappeared—or the way the BLM officer had flinched when Leon Spence's name had been mentioned. That stuff was in the pending file for items of developing interest.

"So my mustache theory about the shooter didn't hold up," Jim said, when Kerney finished. "I guess we can write Steve Lujan off."

"I'm not so sure," Kerney replied. "He was a little too eager to cooperate."

"Want to check his story out?" Jim said.

"I think so."

"I'll do it. There's got to be a record of his injury settlement at the company."

"Get his bank records while you're at it," Kerney advised. "What about Eugene's wife? Anything yet?"

"*Nada*, except for some background. Louise Blanton Cox moved to Pie Town at the end of World War Two and taught school for two years before marrying Gene Cox. She stayed with Gene for fifteen years and walked out on him in the early sixties. I haven't found any record of a divorce, but I still need to check with several more district courts."

"Maybe she never divorced him," Kerney speculated. "Have you traced her family?"

Jim shook his head. "She came here from Ohio or Michigan. All her family was from back there."

Kerney sighed. "Keep on it."

"I will."

Both men were dejected and unwilling to admit it. Kerney watched Jim fidget with the sling that held his arm secure against his chest before resting his own head against the cushion of the chair and closing his eyes. He was almost asleep when he felt a hand shaking him.

Molly looked down at him, a pillow and a blanket in her arms. "You're spending the night," she announced. "The couch in the study makes into a nice bed."

"That's not necessary."

"It is too." She wheeled and faced Jim. "Have you seen the pit he calls a home?"

"Just once."

"He has mice living with him," Molly said, in a tone of voice suitable for castigating heretics.

"That seals it," Jim agreed, laughing. "He stays."

Kerney took the bedding and followed Molly to the study.

DOYLE FLETCHER rose every morning before his wife so he could make the coffee while she showered and dressed for work. At thirty-seven, he didn't need a mirror to know he looked older than his years.

His prematurely gray hair wasn't the worst of it. The bags under his eyes seemed to get bigger every day.

Doyle had hauled logs to the sawmill until the lumber industry got screwed by the spotted owl and he was laid off from truck driving. Two years without regular work had battered his once cheerful disposition into a real bad attitude. Lately he had caught himself bitching about everything, criticizing the wife and kids for minor crap, and throwing temper tantrums for no reason.

It was four o'clock in the morning. His wife worked the day shift at Cattleman's Café. Her job and food stamps were keeping a roof over the family's head and food on the table. Fletcher hated the situation he was in, hated not being able to contribute to his family, and most particularly hated the United States Forest Service.

Doyle had charged Kerney all he could get for the trailer, and slapped a hefty security deposit on top of the rent. He had been counting on the extra income through the end of summer, but the stupid son of a bitch had gone and gotten himself fired from his job. To make it worse, the security deposit was gone, used to pay a bill, and there was no way he could scrape together the cash to give Kerney a refund. Doyle figured cleaning up the mice shit in the trailer would cancel out the deposit. If Kerney didn't agree, he'd have to wait until hell froze over to get his hundred dollars back.

His wife kissed him quickly on her way out the door. He sat at the kitchen table sipping coffee and studying the county health office pamphlet on hantavirus. Cleaning up mice shit was no longer a simple chore; not since the hantavirus outbreak began killing people several years back. Television reporters had yapped endlessly about the mystery killer illness, until the scientists figured out what the hell caused it. According to the pamphlet the disease was caused by airborne particles from deer mice droppings that attacked the pulmonary system in humans.

There were protocols to follow to remove the danger and avoid exposure, and Doyle read them over again carefully. He'd already picked up the rubber gloves, flea powder, traps, bait, paper towels, disinfectant, trash bags, and mask. It looked pretty straightforward.

He put everything in a box and carried it to his truck. In the darkness, he could see a single light on in the trailer window, and he wondered where in the hell Kerney was going so early in the morning. It wasn't like he had a job. Join the club, he thought sarcastically.

He got the kids up, dressed, fed, and ready to go. Both were enrolled in church camp for the summer on scholarships, but that didn't bother Doyle; half the children in the congregation attended for free, and he had tithed every year when he was still working.

He let the kids watch a little television until it was time to drive them to church. Kerney's truck was gone as he passed the trailer. That was fine with Doyle. Maybe he had moved out and forgotten about the deposit.

He dropped the kids off, spent a few minutes chatting with the youth minister, and went to the trailer. It had to be aired out for an hour before he could go after the mice. He unlocked the door, called out to make sure no one was home, waited a minute, and flipped on the light switch. The explosion that followed blew the roof off the trailer and slammed Fletcher across the hood of his truck into the windshield. He shattered the glass headfirst, and the impact broke his neck.

9

Wind-driven plumes of black smoke forced the onlookers back from the ropes that cordoned off the still-smoldering trailer. Kerney watched unnoticed at the back of the crowd. The trailer lay tipped precariously on its side with most of the roof missing. Scorched metal fragments, strewn in random patterns across the field, showed that the blast had been considerable.

On the hood of a truck next to the trailer, a blanket covered a lifeless body. Near a fire engine, Omar Gatewood talked to a woman who wore a yellow firefighter's slicker. Directly behind them police, emergency, and rescue vehicles were haphazardly parked in the open field. A paramedic, bent over next to the open door of an ambulance, consoled an agitated, sobbing woman who huddled on the ground.

The wind died off and the smoke rose vertically, allowing people to move forward against the ropes. Kerney scanned the crowd. He recognized a lot of faces, most of them people he knew only by sight. The gathering had almost a carnival air to it as folks shouted comments at the firefighters, who were smothering patches of smoldering grass with dirt. There were lots of smiles and head-shaking going back and forth. Based on the size of the gathering, Kerney reckoned the event had brought out the entire village.

A voice on his right side spoke. "Bomb."

Kerney glanced at the man. He wasn't familiar at all. "Excuse me?"

The man was in his mid to late twenties, with a long ponytail tied back at the nape of his neck, eyes that were filled with amusement, and broad Navajo features. He took a deep drag on a cigarette before answering. "I said it was a bomb."

"What makes you so sure?" Kerney asked, although he tended to agree with the analysis.

"I spent three years in an Army demolition unit. No exploding water heater can do that kind of damage unless it's been rigged with a charge."

"You think the water heater was rigged?" Kerney asked.

The young man nodded. Dressed in jeans, a plaid work shirt, and a lightweight black denim jacket, he wore a very old coral-and-turquoise Navajo bracelet made of coin silver. "I sure do." He dropped the cigarette and ground it under the heel of a work boot. "See how the roof is torn up? It takes more than exploding propane gas to do that kind of damage."

"What kind of bomb do you think it was?"

"From the blast pattern, dynamite would be my guess."

"Triggered by what?"

"Probably by a spark. It's easy enough to do. You plant your material, short out an electrical switch, and start a gas leak. Whoever turns on the juice becomes a crispy critter."

"Did you do it?" Kerney asked, half seriously.

The young man chuckled and his dark eyes flashed in amusement. With high cheekbones, slightly curved eyebrows, and an oval face that tapered to a round chin, he looked quietly fun-loving. "I wouldn't be talking about it if I did it, Mr. Kerney. You've got a rookie on your hands—probably a virgin—and not a very talented one at that."

"You know me?"

The man laughed. "Hell, man, you're headline news at Cattleman's Café."

"You have me at a disadvantage," Kerney said.

"I'm Alan Begay," he replied, raising his chin in a quick greeting. "From the Navajo Pine Hill Chapter at Ramah."

"What brings you to this party?"

"I'm a surface-water specialist with the state. I work in the Gallup field office. I've been down here for the last three weeks. I heard the explosion and tagged along with the crowd."

"Do you have time to stick around and take a look at the trailer after things calm down?"

"Yeah, I can do that," Begay replied, his smile widening. "It would be fun."

Kerney chatted with Begay for a few minutes to reassure himself that the man was who he seemed before skirting the fringe of the crowd. He found Sheriff Gatewood by the fire engine, occupying his time watching firefighters roll up hoses and shovel debris from inside the trailer.

Gatewood didn't notice Kerney until he was at his side. He cast a glance at Kerney and stifled a reaction of surprise by clamping his mouth shut. It made his chubby cheeks puff out even more. "Damn, Kerney," he said, "we figured you were burned up inside."

"No such luck. Who got killed?"

"Your landlord, Doyle Fletcher, the poor son of a bitch."

"What happened?"

"Fire chief thinks someone planted a device. She put a call into the state fire marshal to send an arson investigator up from Las Cruces."

Gatewood kept talking, and Kerney's attention wandered. The medical examiner and a paramedic were moving Fletcher's body from the truck hood onto a gurney. He stepped over and pulled the blanket down. Fletcher's face, seared and unrecognizable, made Kerney choke down bile. He flipped the cover back over the face and spent a minute considering whether it had been the blast or the fire that had killed Fletcher. He decided it didn't really matter.

The crowd began to thin out. Slowly people walked away in tight, chatty little groups. Gatewood moved off to speak to a deputy. Soon only a few hangers-on and official personnel remained, most with nothing to do. Kerney found himself wondering what had happened to the mice, and decided his sense of humor had gone stale.

At the rear of Fletcher's truck a deputy sheriff was using his bulk to block Alan Begay from getting closer to the trailer.

Kerney intervened. "Sorry for wasting your time," he apologized, as they stepped out of the deputy's earshot. "But the sheriff has sealed the crime scene. I can't get you in."

"Doesn't matter," Begay said. "Let me show you something." He walked Kerney thirty feet behind Fletcher's truck, stooped down, and used a stick to turn over the partially melted remains of a light socket. "Here's your trigger," he said with satisfaction.

Kerney bent over, peered at it, not quite sure what he was looking at, and waited for Begay to explain.

"You take the bulb out and solder filament wire to the hot post. When you turn on the juice it sparks, ignites the gas, and detonates the dynamite," Begay said. "You can see where its been soldered."

"What about fingerprints?" Kerney asked.

"Don't hold your breath." Begay tossed the stick away, brushed his hands, looked at Kerney, and shook his head. "So now you're unemployed *and* homeless."

"I didn't even think about that," Kerney said, as reality sank in.

"I've got a spare bed in my motel room, if you need a place to crash for the night."

Reserve boasted only one motel, so Kerney didn't have to ask where Begay was staying. "I may take you up on the offer."

Begay nodded. "I'll tell the desk clerk to give you a key."

"Thanks."

"No problem, man," Alan said as he walked away.

The television crew arrived. A cameraman unloaded equipment while the reporter—one of those bright-eyed, perky women who smiled at the camera no matter what the subject matter might be—hustled off to find Gatewood. It brought the few remaining onlookers who were leaving scurrying back for more entertainment.

As soon as everyone clustered around Gatewood and the reporter to watch the interview, Kerney took off.

MOM'S SURGERY had gone well—better than expected, according to the doctor—and Karen sat in the waiting room with her father. Even with the good news, his face was filled with worry, and he was fidgety, running his fingers through his gray hair and pacing back and forth across the waiting room, taking big strides with his long legs.

Karen wanted to pass it off as nothing more than Edgar's desire to see Mom as soon as the doctor would let him. She wondered if the love that her parents had—a sweet, absolute devotion—had melted away with their generation and was now nothing more than a cultural icon. The idea of being joined at the hip to a man had always felt stifling to Karen.

Elizabeth and Cody were much calmer than their grandfather. They were playing with a puzzle in the corner of the room with the pieces spread out on the floor between them. Elizabeth was lying on her stomach, knees bent and legs in the air, fitting pieces together, while Cody, stretched out on his side, played tiddledywinks with his pile of the puzzle, trying to vex his sister by skipping shots at her.

The only other person in the room, a woman waiting to take her husband home from outpatient surgery, sat in front of a television at the far end of the room, watching a mindless talk show. The station broke away from the network for a news bulletin.

Karen got to her feet as soon as the anchorman in Albuquerque started talking about more violence in Catron County. A trailer had been bombed and a man was dead. There would be a full report on the evening news.

"Daddy," she called.

Already at her side, Edgar scowled at the television.

"I've got to go," she said.

"Go ahead. I'll take care of the children," Edgar replied.

Karen grabbed her purse, kissed Cody and Elizabeth, and flew out the door.

THWARTED BY MOLLY'S REFUSAL to drive him around because she had to work for a living, *and* because his face would cause a massive traffic accident if she took him out in public, Jim Stiles was forced to do detective work by telephone. The mining company confirmed Steve Lujan's story about his settlement, and the Catron County Bank reported no large amounts of money going in or out of Lujan's accounts. The disappointment continued. No record of a divorce for Eugene or Louise Cox was on file in any of the district courts throughout the state.

Molly came home for lunch, bringing the telephone directories he'd asked for from the library, and questioning his sanity. When he told her what he planned to do, she told him he'd damn well better have the money to pay her phone bill. After sharing a quick, thrown-together sandwich and giving him a smooch on the lips, Molly said he kissed very well for a man with an ugly face and went back to work.

Jim's plan was simple. He would call every damn person who lived in or between Pie Town, Quemado, Magdalena, Reserve, and Luna until he found somebody who knew something about Louise Blanton Cox.

KAREN ARRIVED AT the trailer and quickly grilled Gatewood. She was relieved to learn that Kerney wasn't dead. The devastated trailer had been braced up with scrap lumber so that the crime scene specialists, flown in from Santa Fe by the state police, could work inside the structure. They were laboring cautiously, bagging evidence, dusting for prints, and taking photographs. Karen logged in with the officer in charge and toured the outside area with Gatewood, an arson investigator, and the state police agent assigned to the Padilla homicide. The wall studs of the trailer had been fractured into giant toothpicks, and melted ceiling tiles, warped by heat into bizarre shapes, dangled from the gaping hole in the metal roof. A couch, consumed down to the metal frame, sat next to a badly charred and smoldering mattress.

The arson investigator, in from Las Cruces, took Karen and Omar up a plank board to the hole where the front door had been. His rumpled jacket caught on the sharp edge of a piece of metal, and as he turned to free it, the trailer settled a bit. The movement froze Karen in her tracks.

The man coughed, shook his head, and stepped back down the plank, forcing Gatewood and Karen to retreat. "Maybe I should just tell you what I found," he said.

"That's a good idea," Karen replied.

On solid ground he inspected the tear in his jacket and tried to pull out a loose thread without success before pointing at the trailer. "We've got a dynamite explosion triggered by propane gas." He wheezed, took out a tissue, and blew his nose. "Enough material was used to guarantee nobody inside would survive the blast. Whoever did this wanted to send a message that it was no accident. I'd say the tenant was the target, and revenge or retaliation was the motive."

"Was it a professional job?" Karen asked.

"No way," the investigator replied.

"Does it fit any kind of profile?"

The investigator shrugged. "Sure. My bet is that we've got a male perpetrator. Women tend to use flammables and burn personal objects, like clothes or bedding. Men go for accelerants and explosives. The perp was organized about it. Knew what he wanted to do. This is a flat-out murder case."

"Anything else?"

The investigator nodded. "The landlord probably wasn't the target. I understand the tenant is a single man who worked for the Forest Service. I'd be looking for either an extremist or a jealous husband or boyfriend. Something along those lines."

Karen turned to Gatewood and gave him a searching look. "Where is Kerney?"

Omar looked sheepish. "He was here earlier."

"Find him," she ordered, thinking that maybe the democratic system of electing sheriffs was a stupid idea. "I want a full statement from him on my desk as soon as possible. Does he know anybody angry enough to want to kill him? Concentrate on his investigation. Find out if he has been threatened or harassed. If you come up empty, ask if he has a girlfriend. What was his relationship to Doyle Fletcher? Fletcher's wife?"

Stung by her crisp manner, Gatewood sent two deputies to look for Kerney.

Satisfied that the investigation was a little less scattered, Karen went to her office to call her boss in Socorro. Then she stood at the window for a very long time, looking at the sorry row of buildings across the road. Reserve had no charm other than the natural beauty of the valley and mountains. Most of the tourists stayed in Silver City or at resort ranches when they came to the region. There were no sidewalks or streetlights on the road. In front of an empty house across the way, once used as a real estate office, a pile of trash had collected against the sagging porch. Next door, she could see into the vacant modular building that had housed the weekly local paper before it went belly-up. Waist-high weeds covered the bottom half of the door.

The town felt like it was dying. Maybe they needed to keep track of the population: five hundred and counting—down.

She brushed a strand of hair away from her cheek and thought about the three dead men, Fletcher, Hector Padilla, and his grandfather. How were the deaths connected? What linked them to her family and a sixty-year-old secret? Would Kerney uncover the link before she could prepare her parents for the repercussions?

FAR PAST THE RANCHES along Dry Creek Canyon, at the point where the forest road separated, Kerney took the fork that led away from the Slash Z summer grazing land, where he had first met Phil Cox. The road dipped into a canyon before climbing the slope toward the hog-back ridge.

Jim had discovered engine oil in the mine shaft before he was shot. That meant Padilla Canyon had been used as a staging area to scout out the hunter's prey. Maybe another look would turn up similar evidence on the black bear poaching.

At the ridgeline he shifted the truck into low gear and descended slowly into a second canyon. Bracketed by box elder and walnut trees that thrived in the moisture-rich ecosystem, the canyon was an oasis compared to Dry Springs. The road, or what was left of it, crossed several small springs that trickled over river rock. It seemed to give out as sheer canyon walls closed in and the stream widened. He sloshed the truck through a pool of water three feet deep, past downed trees rotting in the undergrowth, and picked up the bare outline of the route moving sharply upland. Crawling slowly to the summit, he topped out to find a cabin in a secluded hollow, sheltered by pine trees and protected by the mountains that filled the eastern skyline. Made of hand-hewn logs, it had a tin roof that sagged in the middle and a rock chimney that leaned precariously at an angle over the roof. The windows and doors had been boarded up with sheets of plywood.

Kerney made a quick outside inspection before approaching the cabin, and found no sign of human activity. A strong odor of skunk grew as Kerney approached the door carrying a tire iron. He tapped hard and listened for scurrying sounds. All was quiet inside. From the high country above, he heard an elk bugle its presence with a thin, clear whistle that echoed into the hollow. On the plywood covering the door a Forest Service No Trespassing sign was posted.

He wedged the tip of the tire iron under the edge of the plywood next to a nail, yanked hard, and almost fell on his ass as the board pulled easily away from the doorjamb. There were imprint marks in the wooden doorframe, probably from a pry bar. Someone else had been here before him. A padlocked steel grate in front of the closed door barred the way. He gave up on the door and went to work on a boarded-up window, jimmying the plywood free only to discover it was shuttered on the inside. He broke the pane of glass, cleaned out the fragments embedded in the sill, pushed open the shutters, and climbed inside. The structure was a single room with a stone fireplace and four built-in bunks.

Kerney smiled when he saw the four-wheel ATV in the middle of the cabin. He pulled a flashlight out of his hip pocket and took a closer look at the tires. The wear on the rear tires matched exactly with the tread pattern he'd seen on the mesa and at the bottom of the meadows. A carrying rack had been welded behind the rear seat, and some rope was wrapped around the support posts that attached it to the frame. There were animal hairs in the fibers, some from a cougar. He bent low and shined the light under the ATV. The oil pan, crusted with a film of dirty oil, had a small leak. Holding the flashlight between his teeth, he dug into the sticky substance with a finger and rubbed it on the palm of his hand. There were small particles of rock dust and tiny wood chips embedded in the liquid. He put his hand to his nose and sniffed. Mixed with the smell of oil was the fragrance of fresh-cut pine.

Outside the cabin he cleaned up the signs of his forced entry and replaced the plywood over the window and the door, trying to decide who to tell about his find. It wouldn't be Charlie Perry or Omar Gatewood, and after a few minutes of inner debate, he also rejected telling Karen Cox, for now. An anonymous call to the state police was the best bet. At least that way he could hope the information would get to someone who didn't have a personal agenda.

He called the state police from Glenwood. On the highway a few miles south of the village, a surveillance car picked him up again, staying with him all the way to Deming, dropping out of sight only when Kerney waved down a patrolling cop inside the city limits to ask him how he could find Mike Anderson. The officer located Anderson by radio, and Mike agreed to meet Kerney at the entrance to Rock Hound State Park.

The Floridas, a short but prominent range southeast of Deming, broke twenty-five hundred feet above the desert. The road to the state park ran straight toward the stark, arid range. At the turnoff to the park, Anderson was waiting in his Bureau of Land Management truck. The car following Kerney continued on, moving too fast for Kerney to read the plate.

He pulled up next to Anderson's truck and rolled down his window.

"Heard your trailer got bombed," Anderson said, looking at him from inside his vehicle. "You're having trouble making friends up in Catron County, aren't you?"

"I'm not very popular," Kerney agreed.

"Sounds like you've got a war on your hands," Anderson replied. "Who did you piss off so royally?"

"I wish I knew," Kerney answered.

"I hear you. Could be any one of those radical groups that want the government to butt out so they can clear-cut the forests, over-graze the land, and reopen the mines. What do you need?"

"Answers. Tell me what you know about Leon Spence."

"Don't know anything about the man." Anderson shifted his weight and tapped his fingers on the steering wheel. "I already told you that."

"You never met him?" Kerney probed.

"Never."

This time Anderson was telling the truth, but he was also holding something back.

"Come on, Mike, level with me on this. You never met Spence. I believe you, but I've got a situation with three dead men, a wounded partner, and someone trying to kill me. I need help."

Anderson removed his hat, rubbed the back of his neck, and looked Kerney in the eye. "Okay, but I don't know what good it will do you. Spence set up his trailer at that old rock shop about two years ago. Nothing strange about it—people come and go with their trailers on those frontage lots along the highway all the time.

"A few months after he moved in, I started noticing unusual activity. Folks visiting at odd times driving vehicles with Arizona and Texas license plates, panel trucks towing rental trailers—that kind of stuff. I thought maybe it was a drug-smuggling operation, so I did a little snooping, found out what I could, and passed it along to my supervisor."

"And?"

"And nothing," Anderson retorted. "I was ordered to back off, make no more inquiries, and drop it completely."

"Why?"

"Don't know why."

"What did you learn about Spence?"

"Not much. He's in his mid-thirties, supposedly from Louisiana, speaks fluent Spanish, and worked as a salesman. Moved out, lock, stock, and barrel."

"Any theories about what's going on?" Kerney queried.

Anderson shook his head. "I've said enough already. Maybe too much." He put on his hat and gave Kerney a thin smile. "Be careful."

"Thanks, Mike."

Anderson drove away, and Kerney mulled over the new information. Maybe Juan had given him a bum steer about Leon Spence. Kerney dismissed the idea. Spence *was* smuggling, but it wasn't drugs, as Anderson thought, and Mike's reluctance to say more boiled down to one strong possibility: Spence was the target of an undercover investigation. It was the only possibility that made any sense.

Kerney's tail picked him up in Deming and stayed with him until he reached the trailer park on the outskirts of Reserve. The village had returned to a normal rhythm after the excitement of the morning; two people were talking outside of the bank, a few cars were parked in front of Cattleman's, and a cowboy was gassing up a truck at the service station. In the parking lot of the sheriff's office, all the squad cars were lined up in a neat row, joined by two state police units. Probably Gatewood had called a meeting.

Across the street at the motel, done up as a mountain chalet with a frontier motif, he caught a glimpse of Alan Begay unloading canisters from the back of a Chevy Suburban. He went into a nearby grocery store and bought two pounds of sliced ham, before making the short drive to Steve Lujan's house.

The house, at the end of a lane, was somewhat isolated from the neighbors. Kerney saw no sign of activity in the homes he passed. The gate was locked, and the only vehicle inside the fence was the flatbed truck, parked between two mounds of unsplit wood.

The barking German shepherd was off the leash. He backed up as Kerney drew near the gate and growled.

"Come here, Loco," Kerney called.

The dog stopped barking, wagged his tail, and looked at Kerney expectantly. Kerney threw some slices of ham over the fence and watched. After wolfing down the treat, the shepherd approached, looking for more.

"Good boy, Loco." Kerney poked another slice through the gate slats, and the dog took it gently from his fingers. Then he followed along quietly as Kerney walked the outside fence perimeter to the back of the house.

The existence of the fence and gate had raised Kerney's interest. It made no sense to fence off firewood and landscape rock in a community where both were readily available. What else was Lujan protecting?

Behind the house stood a metal toolshed and a storage building. A few truck tires, discarded engine parts, and a rusty oil drum were stacked against a wall of the shed. A patio deck jutted from the back door of the house and stopped at an unfinished rock wall. At the rear of the lot, two clothesline poles and a swing set, rusty and unused, stood in a bed of tall weeds. Part of the fence was covered by a massive thick vine, tangled and wild, that completely hid the river valley from view.

Kerney called Loco to him and tossed him some more meat. "Are you going to let me climb the fence and take a look around?"

Loco didn't respond. He was too busy devouring the ham.

As Kerney climbed the fence, Loco growled once, flopped down on the ground, and put his legs in the air for a tummy scratch. Kerney obliged and gave him the remaining ham.

"Heel, Loco," he ordered, hoping that Lujan had trained the shepherd to do more than bite on command.

Loco took his station at Kerney's side and meekly followed him to the toolshed. The building was locked, so he used his pocket knife to open the window latch. He climbed in and looked around. The shed contained several expensive chain saws, a set of stone chisels, and an excellent assortment of power tools, supplies, and hardware—all ordinary stuff.

The storage building had a thick pine door as the only point of entry. It was secured by a deadbolt lock. It would take an old burglar's trick to break in. While Loco stayed with him all the way, he got a truck jack from Lujan's flatbed, placed it between the joists that framed the door, and cranked until he couldn't ratchet it another notch. The joist sagged back enough to show a half inch of the bolt. He kicked the lock once and the door splintered free from the bolt, swinging on its hinges to reveal a room crammed with old Victorian furniture, including a four-poster bedstead, a carved chest of drawers with brass pulls and marble top, and an oak pedestal dining-room table with matching chairs. The rafters were covered in cobwebs, but the furniture had only a very thin coating of dust. It had been recently moved into storage, probably to make room for all the new stuff that filled Lujan's house.

After a quick search to make sure nothing else was missed, Kerney closed the door, wiped his prints from the doorknob and the jack, and went back to the flatbed. In the rear of the truck some of the wood chips, pine needles, and small twigs left over from Lujan's last load were coated with a sticky substance. He picked up a chip. The underside was gritty to the touch. It was fresh-cut pine, grimy with rock granules, and smelling like motor oil. Lujan had recently hauled a machine with an engine that leaked, Kerney noted with satisfaction. None of the chain saws in the toolshed had a cracked casing, so it could have been that Lujan had hauled the ATV in his truck to the cabin.

Kerney scratched Loco's ear and thanked him for the tour, then climbed back over the fence.

A sheriff's patrol car pulled in behind him just as he was about to back away. Inwardly, Kerney groaned. If he got busted, he wasn't sure how he could explain away the charges he faced. He killed the engine, put both hands in plain view on the steering wheel, and watched the deputy in his rearview mirror, waiting to see what kind of action the man would take. He relaxed when the officer walked casually to him with no hint of wariness.

"Deputy," he said, forcing a smile. It was the same man who had been waiting for him at his trailer the night he returned from dinner with Phil Cox and his family.

"Sheriff needs to see you," the deputy said, smiling in return. In his thirties, the officer had a football player's thick neck, a body about to go to seed, rosy cheeks, and a nose that had been broken at least once.

"What's up?"

"Hell if I know. You can follow me into town." He looked at the locked gate. The German shepherd was barking loudly and sticking his snout in between the gate slats. "I don't think the Lujans are home from work yet."

"I guess not. I'll catch them later," Kerney replied.

"Where you been all day? I've been looking for you since this morning."

"Really?" Kerney answered.

The deputy shrugged. "No matter. You've been found." He walked to his patrol car, called in his discovery, backed out, and motioned for Kerney to do the same.

THE MEETING with Gatewood consisted of the sheriff asking all the usual questions. In Omar's cramped, cluttered office, Kerney watched Gatewood's technique unfold. He talked about the "incident" at the trailer—a soft way to describe a murder bombing—and asked Kerney how well he knew Doyle Fletcher. Kerney answered directly, and Gatewood moved on, asking if he had encountered hostility from anybody during his investigation.

"Not really," Kerney replied.

"Who did you talk to?"

Kerney gave him an abbreviated list of names, and Gatewood wrote them down.

"That's not a lot of people," Omar noted.

"I didn't have much time," Kerney reminded him.

"Too bad about you getting fired," Omar said with false sympathy. "Do you think the bombing was tied to your investigation?"

"What do you think?" Kerney countered.

"It could be. Or maybe you just pissed somebody off."

"I don't think I've been around long enough to make any enemies on my own account."

"Some people don't need a lot of time to piss folks off. And working for the Forest Service is enough of a reason for some folks not to like you," Gatewood replied with a slow grin.

"Do you have particular folks in mind?"

"None in particular." Gatewood leaned back in his chair and stared down his nose. "So tell me something: what's keeping you here?"

"Inertia."

"No lady friend?"

Like maybe Fletcher's wife, Kerney thought. "No," he answered.

"Maybe a lady with a husband or boyfriend?" Omar nudged.

"No."

"Mind telling me where you where last night?"

"I stayed with Jim Stiles and his girlfriend."

Gatewood looked disappointed. "They'll vouch for you?"

"I don't see why not. Do you have any leads at all?"

"Not on the bombing, but we have a small break on the Padilla case," Gatewood answered, getting to his feet and walking to the office door. "The state police got a tip on that ATV you were looking for. Damn thing was stashed in an old Forest Service cabin up in the Mogollon Mountains. The tires match the tread evidence at the Elderman Meadows crime scene."

"Ownership?" Kerney inquired.

"Stolen about two years ago in Las Cruces." Gatewood held the office door open. "But we might get lucky if the lab boys can lift some prints. You'll stick around for a few days, won't you? Just in case we need to talk some more?"

"I will," Kerney replied, joining Gatewood at the door. "Carol

Cassidy told me you have a militia group operating in the county. Do you have any intelligence on them?"

Gatewood guffawed. "The militia is nothing more than a bunch of sword-rattling good old boys who like to play soldier."

"No political agenda?" Kerney prodded.

"Of course they have an agenda. Some time back they circulated—what do you call it?—a manifesto. They want the feds out of Catron County and the land returned to the people."

"Sounds like a good place to start," Kerney suggested.

Gatewood's eyes narrowed. "You just love to tell me how to do my job, don't you? For your information, I know every mother's son in the organization, and I've been talking to them on the telephone all day long. Nobody knows nothing."

"Seems like you've covered all the bases," Kerney said as he left Gatewood.

ALAN BEGAY was in his motel room when Kerney knocked.

"You didn't get a key?" he asked, when he opened the door.

"No. I'm not staying. I just stopped by to thank you for your offer."

"No sweat, man. Come in, if you can stand the mess."

The room had camping equipment strewn all over it. There were half a dozen large ice chests stacked in a corner along with boxes filled with bottles of nitric acid, filters, and unused plastic sample jars. A portable water pump and battery sat on the desk next to an assortment of meters and probes. The bed was strewn with maps, cameras, and lab report forms. At the foot of the bed were a pair of wading boots, a face shield, a lab coat, and lab gloves.

"Tools of the trade," Begay said, as Kerney looked around. He cleared some papers off a chair and perched on the end of the bed. "Have a seat."

Kerney sat.

"You've got some questions you want to ask me?"

"Why do you think I have questions?"

"Because it was pretty dumb of me to be showing off this morning," Begay replied. "Made me look suspicious. I figured you'd want to at least check me out."

"I already have checked you out. I called your boss in Gallup."

"And?"

"You're a choir boy, according to your boss."

Begay laughed, his eyes twinkling. "Sure, he said that. If I'm such an upstanding citizen, what are you doing here?"

"You spend a lot of time in the backcountry. Maybe you've seen something."

"A lot of beautiful country and a few pissed-off ranchers is about all I see."

"What about official personnel?"

"Who do you have in mind?"

"Steve Lujan."

Begay nodded. "I know him. He works with Amador Ortiz. But I don't see him when I'm in the mountains."

"Anybody on an ATV?"

"Nope."

"Who have you seen on this trip?"

"Just one guy I never met before. I was working on the Negrito Creek last week, checking for mercury and zinc seepage from an old silver mine. He was at one of the private ranches in the Gila."

"Doing?"

"He didn't say. He flew in. The owner has a landing strip. I was half a mile downstream when the plane came over, so I hiked in to see what was up."

"It wasn't the owner?"

"No. This guy was much younger. In his thirties. The owner is an insurance millionaire from Detroit. Older man. Fifty-something, at least."

"You've met the owner?"

"Yeah, once, when he was out for an elk hunt."

"Tell me about the stranger."

"Like I said, mid-thirties, six feet, maybe a hundred and eighty. Blond hair with no sideburns. Pale complexion. The guy didn't look like he spent much time outdoors. Didn't say much. Talked with a real thick southern accent."

"Did you get a name?"

"No, I didn't. He was kinda huffy about me being there. I had to show him my ID."

"Thanks, Alan. You'd make a good police officer."

Begay grinned. "Think so?"

"Yes, I do."

Alan shook his head. "I'll stick to protecting natural resources. From what I saw of your trailer, it's a lot safer then being a cop."

Kerney laughed. "How about *helping* a cop for a few minutes?

"What do you need?"

"How well do you know Steve Lujan?"

"Not very well."

"Would he recognize your voice on the telephone?"

"I doubt it."

"Good. Thirty minutes after I leave I want you to call him and say that you saw someone breaking into the shed behind his house this afternoon. Keep it simple. Give him the message and hang up. Will you do that for me?"

"You want me to tell him what?" Begay asked, giving Kerney a quizzical look that didn't completely mask a half-formed smile.

Kerney carefully repeated the message he wanted delivered.

"Did the break-in really happen?" Alan asked.

"Yes."

"Okay, I'll do it, but where will you be when I call him?"

"I'll be watching to see what Steve does."

"That's sneaky."

"That's police work," Kerney corrected.

DUSK CAME, and Kerney wondered if he had completely missed the boat about Steve Lujan. From a fire road in the hills behind the valley he watched Lujan's house through binoculars, waiting for Steve to make a move.

There were a few kids still riding bikes up and down the lane, popping wheelies in the dirt and practicing stunts, and Lujan's nearest neighbor had a barbecue grill going, but that was the extent of activity in the small collection of homes sprinkled in the valley west of the river.

At the Lujan residence, the Pontiac and Ford Bronco were parked inside the open gate. Lights burned inside the house, Loco was on his chain in the front yard, and there were occasional shadowy movements in the windows as people moved about. Finally, the kitchen went dark, a sure sign dinner was over. Ten minutes later, Lujan hurried out the front door, got into the Bronco, and drove away.

Kerney followed, staying a quarter mile back. Lujan traveled through Reserve to the state road that ran down to Glenwood and on to Silver City. Kerney kept an eye out for a tail behind him, but the road was dark and empty.

Lujan passed through Glenwood and didn't slow down again until he reached the turnoff for the Leopold Vista Historical Monument, a wayside rest stop on the highway dedicated to the man who had established the Gila Wilderness.

Kerney watched the taillights of the Bronco make the turn and disappear behind the low hill that concealed the monument from the highway. With only one entrance, Kerney couldn't follow without being detected. He got a microcassette recorder from the glove box and left the truck far enough back from the entrance to avoid suspicion, parked in deep shadows under a cottonwood tree. He jumped the highway fence and walked around the hill to the back of the monument. The site faced a sweeping vista of mountains to the east, and was nothing more than a large parking lot with a sign that told about Aldo Leopold and the Gila. During the daytime, tourists could whip off the highway with camera in hand, snap a picture, and be on their way in fifteen minutes.

Three vehicles were in the lot: Lujan's Bronco, an expensive RV towing a compact car, and a light-colored Chevy Caprice, with the parking lights on.

Hunkered down, Kerney memorized the license number of the Caprice and watched.

At the RV, a man packed up a folding card table and some chairs while his wife waited inside the vehicle. The Bronco and the Chevy, at opposite ends of the lot, showed no signs of movement. Almost nervously, the man at the RV lashed the table and chairs to the back of his vehicle, hopped inside, fired up the engine, and drove away.

Lujan got out of the Bronco and started walking toward the

Chevy. The driver cranked the motor, turned the Chevy directly at Lujan, flipped on the high beams, and froze him in the glare. Lujan yanked a hand over his eyes so he could see against the light.

A man's figure emerged from the car and stood behind the open door. Kerney turned on the recorder.

"What's so goddamn important?" the man said.

"I told you what happened," Lujan answered, moving closer.

"Yeah, you did. So what? Go home, call the sheriff, and report the break-in. That's all you have to do."

"No," Lujan countered. "I've had it. This is too fucking much. People breaking into my house and everything."

The man laughed. "You sorry son of a bitch, they broke into your storage shed, for chrissake, not your house."

"Same thing."

"I'll take care of it."

"How?" Lujan asked.

The man braced his arm on the top of the door and shot Lujan twice in the chest with a semiautomatic. He picked up the spent shell casings, walked to Lujan's body, and, satisfied with his solution, got in the Chevy and drove off.

Kerney checked out Steve Lujan's body. There were two rounds, center mass, in his chest. He turned on his heel and left the monument. When the killer walked into the light to make sure Lujan was dead, Kerney had gotten a good look. He was thirty-something, six feet tall with short blond hair, and he had spoken with a thick southern accent.

10

The sound of hard pounding at the motel door brought Kerney out of a deep sleep. He fumbled for the light, got up, peered out the window, and saw Jim Stiles. He unlocked the door and Stiles slipped inside, a worried look plastered on his face.

"I've been looking for you since midnight," Stiles said snappishly.

Kerney wore only boxer shorts, and the scar on his stomach, a long surgical incision with a puckered entry hole from a bullet, caught Jim's attention. It was a nasty-looking wound.

"What time is it?" Kerney asked groggily.

"Four in the morning," Jim answered. "What the hell is going on?"

"You tell me." Kerney struggled into his jeans, sank down on the end of the bed, and pulled on his boots. "What's up?"

"Steve Lujan's been shot dead, and Gatewood's got an APB out on you. A city cop came by Molly's house looking for you."

Kerney tugged his arms though the shirt sleeves and buttoned up. "What the hell for?"

"I called Omar and asked him the same question. He's prepared an arrest warrant on you for Steve's murder."

Kerney rubbed the sleep from his eyes, snorted, and stood up. "Based on what?"

"He said you were seen at Lujan's house earlier in the day, and Alan Begay told him about the phone call you had him make to Steve."

"That's it?" Kerney replied, shaking his head in disbelief. "Gatewood doesn't have a clue, does he? I think the man has just redefined the meaning of probable cause. Will Karen sign off on the warrant?"

"I don't know," Jim replied. "I called her after I spoke with Gatewood. She didn't know a damn thing about it." Jim paused and made a frustrated face. "Are you going to tell me what happened, or not?"

"Oh. Sure. I saw Steve get whacked."

"By who?"

"I'm not absolutely certain, but he matches the description I got from two different sources. He goes by the name of Leon Spence."

"Who told you about him?"

"Alan Begay and a BLM officer in Deming."

"I know Alan. He's solid. Do you know how to find Spence?"

"Not really. But I know where he's been. Begay saw him at a private ranch on the Negrito Creek. It's owned by some millionaire from back east who flies in. According to Alan, the ranch has a land-ing strip. Does that ring any bells?"

Jim nodded. "The old Double Zero."

"Can you get me there without any fanfare?"

"I think you should talk to Karen first," Jim countered.

"That can wait," Kerney replied. "First, we pay a quiet visit to the Double Zero. What's the most unobtrusive way in?"

"Horseback."

Kerney eyed the sling holding Jim's left arm. "Are you game?"

Jim flapped the sling against his side. "Give me a break. This itty-bitty scratch won't slow me down. Saddle me up and I'll take you there."

"What a guy," Kerney responded with a grin.

Jim smiled back. "Stuff it, Kerney. How did you get into this pile of shit?"

"It was easy: a little breaking and entering, a little criminal damage to property."

"Before or after your trailer got bombed?"

"After. I'll tell you about it on the way."

As they left the motel in Jim's truck, a police cruiser turned into the parking lot and started spotlighting vehicles.

THE STILES FAMILY ranch was directly across the river from Jim's house, where the Negrito Creek drained into the San Francisco. Stiles and Kerney arrived before dawn with the moon still full above the mountains. Jim drove to the horse barn, parked the truck out of sight, and told Kerney to saddle two horses while he paid a visit to his father.

In the paddock were two fine stallions, both about ten years old and built along the same lines, with well-sloped shoulders that would generate a fluid stride. He got the gear out of the tack room, saddled the horses, and sat on the top rail of the paddock waiting for Jim's return. The first light of dawn revealed the ranch house. It was a territorial-style L-shaped adobe with thick wood lintels above the first-floor windows. The sloping roof had a series of dormer windows over a covered porch.

The porch light came on, and Jim hurried out with pistol belts looped over his shoulder, clutching two rifles.

"What did you tell your dad?" Kerney asked. He put the rifles in the gun boots and fastened a pistol belt around Jim's waist.

"I told him we were going after a predator," Jim answered.

"Did you tell him it was the two-legged kind?" Kerney asked, smiling. He buckled on his own pistol belt and swung into the saddle.

"I left that part out," Jim answered.

They followed a sinuous creek bed through a moist, sandy wash into the mountains, cutting back and forth in hairpin turns through the shallow, fast-running stream of a slot canyon. It was slow going as the horses picked their way over smooth, slippery cobblestones. Above them the early-morning sky turned blue, but the gloom of night still hung in the canyon, and rising mist from the stream created the feeling of a dreary winter's day.

At a fast-rushing pool they walked the horses up a steep bank past walnut trees stained dark by water, the limbs weighed down by moisture-laden leaves. Kerney remounted at the top of the bank and stopped to watch a Gila woodpecker light on an exposed rock in the pool. It dipped down for a drink, and the red crown patch flashed at Kerney. Then it dropped into the pool for a morning bath and flapped its striped wings.

Kerney rubbed the stubble on his chin and looked down at the wrinkled, sweat-stained, stinky shirt that badly needed washing. Reality hit: he was unemployed, under suspicion, and wearing all that he possessed. What little he owned had been blown up. Clothes could be replaced, but his grandfather's two Navajo saddle blankets and the pictures of his parents—the only mementos he had of his family—were gone forever. Even the championship rodeo buckle was probably nothing more than a lump of melted metal.

He looked ahead. Stiles had his eyes glued on Kerney's face. He forced a smile.

"Are you all right?" Jim asked.

"Fine and dandy."

"You look ready to pound the shit out of someone."

"That's a damn good idea," Kerney allowed. "I just need to find the right someone."

ALAN BEGAY stood in the ankle-deep Negrito Creek wearing waders and holding a portable pH meter with a probe. The high acidity reading wasn't a surprise, given the closeness of the tailings pile to the streambed. The return visit to the creek had been demanded by the landowner's lawyers as a delaying tactic. Alan already pretty much knew that the readings wouldn't change. He grunted and noted the result in his field book.

Begay's thoughts jumped ahead to the report he would write and the additional shit he would have to face from Sanderson's lawyers. The three mine sites along the creek on the Double Zero property were spewing contaminants into the water and threatening the fish downstream. You'd think that a big-time Detroit millionaire who used the Double Zero as a retreat and hunting lodge wouldn't mind spending some spare change to clean up the pollution. No way. Sanderson was fighting the proposed sanction tooth and nail.

Alan heard a clattering of hooves and turned to find Jim Stiles and Kevin Kerney riding toward him. They reined in and looked down at him.

"Hello, Alan," Jim said.

"Jim," Begay replied. He shifted his attention to Kerney. Kerney was a big man, and on horseback he looked even bigger. The expression on Kerney's face was grim. Alan braced himself for a chewing-out. "I didn't mean to get you in trouble," he said.

"You didn't," Kerney replied gently, reading Alan's dismay, as he slipped out of the saddle. "Tell me what happened between you and Gatewood."

"He came to see me at my room," Alan answered. "He said Steve Lujan had been murdered, and that he knew I had talked to you. He wanted to know about our conversation, and I told him. I didn't know what else to do."

"You did the right thing," Kerney said.

"It didn't feel like the right thing," Alan countered.

Stiles nodded in the direction of the switchback trail that led to the Double Zero headquarters. The ranch sat on a flattop mesa overlooking a confusion of deep gorges and sheer cliffs that slashed north and south. "Any activity up above?"

"A plane flew in a little while ago," Begay answered. "It's still there."

"Did you recognize it?" Kerney asked.

Begay shook his head. "I just heard it. What are you guys doing up here?"

Kerney remounted. "Stay put, Alan," he ordered.

"More cop stuff?"

"Just stay put," Kerney replied genially.

Begay grinned and snapped off an exaggerated salute. "Whatever you say."

THE EDGE OF THE MESA, thick with piñon and juniper trees, gradually opened onto a meadow that stopped at a dirt landing strip. A silver twin-engine Beechcraft was parked next to a pickup truck. Behind the plane, built on a rock outcropping that served as the foundation to the building, was a long stone house. A split-log staircase curved over the rocks and up to the porch. Old-growth pine trees kept the house in deep shade. The place had a rustic, turn-of-the-century feel to it.

They stayed in the trees out of sight watching two men unload crates from the plane and carry them to the truck.

"What do you think?" Jim asked. "Is either one of them your man?"

"Can't tell from this distance. Let's go see. We'll stay in the trees and work our way around back."

They were halfway to the ranch house when the distant sound of choppers cut the silence. Kerney and Stiles looked up at an empty sky and back at the Beechcraft. The two men unloading cargo started scrambling—one to the truck, the other to the plane. A third man came running out of the house and swung himself into the bed of the truck as it started to roll. The Beechcraft's engine caught and the plane turned to taxi down the runway.

Out of the sun, three assault helicopters, all in a line, popped over the east ridge of the mesa, moving at over a hundred miles an hour. The choppers swung in an orbit over the field, one dropping to block the pickup that was running for the cover of the trees. As the chopper touched down, a door gunner fired a burst in front of the truck. Eight men, four from each side, all in black SWAT uniforms, hit the ground running. It was no contest. The team swarmed the vehicle without firing a shot.

A second chopper landed almost simultaneously, cutting off the Beechcraft. Eight more men piled out. Four surrounded the plane, pulled the pilot from the cockpit, and put him in a spread-eagle position on the ground. The remainder of the squad moved in on the house.

The last chopper circled and made a complete pass over the mesa. The pilot spotted Kerney and Stiles, veered away, and landed out of rifle range. Eight more men spilled out and scampered into the trees.

"Nicely done," Kerney said with admiration in his voice.

"Think we should surrender?" Stiles asked.

"That's a good idea. Let's make it easy for them."

Kerney moved his horse into the open, raised his hands, and clasped them behind his head. Jim followed suit, but couldn't get his left arm above the shoulder, so he surrendered with one hand raised.

A short burst of automatic-weapon fire cut into the treetops at the edge of the mesa. Pine cones and needles rained down on Alan Begay, who stepped into view with both arms in the air as high as he could get them.

"I guess Alan wanted to surrender too," Jim said. "No sense letting us have all the fun."

"I like a man who can follow orders," Kerney noted.

A man got out of the third chopper and scanned Kerney, Jim, and Alan with binoculars before talking into a hand-held radio.

The two guys who came out of the woods behind Kerney and Stiles wore Alcohol, Tobacco and Firearms shield patches on their SWAT uniforms. They got Kerney and Stiles dismounted, disarmed, and handcuffed before walking them across the meadow to the man with the binoculars. Another team followed behind with Alan.

The slightly stoop-shouldered man had an FBI shield patch on his SWAT jacket and an angry expression on his face which Kerney had seen before.

"You're a meddlesome son of a bitch," Charlie Perry said to Kerney.

"Let me guess, you're really not Ranger Rick," Jim remarked.

Perry ignored Stiles. "What the hell are you doing here, Kerney?"

"Looking for Leon Spence," Kerney answered.

Spence was stretched out facedown, hands cuffed at the small of his back, with an M-16 muzzle pointed at the nape of his neck.

"I see you found him for me," Kerney added.

"What's Spence to you?" Charlie demanded.

"A murderer," Kerney replied.

"Don't play games with me, Kerney. I haven't got the time."

"I'm serious. Spence whacked Steve Lujan."

Perry laughed. "If you can prove that, I'll personally kiss your ass."

"That won't be necessary. An explanation of what's going on here will do nicely," Kerney countered. "Do we have a deal?"

Perry nodded curtly.

Kerney turned his back to Perry and waited for him to remove the handcuffs. Hands free, Kerney took the small tape recorder from his shirt pocket and played it for Perry. Voices carry in the thin night air, and even the noise of the car engine didn't mask the conversation between Spence and Lujan, and the sounds of the two gunshots. Kerney popped out the tape and tossed it to Charlie.

Spence stared at Kerney with one eye, his cheek ground in the gravel of the landing strip. He tried to lift up his head and spit at Kerney. The man with the M-16 poked Spence with the rifle to keep him still.

"I'm sure your technical people can do a voice-print analysis and match it to Spence," Kerney said. "Plus, I'll testify as your star witness. I saw the whole thing go down."

"That sure sounds like Leon," Charlie said as he pocketed the tape. "You stay here," he ordered Alan Begay. "Kerney and Stiles, come with me." He uncuffed Stiles, turned away, and walked toward the lodge.

As they moved toward the lodge, two large trucks lumbered into view and turned in the direction of a wooden barn a hundred yards from the house. Some of Perry's team were hauling crates outside and stacking them in front of the open barn door.

THE LIVING ROOM of the ranch house, a wide, deep room with exposed rock walls and an oak floor, was richly furnished. Two tan matching Italian leather couches sat on either side of a fireplace which could easily take an eight-foot log. Scattered over the floor were expensive Navajo rugs. The mantel above the fireplace, a good six feet off the ground, displayed a collection of Zuni pots. An antique side table held a Remington bronze that looked authentic.

Kerney and Jim Stiles sat together on the couch that faced the front windows of the room. High up on the wall were mounted heads of elk, deer, and antelope overlooking the room. Charlie Perry sat on the other couch. Behind him was a floor lamp made of deer horns. A bear pelt, complete with head and paws, hung on the wall next to the fireplace.

"Let's have it," Kerney said to Perry.

Charlie pushed his sandy hair up from his forehead and stretched out his legs. "About three years ago the bureau infiltrated the Michigan Militia. Sanderson, the guy who owns the Double Zero, a rich right-wing zealot from Detroit who made his money in insurance, stepped in and helped bankroll the organization. There was nothing illegal about it, but it made Sanderson worth watching.

"He put a hundred thousand dollars on the table and we kept waiting to see how the money would be used. Finally, the money was filtered to a national committee charged with reorganizing state and local militia groups into regional military districts. We have a mole serving on the committee. There are six regional districts already operating. The committee decided to use Sanderson's funds to finance a special project.

"Leon Spence ran a smuggling organization that specialized in bringing exotic birds and animals into the States. The committee approached Spence with a scheme to harvest wild game to supply the Asian market with ingredients for folk remedies. He had an organization in place that could move the product to the right buyers and get top dollar for the goods.

"It was a damn good idea. Hardly anybody knows you can kill a cougar, boil its testicles, and sell the concoction as an aphrodisiac in a third-world country at a big profit. It's been a quiet crime spree that hasn't drawn any media attention.

"Spence targeted two areas for harvesting—Alaska and southern New Mexico. Both fit the criteria: small populations, the right kind of wildlife, and not enough cops to cover the wide open spaces. He's been running the operation for the past two years."

"What were the proceeds to be used for?" Kerney asked.

"What every army needs," Perry replied. "Weapons and guns. Nice little toys for the self-proclaimed patriots."

"The crates," Stiles exclaimed.

"Exactly," Charlie confirmed. "All of them filled with illegal armaments."

"Tell me about Spence," Kerney asked.

Charlie laughed. "He's a blue-eyed, blond-haired, Spanish-speaking Mexican, with a green card. His father is the son of a German who immigrated to Mexico after World War II. His mother is the daughter of the former governor of the state of Nuveo León. He went to a military prep school in Georgia and took a degree at Tulane in New Orleans. He does a great southern accent."

"Steve Lujan worked for Spence," Kerney prompted.

"Exactly."

"I'd sure like to know how he got paid," Jim broke in. "I couldn't find a money trail."

Charlie chuckled and stood up. "The deposits were made to a bank in the Bahamas. We've got the account impounded along with about a dozen more." He looked at his watch. "We have agents picking up the national committee members and Sanderson right about now. Plus we're shutting down two illegal arms dealers and breaking the back of a whole network of illicit exotic animal traders. This is one for the good guys."

"It sounds like a major bust," Kerney said, standing up so he could look Perry in the eye.

"Big-time."

"Did Steve Lujan murder Hector Padilla?"

"I can't answer that."

"I'm real happy for your success Charlie, but it doesn't get us any closer to finding out who shot Jim and blew up my trailer."

Perry chewed his lip for a minute before he answered. "Your assumption about Lujan killing Padilla is reasonable. Maybe we can get Spence to confirm it. But if you think Steve came after the two of you to cover his tracks, you're betting on the wrong horse. I don't think Spence would allow that."

"Would Spence do it himself?"

"No way. He was under full surveillance when Jim was shot and your trailer was blown up. He wasn't even in the neighborhood."

"So who is coming after us?" Kerney demanded.

Charlie shrugged his shoulders. "Your guess is as good as mine."

"What about the Catron County Militia? The People of the West? The Free Range Society?"

Charlie smirked. "Take your pick. Look, Kerney, let me make it clear. This operation wasn't designed to round up every pissed-off, angry white male in Catron County who wanted to join the revolution, rewrite the Constitution, or take a deer out of season. We've got a national militia organization developing that could make the Ku Klux Klan look like a bunch of boy scouts in bed sheets, once it really gets rolling. That's our target, and we plan to cut its head off."

"One more question."

"What is it?"

"Did you put a tail on me?"

"You bet I did. You're a loose cannon. I'll let Gatewood know we've got a suspect in the Lujan murder and tell him to rescind the arrest warrant on you."

"Gatewood got the warrant approved?"

"He sure did. You're a fugitive."

"Don't tell Gatewood anything."

Jim Stiles gave Kerney a quizzical look. "Why not?"

"What kind of hand are you playing?" Charlie demanded.

"Just a hunch."

"Have it your way," Charlie said.

KERNEY SAT down in the easy chair in Jim's living room wearing a pair of blue jeans that were a tad too tight around the waist and a blue cowboy shirt that fit him pretty well. He was just out of the shower and felt a hell of a lot better after a shave and a fresh change of clothes, supplied by his host.

Jim sprawled on the couch, sipped a beer, and waited for Kerney to settle himself. "Why didn't you want Charlie to tell Gatewood to cancel the arrest warrant?" he asked.

"I don't trust Gatewood," Kerney answered. "He's too eager to make me his prime suspect. Besides, I need an edge."

Stiles rested his head on the arm of the couch. "An edge against who?"

Kerney smiled. "That's the question, isn't it? Tell me about the local militia."

"I don't know who runs it," Jim replied. "They keep a pretty low profile. What I've heard is mostly rumors."

"Gatewood said he knew the leadership."

"Maybe he does."

"Is he connected with them in any way?"

"Hell, I don't know."

"Does the name Ulibarri mean anything to you?"

"Sure. Steve Lujan's sister, Ramona Ulibarri. She lives in Southern California with her husband."

"Any kids?"

"Two teenage boys, I think. Maybe a little younger. They visit every summer."

"Do you know the kids' names?"

"No. But the husband's name is Ray. Why are you interested in them?"

"A BLM officer checked with Gatewood after he stopped a kid on an ATV outside of Deming. The kid said he was from Reserve and gave his name as Ulibarri. Gatewood told the officer he didn't know anybody in the county by that name."

"Gatewood knows the family," Jim said. "They only moved to California a short while back."

"Was Gatewood informed of the mountain lion translocation?"

Stiles adjusted his position. "I'm almost certain he was."

"How certain are you?"

"If he reads his mail, he had to know. Santa Fe sends out bulletins to all local law enforcement agencies on every translocation of a cat, with an advisory to inform us if the animal is found dead or killed."

"Then he knew."

"Most likely. Do you think Gatewood's dirty?"

"Gatewood's a politician. He could be anything."

Jim laughed. "That's funny, but I don't think Omar Gatewood would shoot me."

"Maybe he didn't. Maybe he just *helped* get you shot."

"That's an interesting idea. How do we find out?"

"Amador Ortiz. His phone call sent you to Padilla Canyon. Maybe somebody encouraged him to make that call."

"Let's talk to him," Jim said as he got off the couch. "I'll go with you."

Before Kerney could answer, the front door opened and Molly Hamilton flew into the room. She glanced at Kerney, sparks flashing in her eyes, and gave Jim a very nasty look.

"Goddamn you!"

"What?"

She walked to Stiles and poked her finger in his chest. "You were supposed to call me, remember?"

"I'm sorry."

She poked him again. "That's not good enough."

"I think I'll leave," Kerney said, unraveling himself from the chair.

"Stay put, Kerney. I'll get to you in a minute." She poked Jim again. "I've been all over the damn place looking for you, wondering if you'd been shot again, or kidnapped, or something."

"We haven't been anywhere near a phone until just now," Jim explained. "We just got back. We're fine. Stop worrying."

"Shit!" Molly punched Jim in the chest with her fist and dropped her head. When she raised it, the anger on her face had been replaced with tears. "I wish it was that easy to do," she said.

Jim pulled her close in a one-arm hug. Molly didn't resist.

Kerney quietly slipped out of the room and went to the kitchen.

MOLLY SNIFFLED and wiped her nose, still a little red from crying. She sat with Kerney and Jim at the kitchen table.

"Sorry I sounded so bitchy," Molly said.

"You have every reason to bitch," Kerney allowed.

"You're right. I do. I called Karen Cox this morning after I started worrying about Jim." She shot him a dirty look, and he flinched. "She said Gatewood went over her head to the DA in Socorro to get the warrant signed. She wants you to stay out of Catron County and turn yourself in to the police in Silver City."

"I have no intention of going to jail on a murder-one charge," Kerney retorted.

"I'll bail you out," Jim countered.

"I may not be allowed to make bail," Kerney replied.

Molly wrinkled her nose. "Fine. Jim can harbor you, and you can both be fugitives." She took a slip of paper from her purse and passed it to Stiles. "A lady called for you. She got your message on her answering machine asking about Eugene Cox's wife."

Jim read the name and address. "Emily Wheeler. Pie Town. What did she say?"

"She wrote a book about the Great Depression and World War II in Pie Town. It's a history of her family and friends who homesteaded in the area. It sounds like she did a lot of research. Tracking down former residents, searching public records, interviewing folks, and corresponding with old-timers who had moved away. She published it herself and sent copies to all her friends and relatives."

"Did she say anything about Louise Cox?" Jim asked.

"She won't talk about Louise unless you can prove you're really a police officer. She was quite insistent about it."

Kerney raised an eyebrow. "Go and see her," he said to Jim. "Take Molly with you."

"Right now? It's too late."

"Get her out of bed if you have to."

"It can wait until morning," Stiles argued. "I'm going with you."

"No, you're not. Take Molly and go to Pie Town."

Jim gave him a stormy look.

"I don't want you with me," Kerney added.

"I think we should do what the man asks," Molly said.

Jim's expression softened when he looked at Molly. "Okay. Pie Town it is."

"Can I use your truck?" Kerney asked.

Jim tossed him the keys. "Don't get busted, for chrissake. At least not until we get back."

"If I'm caught, I'll tell Gatewood I stole the truck," Kerney replied.

AMADOR'S HOUSE was dark, but a quarter mile up the road the Lujan house was filled with people, and a large number of vehicles were parked in front of the chain-link fence. Kerney debated delaying a confrontation with Ortiz and decided to wait and see how long the gathering of mourners would last. He parked Jim's truck out of sight, walked back to the road, and settled under a tree halfway between the two houses. With moonrise several hours away, the night was dark. Above him the Milky Way cut a swath across the sky and sprinkled out into a vast, random pattern.

He heard a car engine fire up, and soon it passed him, traveling to the blacktop highway and turning toward town. More cars began to leave, along with a few people on foot, walking down the dirt road to their houses. Finally all the cars were gone, except for the Lujans', but Amador had yet to appear. Half an hour later, Amador and his three children came out, walked slowly down the road, and veered up the path to their house.

Kerney waited, wondering if Amador's wife was staying with

Yolanda. He tried to think of a way to separate Amador from the children without announcing his presence, but no ideas came, short of breaking in and yanking him out.

Amador supplied the solution. The bedroom lights were doused, and within minutes Amador was on the porch lighting a cigarette. Kerney waited until Amador walked into the yard before making a long, looping circle behind the house.

Amador flicked his cigarette away, turned to go inside, and felt the muzzle of a gun pressed against his ear.

"Walk across the road," Kerney whispered.

"You motherfucker," Amador said.

Kerney slapped the barrel against Amador's temple, just hard enough to get his attention. "No talking," he hissed. "Move."

In the darkness under the trees, he ordered Amador to turn around. Ortiz spun quickly, and Kerney hit him hard across the bridge of the nose with the pistol. Amador's hands flew to his face.

"You broke my fucking nose," he gasped.

"Isn't this fun?" Kerney replied, as he backed up a few steps, out of Amador's range. "Now, very slowly, I want you to drop to your knees and lie facedown on the ground with your arms and legs spread out at your sides. You know the drill."

"Are you going to kill me?" Amador whined. His stomach heaved and his breath came in quick gasps.

"Do it!" Kerney snapped.

Ortiz sank down and assumed the position.

Kerney walked behind him, cocked the pistol, and patted Amador down. He had no weapons.

"I had a little chat with Steve last night before he died," Kerney said. "He told me you knew about his freelance poaching job. In fact, he said you let him take time off from work to go hunting."

Amador grunted.

"Is that a yes or a no?"

"I knew about it."

"That makes you an accessory to murder."

"You're a fucking murderer yourself."

"I guess we're both in a shitload of trouble. Who told you to call Jim Stiles and tell him about Padilla Canyon?"

"Nobody."

"Don't lie to me, Amador."

"Let me get up," Amador begged. "My nose hurts real bad."

"Come slowly to your knees and keep your arms outstretched."
Amador complied.

"Who told you to call Jim Stiles?" Kerney repeated.

"Gatewood has me by the balls, man. I did a burglary three years ago. I needed money, so I hit one of the vacation cabins. The owner had it wired with a silent alarm. Gatewood got a call from the alarm company and caught me on the road with all the goodies."

"So you're Gatewood's snitch," Kerney said. "Did he tell you to call Jim Stiles?"

"That's what I'm saying, man."

"Thanks, Amador. You can go home now."

"You mean it?"

"I sure do. Get that nose looked after."

As Amador started to rise, Kerney cold-cocked him.

11

Kerney left Amador where he fell. A bad feeling about beating up the man left a sour taste in his mouth. He cursed himself for giving in to the anger and drove away.

From the number of the squad cars patrolling the streets of Reserve it looked as though Gatewood, all his deputies, and the state police were out searching for him. Fortunately they weren't looking for him in Jim's truck. On the highway to Silver City, Kerney considered his options. With a murder-one APB out on him, playing hide-and-seek with Gatewood and his cronies wasn't an appealing idea. He could go to ground, stay in the open and risk the possibility of the danger inherent in a felony arrest, or turn himself in to the Silver City police and deal with Karen Cox. He had no place to hide and no desire to get conveniently shot for resisting arrest—which was a distinct possibility, given Gatewood's culpability. That left jail as his only option. He would have to gamble that Karen Cox would play by the rules.

In Silver City he called Charlie Perry from a pay phone, told him what he planned to do, and asked him to get in touch with Karen and fill her in on the facts about Steve Lujan's murder. Perry was willing to oblige: Spence's handgun had been recovered, ballistics had matched the weapon to the slugs in Steve Lujan's body, and Spence's fingerprints had been lifted from the gun.

"I'll tell Gatewood to cancel the APB and void the arrest warrant," Perry added.

"Leave Gatewood out of it," Kerney snapped. "According to Amador Ortiz, it was Gatewood who told him to set up Jim Stiles for the ambush at Padilla Canyon."

"That's serious shit," Perry said.

"You bet it is," Kerney replied.

"Where's Ortiz now?" Perry asked.

"I had to beat the truth out of him. He's probably home with a broken nose."

Perry sighed. "You're some kind of hot-dog cowboy, aren't you?"

"Whatever," Kerney said. "One more thing: talk to Karen Cox in person, okay?"

"Are you paranoid, Kerney?"

"No, cautious," Kerney answered. "Paranoia is an FBI trait."

"Not anymore. J. Edgar Hoover is dead," Perry replied and hung up.

It was well into the graveyard shift when Kerney turned himself in to the on-duty commander at the police department. He was photographed, fingerprinted, booked, and placed in a holding cell. After about an hour, the commander, a young lieutenant with a washed-out complexion, tired eyes, and a weight lifter's body, returned and squinted at him through the bars of the cell.

"Looks like you've had a busy night," the lieutenant said. "There are additional charges pending on you out of Catron County. Seems you forced some guy off his property at gunpoint and pistol-whipped him. Do you want to call a lawyer?"

"No," Kerney answered without hesitation. For now, he was in the safest room in town, and it wasn't costing him a dime. "Call the ADA in Catron County for me and tell her what's happening. Her name is Karen Cox."

The lieutenant nodded. "I'll give her a call." He passed a brown bag through the bars. "Sack lunch," he explained. "Left over from the morning prisoner run to the courthouse."

Kerney took the bag and opened it. It contained a bologna sandwich on white bread, an orange, and a cookie. "Thanks."

"No problem."

The lieutenant stayed put and watched Kerney eat his meal. When he'd finished, Kerney crumpled up the bag and gave it back to the officer.

"I hear you were a good cop in your day," the lieutenant said.

"I like to think so," Kerney allowed.

"That guy you cold-cocked must have really pissed you off."

Kerney laughed and stretched out on the cot.

"Did I say something funny?"

"Yeah, in a way, you did. It reminded me of the old saying 'There's no such thing as a free lunch.' Nice try, Lieutenant."

The lieutenant shrugged lazily. "You can't blame me for trying."

"I don't. But a stale sandwich, a cookie, and a piece of fruit won't get you a confession."

"It might help if you talked about it. I'm a good listener."

"And I'm an innocent man," Kerney said. He waited until the lieutenant gave up and walked away before closing his eyes. He was asleep within minutes.

"I WANT TO MAKE SURE I'm doing the right thing," Mrs. Wheeler said.

Emily Wheeler, age eighty-five and the author of *The People of Pie Town: The Last of the Frontier Homesteaders*, smiled at Jim Stiles and Molly Hamilton as they sat close to each other on the sofa. A nice-looking young couple, she thought to herself, but the young man would look better without those nasty scratches on his face, the eye patch, and his arm in a sling.

"I understand, ma'am," Jim replied.

The front room of the small house had pictures everywhere: in frames on the bookcases, in carefully placed arrangements on the walls, and lined up on the top of an upright piano. Many of the photographs were old, dating back to anywhere from the turn of the century through World War II. Emily Wheeler kept her memories right where she could see them.

"What can you tell us about Louise Cox?" Molly asked.

Mrs. Wheeler, perched at the edge of a Victorian chair, placed her hands firmly in her lap. A slight woman, she sat as erect as a young girl. She wore a housecoat and slippers. Her round face, widely spaced eyes, button chin, and full lips gave her an appearance of perpetual cheeriness.

"She was just a sweetheart," Emily said. "The schoolchildren absolutely adored her. She was an excellent teacher."

"I'm sure she was," Jim said. "When was the last time you had any contact with her?"

"I'm not sure Louise would want me to tell you anything more. Is she in some kind of trouble?"

"No, ma'am. We just need to talk to her."

Emily eyed the young man cautiously.

"Can you tell us how to contact her?" Jim prodded.

"I really don't feel comfortable betraying a confidence," Emily replied.

On the end table next to the sofa was a copy of Emily Wheeler's book. Molly picked it up. "What fun it must have been to write this book," she said.

"Have you seen it before?" Emily asked.

"Oh, yes. We have the copy you donated to the library at Western New Mexico University. I keep it in the reference section."

Emily smiled at the young woman. "I'm pleased to hear that. Do you work at the library?"

"Yes. You did an amazing amount of research. You must have spent a lot of time tracking people down."

"It was a lot of work. I spent a great deal of time trying to locate people who had moved away. I had some luck, too." Emily hesitated.

"What sort of luck?" Molly asked.

"Oh, it was very serendipitous. Once or twice I heard about the whereabouts of somebody from one of the folks I had contacted."

"Did that happen with Louise?" Molly asked.

"Yes. Some old Pie Town residents ran into her shortly after they moved from New Mexico to a retirement community in Arizona. They sent me Louise's address."

"Did you write to Louise?"

"I did. She sent me a short note back saying it would be better if she left the past alone. She asked me not to tell anybody where she was living."

"I wonder why she felt the need to do that," Molly said.

"I have no idea. I never saw her again after she moved away and married. Nobody did. That was a very long time ago."

"If we can find her, it would be a great help," Molly urged. "We need to speak to her about her ex-husband. It is really nothing more than a family matter. Do you have her address?"

"I believe it would be best if you found her on your own."

"There is some urgency," Molly countered. "And if we can find Louise, she may be able to help her family."

Emily Wheeler considered the young woman for a long moment before reaching for her address book from the side table. "I hope I'm doing the right thing."

"I think you're a dear to trust us," Molly replied.

"She lives in Green Valley, south of Tucson. It's a retirement community." Emily Wheeler put on her glasses and slowly read Louise Cox's address so the young man could write it down accurately.

"Thank you for your help," Molly said.

MOLLY BACKED HER CAR, a year-old Mustang hardtop, out of the driveway and headed for Reserve.

"You're going the wrong way," Jim said.

She braked and pulled to the shoulder of the road. "I have to be at work in the morning. I have a job, Jim. Remember?"

"Call in sick and go to Green Valley with me," he proposed.

"I don't have a change of clothes or anything I need."

"I'll use my credit cards. We can drive straight through, get a room, catch a few hours' sleep, and buy some fresh duds in Tucson."

"Are you serious?"

"You bet I am. Besides, I may need you to sweet-talk Louise Cox the way you did Emily Wheeler."

"I was pretty good, wasn't I?"

"More than good. You were great."

"Green Valley it is," Molly replied, after a momentary pause. "But it's going to cost you."

"I certainly hope so."

A PREDAWN RAINSTORM, usually a delight to Karen, only served to reinforce her bitchy mood. She hated saddling her father with Elizabeth and Cody and breaking her promise to visit Mom at the hospital, but three phone calls—one from Omar Gatewood, one from a police lieutenant in Silver City, and one from Charlie Perry, asking her to stop by his office—made it necessary. She started with Gatewood. In the sheriff's office, she stood in front of his desk and read Amador Ortiz's sworn statement accusing Kerney of an unprovoked attack. Omar watched her from his chair with a look of satisfaction on his face, then pushed an arrest warrant across the desk.

"I'm not signing it," Karen said, looking down at the document.

"What's the problem?"

"You went over my head on the murder warrant. I don't appreciate your little bullshit game."

"I had sufficient probable cause," he argued, stung by Karen's bluntness.

"Maybe so, but you still went around me."

Gatewood waved the paperwork at her. "This is a solid criminal complaint."

"That's my decision to make. I want to talk to Kerney before I decide. I want to make absolutely sure the complaint is reliable."

"Amador has no reason to lie," Gatewood rebutted.

"It's one man's word against another," Karen replied, "and it's my call to make."

"Whatever you say," Omar replied, forcing a compliant smile.

"Don't even think about blindsiding me this time, Omar," Karen said, her eyes locked on his.

She left Gatewood, his frozen smile still plastered on his face, and headed down the road to find out what Charlie Perry wanted to see her about.

OMAR GATEWOOD sank against the cushion of his chair, stared at the ceiling, cracked his knuckles, and rubbed the back of his neck. Karen Cox was turning out to be nothing but trouble. He didn't know if she was fucking with him or just acting like a gung-ho, know-it-all rookie who wanted to do everything herself. He did know that there wasn't a damn thing wrong with the arrest affidavit.

He stood up, took his handgun from the desk drawer, and slipped it into the high-rise holster. Maybe he'd better talk to Amador one more time, just to make sure he really hadn't told Kerney anything.

The phone rang, and he grabbed it. "What is it?"

"What happened?" a voice asked.

"She wants to talk to Kerney first before she signs the warrant. Don't sweat it—Silver City will hold him on the murder-one charge. He's not going anywhere."

"See that he doesn't. What does Kerney know?"

"Nothing," Gatewood replied.

"Are you sure?"

"I'm going to talk to Amador again."

"If Amador lied to you, get him out of town until this blows over."

"This is turning into a real pile of shit," Gatewood hissed into the telephone.

"Talk to Ortiz and call me when you're finished. We'll meet at Whitewater Creek."

"What about Kerney?" Gatewood demanded.

"I'll bring your orders with me."

The line went dead.

CHARLIE PERRY, dressed in a three-piece suit, sat in his office sorting papers and putting stuff he wanted to take with him in a box. It felt damn good to be closing the assignment out, and he looked forward to returning to the Beltway civilization of Washington and a headquarters job. Two years undercover in the boondocks of New Mexico had seemed like living in a nineteenth-century time warp. He was glad to be done with it.

He looked up to find Karen Cox standing in the doorway.

"You wanted to speak to me, Charlie?" she asked, eyeing his suit.

"I do." He stood up and gestured at an empty chair. When Karen was settled, he showed her his FBI credentials.

"What's this all about?" she demanded, giving Charlie another appraising look.

Charlie perched on the edge of his desk. "Kerney turned a smuggling bust into a murder-one case for me," he explained, "and for that, I owe him. I have hard evidence that exonerates him in the Steve Lujan shooting, and he has information that your sheriff may be a dirty cop. He wants you fully briefed on the situation."

"I'm listening," Karen said.

AT THE SILVER CITY POLICE DEPARTMENT, Karen used a vacant interrogation room to meet with Kerney. Even though Charlie Perry had walked her through the facts of the Steven Lujan murder, she let Kerney tell his story. He finished up with Amador's admission that Gatewood had ordered him to give the Padilla Canyon tip to Jim Stiles.

"Do you think Gatewood did the shooting?" Karen asked, making a final entry in her notebook.

"I doubt it. But I've been wondering if Jim was a target of choice or a target of opportunity."

"Meaning?"

"Jim should have waited and turned the information over to me. Padilla Canyon is Forest Service land and on my patrol route. Amador knew that and probably told Gatewood."

"So you think you were the target?"

"Maybe I have been all along."

"That would make the trailer bombing a second attempt to kill you," Karen noted.

"Which makes me very nervous."

Karen closed her notebook and stood up. "Let's go."

Kerney stayed seated. "There's the small matter of murder charges against me."

"Not anymore. The charges have been dropped."

"Why didn't you tell me that up front?"

"We don't have time to bicker. Let's go."

Outside the police station the drizzle continued, but the sky promised a heavier rain. Rolling thunder rumbled in overcast, thick clouds. Kerney stepped off in the direction of Jim's truck.

"Where do you think you're going?" Karen demanded, standing in the drizzle.

"I've got to find a way to get to Omar Gatewood and rattle his cage."

"Not without me you don't," Karen said sharply.

"That's not a good idea."

"If you're concerned for my safety, don't be," Karen said sarcastically.

"This could get ugly."

"Either you work with me or I'll put you back in the slammer under protective custody."

"That's illegal," Kerney said.

"I'll do it anyway," Karen countered. "Your chances of getting to Omar are nil, if you try it by yourself. He's probably pulled in every IOU he has to get to you before you can get to him. If you want to solve this case, get in my car."

Kerney studied Karen's icy expression and decided arguing with her would do no good. "What's your plan?" he asked as he opened the passenger door to Karen's station wagon.

"Our best bet is to isolate Omar. I'll call Gatewood from home, tell him that I'm approving his warrant, and ask him to personally bring it by the house for me to sign. When he shows up, we'll Q-and-A him."

"That might work."

As they drove away, the skies opened and hail began to fall, clattering loudly on the roof of the station wagon.

"Would you mind making a couple of stops along the way?" Kerney asked, raising his voice above the din to be heard.

"Where do you need to go?"

"Jim loaned me a shirt and a pair of jeans, but I'd like to buy some new clothes and some shaving gear."

Karen's eyes softened as Kerney's predicament hit home. "You lost everything in the trailer, didn't you?"

"It wasn't much," Kerney admitted. "But it was everything I cared to keep."

She looked at his waist. He wasn't wearing the rodeo championship belt buckle. He wasn't wearing a belt at all.

Kerney followed her glance. "Melted," he announced.

"That stinks. We'll stop at a couple of stores and get you squared away."

When Kerney had finished buying what he needed, the backseat was filled with shopping bags and a large canvas carryall to put everything in. Halfway back to Glenwood, with the skies clearing, Karen took her eyes off the road and glanced at Kerney.

"You're staying with me," she said, "until we get things sorted out."

"I'm staying with you?"

"There's no other option. You haven't got a place to live, and bunking with Jim Stiles is too risky."

"I guess house arrest is better than jail," Kerney noted.

"You'll have to sleep on the floor." She glanced at Kerney again. "Where is Jim?"

"I wish I knew," Kerney answered.

IN SPITE OF Jim's attempts to hurry Molly along, she took her own sweet time shopping for a new outfit in a Tucson clothing store that opened early. His stomach was grumbling for breakfast by the time she finished and came out of the dressing room wearing a dark green blouse with an embroidered yoke, a pair of white jeans, and new Tony Lama cowboy boots.

"Now you have to feed me," she announced, as she spun around to give him a full view of the outfit.

He grinned, nodded in agreement, and paid the bill without complaint.

They arrived in Green Valley in the middle of the morning, with the temperature already in the three digits. Halfway between Tucson and the border town of Nogales, Green Valley paralleled the interstate that ran through the high Sonoran Desert. Except for a few businesses at the northern end of the town and one large strip mall on the main drag, there was very little commercial development, but there were a hell of a lot of churches. Cars along the wide boulevard moved slowly in spite of the absence of heavy traffic, and most were late-model American-made land yachts driven by gray-headed motorists. There wasn't a baby boomer, adolescent, or thirty-something person in sight.

Molly turned off the main street and passed row after row of single-story apartment condominiums that looked like cheap budget motel units. The native landscaping of saguaro cactus, paloverde trees, desert ironwood, brittle bush, and yucca didn't completely hide the cut-rate construction of the cement-block buildings.

After the condominiums petered out, the neighborhood changed into modest single-family ranch-style tract homes on small lots. Recreational vehicles, pickup trucks with camper shells, and travel trailers filled about every other driveway. Finally they entered an upscale area of multilevel homes with brick exteriors and tile roofs that surrounded a golf course. Molly parked in front of a house that backed up to a fairway. It was expensively landscaped with crushed rock, native plants, flagstone walks, and a border of blackfoot daisies that covered a low stone wall.

With Molly at his side, Jim rang the doorbell. A tall woman, about seventy years old, answered. She had an angular face, a high forehead, and a long nose that gave her a birdlike appearance.

"Yes?" the woman said, glancing from the man to the woman. The young man's face looked as if it had been peppered with birdshot, his eye was covered with a patch, and his left arm was in a sling. The young woman was wholesomely attractive with lively blue eyes that sparkled with vitality.

"Louise Blanton Cox?" Jim asked.

"Yes."

He introduced himself and showed his deputy sheriff's commission to the woman. "I'm with the Catron County Sheriff's Department. We'd like to talk to you about your husband and brother-in-law."

Louise Cox began to close the door as he spoke. Stiles blocked it with his foot.

"I have nothing to say to you," Louise Cox said.

"We can talk informally, or I can get a subpoena," Stiles bluffed.

Louise Cox hesitated and opened the door, her mouth drawn in a thin, anxious line. "Come in."

She ushered them into a vaulted-ceiling living room and sat them in a conversation area in front of a freestanding natural-gas fireplace with fake logs. She looked warily at them across a low glass coffee table centered on an off-white area rug. Next to the front picture window stood a grand piano. An accent table which held a vase of fresh-cut flowers was close at hand.

"What is this all about?" Mrs. Cox asked.

"Don Luis Padilla's son and great-grandson were murdered at Elderman Meadows," Jim explained. "They had returned to New Mexico to investigate the death of Don Luis."

"Luis Padilla died long before I arrived in Catron County."

Jim smiled. "But you do know about his death. What can you tell us about it?"

"Talk to Eugene," Louise said flatly.

Molly leaned forward. "Mrs. Cox, please help us. We came a long way to see you."

Louise's hand fluttered to her cheek. "I can't."

"You have a beautiful house," Molly said. "How long have you lived here?"

"Ten years. I had it built when I moved from Sedona. My doctor said I needed to move to a lower altitude. My heart isn't very good."

"Were you teaching in Sedona?"

Louise shook her head and relaxed a bit. "No. I haven't taught since I married Eugene and left Pie Town."

"You're still married to Eugene, aren't you?" Molly asked, looking at the wedding ring on Louise's left hand.

"Technically."

"After so long?" Molly probed.

"I have no desire to talk about my personal life," Louise said, caution creeping back into her voice.

"Sorry," Molly said quickly with a disarming smile. "We're not here to pry."

"We came to ask you about Eugene," Jim said. "Did he ever talk about what happened when he was shot on Elderman Meadows?"

"Not really."

"What did he say?"

"He talked about revenge."

"Against who?"

Louise hesitated for a moment, brushing an invisible bit of lint off her sleeveless polo shirt. Satisfied, she crossed her legs and adjusted the drape of her poplin skirt.

"Eugene is an angry man, Mr. Stiles. An unforgiving, angry man."

"Was he angry with you?" Molly inquired.

Louise laughed in harsh agreement. "Always. I could never do anything right. It was a loveless marriage. It became intolerable for me."

"You gave him custody of your sons," Molly said softly.

Louise's eyes blinked rapidly. "I had no choice. I don't want to talk about it anymore." Stiffly, she stood up.

"Please sit down, Mrs. Cox," Jim said.

Louise hesitated and complied.

"You said you had no choice," Jim restated.

"I had to protect myself."

"From who?" Jim asked.

"I've said enough."

"You can't be forced to testify against your husband. I'm not asking you to do that."

Louise's eyes flashed at Jim Stiles. "I want you to leave."

Jim pushed on. "Did Eugene tell you things he wanted to make sure remained secret?"

"Absurd." Her voice rose a few notches.

"From where I sit, it looks like whatever happened to you still hurts."

Louise turned her face away and stared off into space; the corner of her mouth turned down in a dour grimace.

Jim continued, "It must be hard to live with those memories."

Louise Cox looked ashen. "It is," she said weakly. She licked her lips, clasped her hands, and pulled herself together before continuing. "But I don't want to be dragged into a police investigation of something that I had nothing to do with."

"You're a victim, not a criminal," Jim responded gently. "Did Eugene mistreat you? Did he beat you?"

Louise took in Jim's words as if they were slaps across her face.

"Did he force you to give up your children?" Molly asked.

The breath rushed out of Louise, and her lip quivered. "I've feared this moment ever since Emily Wheeler wrote to me. It was like opening a door and getting hit in the face with a past I wanted to forget." She looked from Jim to Molly with a taut smile.

Molly slipped out her chair, sat next to Louise, and took her hand. "You don't have to be afraid," she said.

"But I am. I am not a brave person."

"I think you are," Molly said.

Louise swallowed hard and looked at Molly. "What would you do?"

"Maybe it's time to let it go," Molly replied.

Louise nodded her head and stood up slowly, still clutching Molly's hand. "Maybe it is. Wait here."

She returned promptly with an old leather diary and resumed her position on the couch.

"When I decided to leave my husband, I knew I needed something to keep him away from me. Don't let the wheelchair fool you— he is a vicious man. He was tremendously strong back then. His chest and arms were as hard as rocks. He frightened me. Just the thought of him still does. When I told him I was leaving him, he threatened to kill me if I took Cory and Phil with me. He forced me to my knees, put a pistol to my head, and made me promise to leave the boys with him."

"How terrible," Molly groaned. "Wasn't there someone you could turn to for help?"

"No one. Eugene kept me isolated from everybody. After I had his children—my sons—I was nothing but a maid and a prisoner."

She patted the book in her lap. "All I had when I left was the clothes on my back, my grocery money for the month, and his father's diary. After some time had passed and I was far enough away, I copied pages from Calvin's diary and sent them to Eugene. I told him if he ever came near me again I'd make his father's diary public. It's been the only protection I've had over the years."

Louise held out the book. "Read it for yourself. The interesting entries are marked. It won't answer all of your questions. Only Eugene and Edgar can do that. But I'm sure you can piece together part of the puzzle."

Jim reached out and took the book from Louise's outstretched hand, and with Molly looking over his shoulder, they read excerpts from Calvin Cox's diary.

"YOU'RE A PRETTY GOOD detective," Molly said.

"You're not too bad yourself," Jim replied.

Stiles drove while Molly sat next to him. She had taken off the new boots and socks and put her bare feet on the dashboard. She wiggled her toes, and Jim decided that even her feet were beautiful.

Molly gave him a winning smile. "If we get married . . ."

"Pick the date," Jim interrupted.

"I said *if*." Molly poked him gently in the ribs with a finger. "Anyway, *if* we get married, you'd better not turn into an asshole like Gene Cox."

"That's unlikely," Jim replied.

Molly nodded in agreement and stared out the window, thinking about Louise Cox. The heat of the sun and the windblown sand rolling off the desert distorted the distant Superstition Mountains into vague, shimmering shapes.

"What a sad, sad lady she is," Molly said with a sigh. "If someone put a gun to my head and threatened to kill me if I walked out on him with my kids, I'd shoot the son of a bitch myself."

"I believe you would. How many kids would you like to have?"

"That's not the topic under discussion, but the answer is two." She took her feet off the dashboard and faced Jim. "What do we know for sure?"

"We know that Edgar and Eugene went to the meadows together. That they were sent there by their father, and that Edgar brought Gene home badly wounded. Also, that Calvin bribed the doctor, who was a drunk, to change the date that he treated Gene for the bullet wound, and that the same doctor later ruled Don Luis Padilla's death was accidental, for which he received an additional sum of money."

"Which means that Calvin Cox engaged in a cover-up," Molly added.

"So who killed Don Luis?" Jim asked.

"And shot Gene Cox?" Molly added.

"And rustled Padilla's sheep?" Jim noted.

Molly nodded. "At a place called Mexican Hat, that nobody can find?"

"We're down to two suspects. Who do we start with first? Gene or Edgar?"

"Good question." Molly put her feet back on the dashboard and wiggled her toes.

"Do you think Louise has been milking money out of Gene over the years as a payment for her silence?" Jim asked.

"It's possible. She didn't act like a woman who had moved on with her life and made her own way. And that house she lives in certainly isn't a low-end little retirement cottage."

Jim gave her an agreeing look. "We need to find Kerney and fill him in."

"There's a lot of horses under the hood," Molly replied. "We'll get back to Reserve a hell of a lot faster if you goose it a little. Besides, creeping along at the speed limit is boring."

OMAR TURNED east on the paved state road that led to the picnic grounds at the Catwalk National Recreation Trail and stopped at the side of the road when he reached the old mine that jutted out of the hill on the far bank of Whitewater Creek. Cars traveling in both directions slowed as they passed his patrol unit. He waited a good fifteen minutes before a truck pulled in behind him.

Omar unlocked the passenger door and Phil Cox got in, his long legs bumping up against the dash. Omar moved the bench seat back.

"What took you so long?" Phil demanded. "I thought you were going to talk to Amador right away."

"I had to find him first," Gatewood answered. "Which wasn't easy. He was in Silver City helping the family make funeral arrangements for Steve."

"What did he say?"

Gatewood grimaced and looked out the side window at an RV that slowed as it passed by. "He ratted me off to Kerney, the little fucker. Told him everything. I almost kicked his ass in the parking lot at the funeral home."

"Did you get him to agree to stay out of town?"

"That's not a good idea," Omar answered, turning back to Phil. "The funeral service for Steve is tomorrow. Wouldn't look right if Amador wasn't there. I've got a deputy covering him."

"That's not what you were told to do," Phil snapped, his gray eyes narrowing.

"Save the orders for somebody else, Phil," Gatewood said wearily. "It's your daddy we elected commanding officer of the militia, not you. I'm still the goddamn sheriff and I made the call on this one. Amador stays put. I don't want any more attention drawn to him."

"Okay, Omar, relax."

"I put a tail on your sweet little cousin after she left my office. She got Kerney released, dropped the murder charges against him, and took him home with her."

Phil slapped the dashboard with his hand. "Shit."

"You said you would bring a plan with you, Phil. I hope it's better than your last fuckup that got us into this mess."

"Don't lay that on me," Phil retorted. "Every ranking officer in the militia voted on the plan."

"But Kerney's still out there walking around. You shot the wrong man and blew up Doyle Fletcher."

"Fletcher was an accident, and I didn't shoot the wrong man."

Gatewood snorted. "Kerney was the target, not Stiles. It was your idea in the first place to whack somebody who worked for the Forest Service that nobody gave a rat's ass about."

Phil laughed sharply. "You need to listen more carefully to what people say. Kerney was discussed as a target, but the decision we reached was to take decisive action."

Gatewood rubbed his chin. "Jesus. And Gene took that to mean you should go after Jim Stiles?" he asked in disbelief.

"He told me to take out whoever jumped at the bait. Kerney. Stiles. Charlie Perry. Whoever. It didn't matter. It was time to send a message."

Omar ran his tongue behind his teeth before reacting. "I think your old man went over the edge on this one."

Phil lunged across the seat and grabbed Gatewood's throat. "Don't ever say that again," he snarled.

Omar pried Phil's hand free and gasped for air. "I'm not picking a fight with you, for chrissake." He waited until Phil stopped glaring at him. "I'm only saying Kerney was the target. No one else."

"That's not the way my father saw it," Phil replied tightly.

Gatewood grunted, gave Phil a sharp look, and let it pass. It was too late to split hairs with Phil, and the way he was acting maybe both Eugene *and* his son had a screw loose. "What does Gene want done now?"

"We have to clean up the mess."

"That's what I thought," Gatewood replied, pulling a paper from his shirt pocket. "So I did us a favor."

Phil took the paper and read it. "You got the assault-and-battery warrant signed."

Gatewood smiled and nodded. "You bet. I know a very obliging judge. Everything is legal again. All we have to do is go get them. After that, we can improvise."

"Them?"

"That's right. I talked to your daddy after I called you. He wants both Kerney and Karen taken care of, and I agree. That's the only way we can handle it. We can't let Karen off the hook. She could fry our asses. We're looking at first-degree felony murder charges if we don't contain the problem now."

"Kill them both?" Phil asked.

Gatewood nodded. "Are you all right with that?"

Phil's eyes were empty of emotion. "Why not?"

"Good," Gatewood said, exhaling slowly. "But it ain't gonna be me who does it. You get my meaning?"

Phil gazed at Gatewood unemotionally. "I'll make them disappear, Omar. But we leave Karen's children alone, understood? We're patriots, not terrorists."

"Shit, Phil, I know that." He cranked the engine. "Edgar took his grandkids to Silver City. If we get our butts in gear, we can pick up Kerney and Karen and be gone before he gets home."

"Where do we take them?"

"The Slash Z." Gatewood reached across Phil and opened the

passenger door. "I'm taking out an insurance policy on this one. I want your daddy to help you make them disappear, Phil."

Phil got out of the patrol car, stuck his head back inside, and gave Omar a wicked smile. "He'll like that. This will all work out, Omar."

"It better. Otherwise, we'll have to declare open season on every fucking federal and state cop the government sends after us."

12

After treating his grandchildren to an early lunch and a matinee movie in Silver City, Edgar met briefly with Margaret's doctor, while Elizabeth and Cody waited in the hospital lobby. The doctor reported the cancer had not spread and Margaret would be discharged in the morning. The good news put a smile on Edgar's face. He took the elevator to the third floor and hurried to Margaret's room.

He found his wife sitting in the bedside chair with her hair done up in a bun, her makeup on, and wearing a pretty summer dress. She smiled and stroked his cheek when he bent down to kiss her.

"Karen couldn't come?" Margaret asked.

"She's working, and I'm looking after Cody and Elizabeth.

They're in the lobby waiting to see you. The doctor said I could take you down for a short visit."

"I can't wait to see them." She studied Edgar's face. "You look tired."

"I feel fine," he replied. "You look beautiful."

Margaret beamed. "I hoped you'd notice. I had quite a bit of help from the nurses to get gussied up for your visit. Have you kept your promise?"

Edgar's smile faded and his gaze shifted away. "Not yet. I've decided I want to talk to Eugene before I tell Karen."

"What on earth for?"

Edgar grimaced. "I want him to know that the truth is something neither of us can avoid any longer."

Margaret stood up and took Edgar's arm. "I don't think talking to Eugene will make one bit of difference."

"Maybe not," Edgar replied as he walked Margaret to the door. "But that's the way I want to handle it."

"When?" Margaret asked.

"Today. After we leave here, I'll drop Cody and Elizabeth off at home with Karen and drive to the Slash Z. I'll tell Karen this evening. Everything will be taken care of by the time you come home tomorrow."

Margaret patted her husband's hand. "I love you very much, Edgar."

"I love you, too," he replied. "More than you know."

THE SCREENED PORCH to Karen's house was filled with empty packing boxes stacked in neat piles. Behind the porch was the living room, a rectangular space with doors opening to back bedrooms. The room held an astonishing number of books arranged in modular shelves along the walls. The only furniture was a love seat with a curved back that faced a small television and VCR on a portable cabinet next to a fireplace, and a Shaker rocking chair that sat next to the fireplace. An assortment of potted houseplants was arranged on the outer lip of the hearth. Several indoor trees, including a Norfolk pine in a large tub, sat on the floor. In front of the love seat, two sleeping bags were spread out on a Persian rug that matched the deep red color of the flagstone floor. The room had the feel of a sheltered garden library.

Kerney scanned the spines of the books. Karen had an excellent collection of art history, architecture, biography, good fiction, and classic literature. The wide range of interests the collection contained impressed Kerney. He spied a biography of Vincent Van Gogh that he wanted to read.

Karen offered him the use of the bathroom to clean up. He jumped at the suggestion, and with a fresh towel and some new clothes he found his way to the bathroom. It was a cramped space in a corner of the oversized kitchen adjacent to the living room. All the water lines running to the old pedestal sink and cast-iron tub were exposed. It was clearly a renovation done when indoor plumbing was still a recent innovation. It reminded Kerney of growing up in the ranch house his grandfather had built on the Tularosa.

He closed the door and stripped tags and labels off his new clothes while hot water filled the cast-iron tub. He shucked off Jim's hand-me-downs and sank into the steaming hot water, letting the heat work on his knee. The leg had been bothering him more than usual. He needed to get back to his daily workout and jogging routine.

Shaved, clean, and dressed in stiff jeans and a shirt that still had the package creases in it, he went into the living room. Karen sat on the love seat with her shoes off and her feet on the cushion, studying a case file. Reading glasses were perched on her nose, and an open briefcase was within arm's reach. Still wearing her work outfit, a loosely shaped wool crepe suit, she smiled at him, put the file in the briefcase, and snapped it closed.

"You look better," she remarked.

"I feel better. Did you get in touch with Gatewood?"

"He's out of town. I left a message for him to call me." She unwound herself from the love seat and stood up. "Now it's my turn to change. Make yourself comfortable."

He browsed through the Van Gogh biography and inspected a painting on the only wall of the room not completely taken over by Karen's library. The large watercolor had a Chagall feel to it. A woman dressed in a simple frock held a child in her arms while a small girl stood at her side, her hand clasping the hem of the skirt. All were smiling at something out of view.

Kerney looked for the artist's signature and found the initials KC hidden in a clump of flowers at the bottom of the painting.

"I did that right after I kicked my ex-husband out," Karen said as she reentered the room.

"It was a happy event, I take it," Kerney replied, turning to face her. Barefoot, Karen wore jeans and a ribbed red-and-white-striped T-shirt.

Karen laughed. "You noticed that."

"The feeling of the painting is hard to miss."

"I keep it conspicuously displayed to remind me how unsuited I am for married life."

"Not your cup of tea?"

"Hardly."

The painting had an accomplished feel to it. "Did you study art?" Kerney asked.

"I was a delinquent in the undergraduate fine arts department for a time," Karen replied.

"You were very good."

"Thank you."

"From fine arts to law is quite a switch," Kerney said.

Karen cocked her head. "I'm not very predictable. Would you like some iced tea? The dispatcher said it would be a while before he can contact Gatewood."

"That would be nice."

Over iced tea and a platter of fruit, Karen and Kerney sat on the living-room floor and talked.

"Whatever made you take a temporary job with the Forest Service?" she asked, nibbling on a slice of honeydew.

"Money," Kerney replied.

"It can't be that much."

"Every little bit helps."

"Don't you have a pension?"

"Yeah. It pays the bills."

"So what do you need more money for?"

"Land. Enough to start a small ranching operation."

Karen picked up a piece of watermelon and cleaned out the seeds. "That's what you want to do?"

"You bet. I have my eye on a section just north of Mountainair on the east side of the Manzano Mountains, south of Albuquerque. It comes with BLM grazing rights. The owner will carry the mortgage if I can come up with the down payment."

Kerney was surprised at himself; talking about dreams sometimes vaporized them into extinction. "Do you know the area?"

Karen finished the melon slice, licked her fingers, wiped her hand on her jeans, and nodded. "I've driven through it. It's pretty country. What fun it would be to build a house just where you want to. I bet you're looking forward to it."

"I am."

"I hope it happens for you."

"Me too." Kerney heard a board creak and looked at the open door to the porch. Omar Gatewood stood in the doorway with a revolver in his hand and a nasty smile on his face. Kerney pushed Karen to the floor, flung himself across her, and reached for the pistol under the belt at the small of his back.

"What in the hell do you think you're doing?" Karen snapped, her fist balled, ready to punch him in the chops.

Before Kerney could free the weapon he felt a muzzle dig into his neck.

"Don't," Phil Cox warned, standing over Kerney.

Slowly, hands empty, Kerney moved both arms away from his body. Pinned under him, Karen's expression changed from a look of indignation to one of incredulity.

"Are you totally fucking nuts, Phil?" she yelled.

"I know exactly what I'm doing," Phil answered. He poked the rifle barrel against Kerney's neck, secured the handgun, and stuck the weapon in his waistband. "Get up real slow, Kerney," he ordered.

"The charges against him have been dropped," Karen snarled.

Kerney pushed himself upright. Gatewood had a clear shot at him from across the room. He was boxed in nicely.

"Stay where you are, Karen," Gatewood ordered. He covered Kerney while Phil Cox cuffed him, hands at his back.

With Kerney secured, Omar reached down and pulled Karen

to her feet. "I decided not to take your advice, Karen. I got that warrant you wouldn't approve signed by somebody else," he explained. "Everything's nice and legal."

"Are you crazy, Omar?" Karen snapped. "Or just plain stupid? I'll have your badge for this."

"I don't think so."

She struggled to pull free of his grasp, but Gatewood held her tightly. "Get that gun out of my face."

"Can't do it," Omar answered, wrapping his arm around Karen's waist and pulling her closer. "You both need to come with us."

"Where?" Karen demanded.

"You'll see," Gatewood answered.

"Why?"

"You'll find out." Gatewood backed up to the door, taking Karen with him.

"At least let me leave a note for my children," Karen pleaded.

"No," Gatewood said.

"Phil?" Karen implored.

Phil looked at Gatewood over Kerney's shoulder. "It might be a good idea," he said. "It could buy us time."

Omar considered it. "All right." He holstered his weapon and tossed a pair of handcuffs to Phil. "I'll take Kerney on ahead. It's best if we don't travel together. Cuff Karen after she writes the note and bring her along."

With Karen pinned to his side, Gatewood walked to the middle of the room and exchanged her for Kerney.

Karen searched Kerney's face for a reaction as Gatewood walked him to the door. He remained expressionless except for a slight shake of his head that was barely noticeable. It told her to do nothing foolish.

"Write your note and give it to me," Phil told her as soon as Gatewood and Kerney were gone.

"Can I put some shoes on first?"

Phil waved the rifle toward the bedroom. "After you, cousin." He followed her and watched as she slipped on socks and cowboy boots.

Finished, she sat on the edge of the bed and looked up at him. "Why are you doing this?"

"According to the sheriff, you've been harboring a fugitive. It's my civic duty to help him, isn't it?"

"Help him do what?"

"Just write the fucking note," Phil replied.

She found pencil and paper in a nightstand drawer. "If I tell them I'll be working late, will that do?"

"Fine. Just do it."

Karen wrote quickly and held up the note for Phil to read. He had his rifle pointed at her stomach, his finger on the trigger.

He scanned it and nodded an okay. "Put your hands out," he ordered.

She stuck her hands out hoping Phil would be dumb enough to cuff her to the front. He complied and double-locked the cuffs with a key that he dropped into his shirt pocket.

"If I don't leave the note on my mother's refrigerator, my father won't see it," Karen explained.

"Let's go."

Phil marched her to her parents' house and into the kitchen, where he watched her attach the note to the refrigerator with a magnet. Karen held her breath, hoping he wouldn't read it again. He didn't.

"What this all about, Phil?" she asked, trying hard to sound innocent and obliging.

He prodded her with the rifle barrel. "Get going."

MOLLY TOOK over the wheel just west of Lordsburg near the Arizona border. Off the interstate, on the state road to Silver City, she punched the car hard through the Big Burro Mountains and slowed only when they hit the city limits. Once rid of the city traffic, she floored the Mustang again and passed everything in sight, driving with superb coordination.

She loved to make the Mustang fly when Jim was with her to take the heat in case she got stopped. He had saved her from many speeding tickets during the two years they had been dating. It was, according to Molly, one of the few benefits of dating a cop.

Flying along the road to Glenwood, Jim quietly watched her drive. Molly said nothing until they reached the last long curve before the village.

She slowed the car and flashed him a brilliant smile. "We made pretty good time, wouldn't you say?"

"You are good behind the wheel," Jim admitted. "Swing by Karen's house." He gave her directions. "We'll see if she knows where Kerney is."

Molly hit the turn signal as they approached the turnoff to Dry Creek Canyon. A truck entering the highway swerved onto the road in front of them, then accelerated quickly.

Stiles sat upright, his eyes riveted on the truck. "Keep going," he said.

"Why?"

Jim nodded at the truck as it pulled away. "That's Phil Cox up ahead, and Karen is with him."

"What's so strange about that?" Molly asked.

"I'm not sure, but he's in a hell of a hurry. Stay back a little. Do you have that handgun I gave you?"

"It's under my seat."

Jim reached and got the holstered 9mm semiautomatic.

"What do you need a gun for?" Molly demanded.

"I don't know if I need it," Jim answered. "Drop back a little more."

"He doesn't know my car," Molly said.

"He knows me," Jim answered. "Let's see where he's going."

Molly slowed down to almost the speed limit.

They followed Phil to Old Horse Springs and barely got there in time to watch him turn in on the Slash Z ranch road.

"What do we do now?" Molly asked as she parked on the shoulder of the highway.

"We wait," Jim said. "It's five miles to the ranch from the highway, and I don't want to jump to any conclusions. Damn, I wish I could get to a telephone."

"Why?"

"So I could call around for Kerney. This may be nothing more than paranoia on my part."

"Open the glove compartment," Molly suggested.

Jim punched the button and found a cellular phone. "When did you get this?" he asked, holding up the telephone.

"A couple of months ago."

"And you didn't tell me?"

"Was I supposed to? It's only for emergencies. I hardly use it." Molly smiled winningly. "Isn't it handy?"

"You are amazing."

"I know it."

Stiles flipped open the phone, dialed Karen's home number, and got no answer. He tried Edgar Cox with the same results. He called the sheriff's office and asked for Gatewood. The deputy who answered said Omar was out of town and not due back until morning.

"What's the status on Kerney?" Jim inquired. "Has he been picked up? Have the charges been dropped?" It took longer than necessary to get a reply.

"I haven't heard a thing," the deputy said.

Stiles snapped the cover closed and shook his head.

"What?" Molly asked.

"Something isn't kosher. We'll give Karen and Phil some time to get to Phil's house and then I'll call," he said. "I hope this is just a wild goose chase."

"Is that what you think?"

"No. That's why we're going to sit here and wait."

THE CHILDREN PILED OUT of Edgar's truck as he parked behind Karen's station wagon. He was glad to see her car. It meant Karen was home and he could take a break from his baby-sitting duties. He waved as Cody and Elizabeth called out their thanks and told them to send Karen down to see him. They ran around the side of the house and out of sight.

Inside, the house was too damn quiet without Margaret to fill the place up with the sounds of her presence. Edgar shed his boots in the living room and padded to the kitchen, thinking it was time to start thawing one of the meals in the freezer so he could have it for dinner. On the refrigerator door was a note. He removed the magnet and read it. All it said was that Karen might be working a little late, but would be home soon. She must have forgotten to take it down after she got back. He crumpled it up and threw it in the trash under the kitchen sink.

He got a meal out of the freezer, put it on the counter, and started back to the living room when Elizabeth slammed through the back door.

"Is my mom here?" she asked breathlessly.

"No, sweetie. Isn't she at your house?"

"No," Elizabeth replied. "Where could she be?"

Edgar rumpled Elizabeth's hair. "Don't worry. She left a note for us that she might have to work late."

"But our car is here," Elizabeth replied. "Mom should be home, if the car is here."

"Not necessarily," Edgar answered. "Listen, you go get Cody and we'll drive to Uncle Phil's."

"Right now?"

"Sure. By the time we get back, I'm sure your mom will be home."

"Promise?"

"I promise."

After Elizabeth left, Edgar thought about Karen's note and fished it out of the trash. She had signed it "Peanut." Now that was kind of strange. He couldn't remember a time when Karen had appreciated his nickname for her. He used it in spite of his best attempts to break the habit, and she almost always reacted with a frown when it slipped out.

He read the note again. Even the handwriting looked slanted

and jerky, not at all like Karen's fluid script. There was a crossed-out Z before the word "soon" at the end of the note.

Slash Z, Edgar thought, stuffing the note in his pocket. It couldn't mean anything else. He hurried to get his boots and round up the children. Something was wrong, but for the life of him, he couldn't imagine what it could be.

KAREN PROBED PHIL on the ride to the Slash Z, using the humblest attitude she could manage, trying to match the obsequious demeanor of Phil's wife, Doris. The ploy worked; Phil got puffed up with self-importance and started talking. The garbage that poured from his mouth was truly amazing. He talked about the Catron County Militia with a zealot's passion, and he described his attempt to kill Jim Stiles like a schoolyard bully bragging on himself.

She tried to maintain a servile tone, while her mind raced over the implications of Phil's confession. "What are you going to do to me?" she asked meekly.

Phil guffawed. "You're going to have to disappear."

Karen dropped the charade, and her voice cracked with hostility. "In other words, you're going to kill me."

"It's a family tradition," Phil replied.

"What does that mean?"

He looked at her like a hawk that had spotted its prey. "I'll let my father explain."

"If I'm reported missing, Catron County will be crawling with cops from all over the state. It isn't going to be that easy."

"Omar can handle them."

Karen laughed. "In your dreams he can. Omar isn't smart

enough to take the heat. It won't take much to crack him wide open."

"You're only going to be *missing,* Karen. That's the key word." Phil smiled. "All Omar has to do is put everyone to work scouring the countryside for you."

"A missing ADA is a whole different matter from a lost tourist."

Phil made the turn onto the Slash Z road before answering. "You know what? I have half a mind to strip you naked and stuff a sock in your mouth before we get to the ranch. Hell, I just may do it. Pop would get a big kick out of it, I bet."

Phil's raw sexual glance sent a shiver up Karen's spine. She leaned against the seat and stared at her cuffed hands. Phil's rifle was in the gun rack, but she doubted she could get to it before he could react. She needed to hit him with something, but there was nothing substantial in sight to do it with.

After a mile on the flats, the ranch road cut through some low hills. Phil drove with one eye on the road and the other on her, shifting his gaze back and forth before each curve. There were pools of standing water in the ruts from the heavy morning rain, and Phil slowed down a bit going through them. Silently, Karen started counting seconds between Phil's glances. There was about a ten-second break in eye contact.

The next curve came up, and Phil's eyes moved back to the road. Karen pivoted on the seat, brought her legs up, and kicked at Phil's face with her boots.

He saw the blow coming and threw up a hand to deflect it. Karen's foot slammed into the steering wheel. Phil clamped his hand on her calf and lost control of the truck. They lunged off the road into an arroyo. Phil wrenched the wheel as they slid sideways down the slope.

Karen kicked Phil in the cheek with her free leg. The truck fish-tailed into a tree, bounced, and landed on its side. Phil's head snapped against the doorpost, and Karen landed on top of him, her knees grinding into his ribs.

She waited for him to move, but he remained still. She pushed herself upright until her head bumped the passenger door. She swung the door open, gripped the roof with both hands, pulled herself free, and landed hard on her feet. Unsteadily she walked to the front of the truck. Through the cracked windshield she could see that Phil was out cold. She had to get the handcuffs off before he regained consciousness. She shattered the glass with a large rock, reached in, and fumbled in his shirt pocket for the handcuff key.

Her hands were shaking, and it took several attempts to get the key in the lock. Wooziness hit her, and she stopped until it passed. She got the cuffs off, wrapped Phil's arms through the steering wheel, cuffed him, and threw away the key. She crawled halfway into the cab, picked up the rifle from the floorboard, and scrambled out.

She sat on the ground and trembled, her eyes locked on Phil's unconscious face, wondering where the insanity in him came from and why she hadn't seen it before. Maybe it had been there all the time, lurking under the surface. Maybe it was the legacy of bitterness and rage passed on from father to son.

Finally calm, she considered her options. She could walk to the highway and try to flag down some help or head to the ranch. There wasn't enough time to turn back. It would be the ranch, she decided, even if she had face down Omar Gatewood and Uncle Eugene by herself to free Kerney.

She checked the Winchester, found it fully loaded, and set out for the Slash Z.

IMPATIENTLY, Stiles checked his watch every few minutes. The thought that Kerney and Karen might be in trouble gnawed at him, but he didn't have anything solid to back up the feeling. He gave in to his anxiety and started punching in Phil Cox's number on the cellular phone when a pickup truck sped by and braked quickly for the turn to the Slash Z. Jim dropped the phone in his lap and hit the car horn repeatedly. The truck stopped at the cattle guard.

"What is it?" Molly said, somewhat startled.

"That's Edgar Cox. Drive over to him."

Edgar Cox waited for the car to pull up, wondering who in the hell had flagged him down. Cody crawled into his lap, rolled down the window, and leaned out. Elizabeth, kneeling on the bench seat, stared out the rear window.

Jim got out of the Mustang and stepped over to Edgar's truck. "Mr. Cox," he said.

"I'm in a hurry, Jim," Edgar replied.

"Looking for Karen?"

"How did you know?"

"We saw her drive in with Phil."

Edgar relaxed a bit. "That's a relief."

"Why do you say that?"

"She left me a note. It threw me for a loop. Maybe I'm getting too suspicious in my old age."

"Can I see it?"

Edgar handed Jim the note.

"I thought maybe she was in some sort of trouble," Edgar said.

Jim read the note. "What makes you say that?" Molly was at Jim's side. He passed the note to her.

"The way it's written, the words she used, the little squiggle near the end of it. I thought it looked like a Z with a slash through it."

"It does," Jim replied.

"I agree," Molly said as she returned the note to Edgar.

"Who is this woman?" Edgar asked, as he put the note away.

"My partner, Officer Hamilton," Jim replied.

Edgar nodded a greeting at Molly and turned his attention back to Stiles. "It's just as well Karen is with Phil. I can kill two birds with one stone."

"Meaning?"

"Family business, Jim." He clutched and put the truck in gear. "It's not your concern."

Jim reached in, killed the engine, and took the key from the ignition.

Edgar gave him a hard look. "Why did you do that?"

"What if Karen is in trouble?"

"Sitting here jabbering with you and your partner won't answer that question," Edgar snapped. "I'm sure it's just a family visit."

"Don't bullshit me, Edgar. Karen hasn't stepped onto Slash Z property in over twenty years, if ever. And we're just back from Arizona, where we had a nice chat with Eugene's wife, Louise. So whatever is going on, we're in on it. Now, I'm going to call and talk to Phil before any of us move down that road."

"What for?"

"Because I've got a bad feeling about this. Was Kevin Kerney with Karen today?"

"I don't know. I haven't seen my daughter since early this morning."

Jim stepped back to the Mustang, grabbed the cellular phone, and dialed the number. Phil's wife, Doris, answered.

"Doris, this is Jim Stiles. Is Phil home?"

"Jim! I was so very sorry to hear what happened to you. Are you up and around now?"

"I'm much better, thanks. Is Phil there?"

"Not yet."

"Do you know where he is?" Jim asked.

"I have no idea."

"Is he with Eugene?"

"No. But Sheriff Gatewood is. His police car is parked outside."

"Is anyone with Omar, Doris?"

"I think so. PJ said he saw a man with him. I don't know who it is."

"Let me talk to PJ."

"He's down at the barn doing chores," Doris said. "If you miss Phil, I'll let him know you called when he gets home."

"Thanks, Doris." Jim hit the disconnect button. "Phil and Karen haven't showed up yet, and Omar Gatewood, who was supposed to be in Silver City, is with Gene. He brought somebody with him. I think it may be Kerney.

"I'm going to give you some lawful orders, Edgar, and I expect you to follow them," Jim continued. "Officer Hamilton and I are going to ride in the back of your truck. If we see anything unusual at all, I'll order you to stop. Do it right away. If not, just before you reach the ranch, there's a slight downgrade as you come around the last hill."

"I grew up here, damn it!"

"Yes, sir. I know that. Stop the truck before the curve and stay in the vehicle until I do a sweep, just to make sure everything is all right."

"Is all this necessary?" Edgar demanded, as he took the truck keys back from Stiles.

Cody looked at Jim with wide, excited eyes. Edgar pulled him away from the open window and sat him down on the seat.

"Just do as I say, Mr. Cox," Jim said in exasperation. "Understand?"

"I can follow orders."

"Good. Are you carrying any firearms?"

"There's a Colt thirty-eight in the glove box."

"Grab it by the barrel and hand it over."

Edgar gave Jim the pistol, and he handed it to Molly. "Hold on to this for me."

"This is ridiculous," Edgar said.

"Maybe so, but Padilla Canyon taught me a lesson. I'm not making any more assumptions about what is safe and what isn't until I check things out."

"You'd better know what you're doing," Edgar warned.

Bouncing along in the back of the truck, Molly sat with the pistol cradled in her hands. She looked at the gun and glanced over at Jim, who was resting against the wheel well.

"*Officer* Hamilton?" she whispered.

Jim grimaced. "I didn't want to tell him you were my girl."

"Do you know what you're doing?"

"I think so."

"It turns you on, doesn't it?"

"What turns me on?"

"Cop stuff."

Jim chewed his lip before answering. "Yeah, sometimes it does. Does that bother you?"

"No. What bothers me is that maybe you'll get hurt again."

EUGENE COX sat in his wheelchair in the front room dressed in starched military fatigues. An AK-47 rested against the side of the chair. On the collar of his shirt were the eagles of a bird colonel, and on the left sleeve he wore a Catron County Militia unit patch. Freshly shaved, Eugene had combed his hair straight back over his ears.

The room was trashed with newspapers, magazines, military training manuals, maps, and a clutter of old household appliances that would make an antique dealer drool. There was a floor-size Emerson radio against one wall with a Polar Cub oscillating fan on top that pushed warm air around the room, fluttering the piles of newspapers.

Gatewood forced Kerney to sit on the floor and stood behind him. Kerney smiled up at Eugene Cox. The old man ignored him. Caressing the barrel of the AK-47, he spoke to Omar.

"Where is Phil?"

"He'll be along shortly with Karen," Gatewood replied. "We thought it best not to travel together."

Eugene nodded.

"I'll tell you what I told Phil," Omar added. "You'll have to do your own dirty work on this one."

"Covering your ass, Omar? Or are you just a pantywaist?"

"You figure it out."

Eugene grunted. "Sometimes I think you're just another dumb-ass politician."

"Think whatever you like," Omar replied. "You still have to kill them if you want them dead."

"Fine." Eugene shifted his gaze to Kerney. "Why are you smiling at me like a jackass? What's so damn funny?"

"Was I smiling?" Kerney answered.

Eugene's eyes bored into Kerney. "Don't be a smartass. Answer the question."

Kerney considered the man in the wheelchair dressed in combat fatigues with his useless legs dangling to the floor. "I was admiring your uniform."

Eugene sneered. "You like it?"

"Not really. But I'd love to hear about the militia."

Eugene threw his head back, smiled widely, and showed his stained teeth. "I bet you would."

"Why did you go after Jim Stiles?"

"Because he's the enemy, just like you. He's a diehard conservationist who doesn't understand history."

"What history is that?" Kerney asked.

"The history of revolution. The history of this country. The history of the men who settled the west. Who in the hell do you think preserved the land before the environmentalists began beating the drum? Ranchers. Ranchers brought the elk back. Ranchers protected the antelope. Ranchers saved the white-tailed deer."

"What's your point?"

"Blind, stupid government," Eugene roared. "That's my point. When a man can't manage his land as he sees fit, something ain't right. The government forces us to move fences so elk can migrate, tells us to keep our cattle away from streams to protect the fish, orders us to shut down winter pasture that can't be replaced because it's a habitat for some worthless, disease-carrying rodent or an exotic butterfly nobody gives a damn about. It doesn't make a fucking bit of sense."

Eugene warmed to his speechifying. "We pay taxes, higher

grazing fees, and we still can't use the land the way God intended it to be used. We get shit on, and shit for it."

"It's a tough life," Kerney noted with sarcasm.

"Government interference *will* stop. That's what the militia stands for. That's what we're all about."

"Killing people will certainly get the government's attention," Kerney said, tired of Gene's harangue. He changed the subject. "Who shot Jim Stiles?"

"Phil," Eugene said proudly. "He volunteered. Is there anything else you're dying to know?"

"Tell me what happened between you and Edgar at Elderman Meadows."

Eugene chuckled. "It's a good story."

"I'd love to hear it."

Eugene thought about it for a minute. "Why not?" He grinned. "But you've gotta promise you won't tell."

"I promise," Kerney replied.

Eugene slapped his thigh and chuckled. "I like a man with a sense of humor. Back when Edgar and I were boys, our daddy sent us to Mangas Mountain to herd Padilla's sheep down to where some trucks were waiting to load them up. Now, Edgar had this real deep moral, do-right streak to him—he still does, far as I can tell—so Daddy told him we were just gonna be helping Padilla move his stock out of the mountains.

"Of course, we were rustling, but Daddy knew Edgar wouldn't stand for that, so he made up a helping-hand story for Edgar to swallow, figuring when it was all over the damage would be done and Edgar would have to put up with it or get the shit kicked out of him. He got the shit kicked out of him a lot back in those days."

"But not you, I bet," Kerney proposed.

"Hell, no, not me. My daddy and I thought alike in a lot of ways. He trusted me. Relied on me as I got older.

"We got the herd delivered and were coming back home when snow started falling. When we reached the meadows we heard sheep bleating off on one of those little fingers where the open land snakes into the forest. It sounded like a goodly number, and we were short about twenty-five head on the drive down, so Edgar and I went looking.

"About a quarter mile in from the last stretch of meadow we found them in this craterlike field that was ringed by trees and a rock cliff. Never would have found it if it hadn't been for the bleating. The tree canopy looks unbroken until you get right under it. You could tell it had been used for a long time as a natural corral. Grass was scant, and there were old campsites all over the place.

"Well, Edgar wanted to take those sheep right to Don Luis, but I knew Daddy wanted every last one of them gone. He got real riled when I started shooting those lambs and ewes. I had to stand him down with my rifle until the job was done.

"When I was finished, we walked out of that crater to our horses. Edgar was crying like a baby. We ran smack into Don Luis, who wanted to know where his sheep were, and what the hell all the shooting was about. I had no choice but to kill him. Just as I pulled the trigger, Edgar shot me in the back with his pistol."

Edgar threw back his head and laughed bitterly. "The poor son of a bitch couldn't even kill me. Being the moral, self-righteous little pussy he is, he carried me home. My daddy beat him within an inch of his life before the doctor came."

"Didn't anyone raise a question about the slaughtered sheep?"

Euenge snickered. "There wasn't anyone left who gave a damn enough to ask questions. The Padillas had all scattered. Besides, by the time the spring thaw came, coyotes had picked those sheep clean."

"Still, Calvin had to hush it up," Kerney proposed. "How did he do it?"

"With money. How else? Besides that, there wasn't a white man in Catron County who would side against us with the Padillas. I doubt there are many today who would." Eugene switched his attention to Gatewood. "Omar, are you going to arrest me now that you've heard my confession?"

"I don't think so," Gatewood answered.

Eugene nodded his approval at Omar's reply. "See what I mean?"

"Does killing Karen even the score with Edgar?"

Eugene showed his stained teeth and smirked. "It doesn't even come close. Why are you sneering at me?"

"Wearing army fatigues with eagles on your collar doesn't make you a colonel," Kerney said. "Your brother won his rank in battle. All you are is a sick, crazy old man playing soldier."

Eugene snarled, picked up the AK-47, rolled the wheelchair within striking range, and slammed the butt on Kerney's gimpy knee. The pain sent shock waves through him.

THEY FOUND PHIL COX in his wrecked truck, chained to the steering wheel, barely conscious, and incoherent. He had a smashed cheekbone and an ugly bruise on his left temple. Jim checked his vital signs while steam hissed out of the cracked truck radiator. Edgar Cox leaned over Jim's shoulder with panic on his face, demanding that he ask about Karen.

Phil's eyes were unfocused. All he did was grunt when Jim

grilled him about Karen. Stiles got everybody back in the truck, took over the driving, and kept his eyes peeled, hoping Karen would come into view. They caught up to her at the last curve in the road that dipped down to the ranch. Jim killed the engine, and with Edgar at his side he ran to her.

Jim had to pry the Winchester from her hands. Karen grudgingly let it go, looking at him with smoldering eyes that were as dangerous as any he had ever seen.

Edgar enveloped her in a hug. Karen remained immobile, her arms locked against her side. Some of the tenseness faded, and she raised a hand and patted her father reassuringly on the back.

Molly and the kids surrounded her, the children jabbering and scared. Karen's expression softened. She let go of Edgar, dropped to one knee, and wrapped Cody and Elizabeth in her arms. Jim hushed everybody up and corralled them back to the truck. With Cody on her lap and an arm wrapped around Elizabeth, Karen sat on the tailgate and answered Jim's questions.

When Jim had heard enough, he gently squeezed Karen's hand in appreciation. "That was one hell of a thing you did."

"It wasn't half what I should have done," Karen said hotly.

"You did enough. Now we know what we're facing." He turned to Edgar. "We need a new plan."

"I'm going with you," Edgar snarled.

Jim nodded. "I'll take the point on this one." He looked at the sky. Thick clouds were gun-metal gray. "Molly, stay here with Karen and the children. If anybody comes anywhere near you in a threatening manner, shoot him. We'll sort it out later."

"I'll do it," Karen said flatly.

Karen's eyes were smoking again. An argument wasn't worth the time. "Fine," he said. "Both of you can do it. Take turns." He swung back to Edgar. "You're going to be my distraction. Give me ten minutes to get into position before you drive down there. I want to be inside the house when you pull up."

Edgar glanced at Jim's sling. "You're wounded. I should be the one going in."

Jim pulled his arm free and felt the stitches in his biceps start to pop. "I want you under cover at all times."

"I'll use the truck."

"Good enough. Put a couple of rounds into the house to get their attention. And for chrissake, don't shoot me or Kerney."

"Don't worry, son. I know how to take fire and put steel on a hard target."

"I believe you do, Colonel Cox."

Jim looked at the group. Molly and Karen seemed solid. Cody and Elizabeth were wide-eyed with apprehension.

"Nobody here is going to get hurt," Jim said to the children. "I want you both to do exactly what your mother and Molly tell you."

The children nodded gravely.

"Are you set?" he asked Edgar.

"Ten minutes and counting," Edgar replied, looking at his wristwatch.

Jim kissed Molly.

"I thought she was your partner," Edgar said.

"I lied."

"I am," said Molly.

Jim flashed her an enormous smile and kissed her again. "I partially lied," he said to Edgar.

With Molly's 9mm in his waistband, Jim trotted down the hill and started a curving loop toward the ranch house. Behind him he heard Cody announce in a loud voice that he wanted to go with Grandfather.

"You're staying right here, young man," Karen said, holding Cody back with a hand clamped firmly on his shoulder. He pouted, stomped his foot, and tried unsuccessfully to pull free. She didn't let go until Edgar drove around the bend and out of sight.

Cody waited until the other lady said something to his mother that made her look away. Then he darted into some bushes at the side of the road and started running full-tilt down the hill to catch up with Grandfather.

OMAR DIALED KAREN'S NUMBER and let it ring for a long time before hanging up. He put the receiver down and stared at Kerney as though he were responsible for Phil's lateness.

Kerney sat in the middle of the floor where he'd been dumped. The cuffs cut into his wrists, and his knee felt as if it had been blown out.

"They should have been here by now," Gatewood said, walking back to his position behind Kerney.

Eugene Cox had the AK-47 resting on both arms of the wheelchair, his fingers near the trigger housing. It was loaded with a full clip. "Go find them," he ordered. "I'll take care of Kerney."

Gatewood hitched up his belt and puffed out his cheeks. "Are you sure you'll be all right?"

Eugene gave him a scornful look. "Don't treat me like a cripple. Get going."

As Omar turned for the door, he heard the sound of an engine and tires on gravel. "No need to," he said as he walked to the window to look out. "Phil's here."

"That's not Phil's truck," Gene said. "I know the sound of it."

Two shots shattered the window high up and bits of glass rained down on Gatewood. He ducked beneath the sill and looked over at Eugene.

Kerney lashed out with a foot and kicked the wheelchair. It spun Cox around. Eugene pulled the trigger, and slugs dug into the wall, gouging holes and sending plaster fragments flying about the room.

Omar yanked his sidearm as Kerney swiveled to face him. Before Gatewood could pull off a round, Jim Stiles stepped into view and put two bullets in Omar's head, blowing his face into a bloody mess. Kerney lunged to his feet and made for Stiles, AK-47 rounds tearing up the floor behind him as Eugene spun the chair back, firing with one hand.

The AK-47 stitched Omar as he was falling. Kerney slammed into Stiles as Jim swung the pistol in Gene's direction. He knocked Jim sprawling on his back in the hallway and landed on top of him. AK-47 rounds blew through the wall above their heads as Jim pulled Kerney down the hallway into the kitchen.

"Get us the fuck out of here," Kerney hissed.

Stiles got Kerney on his feet and ran him out the back door into the yard behind a cord of stacked firewood. Kerney fell awkwardly over a power lawn mower and banged his head against a gasoline can.

"Who is at the front of the house?" Kerney demanded as he untangled himself.

"Edgar Cox."

"What are his orders?"

"Distraction only."

"Do you have a handcuff key?"

"In my wallet."

Kerney turned his back and held out his hands. "Get these damn things off me."

Jim released him. Kerney rubbed his wrists and shook his hands to get the circulation going. Another burst came from the house. Eugene was firing out the front door. There were two sharp cracks from Edgar's rifle as he answered back.

"Stay here and cover me," Kerney said.

"What are you going to do?"

"Get Gene out of there. Alive, if I can."

"How are you going to do that without a gun?"

Kerney grabbed the gas can, and the liquid sloshed inside. It felt half full. He opened the cap and took a whiff to make sure it was gasoline. It was.

"That's not very sporting," Stiles said.

"Got a match?"

"No."

"Give me a round from your gun."

Jim ejected the chambered bullet, and Kerney pried the cartridge apart with a penknife. "You're a good shot, I hope," he said, as he poured the powder into the gas can.

"I hit Gatewood, didn't I?" Jim answered.

"At close range, but remind me to thank you later." Kerney recapped the can and dragged it along as he crawled on his belly to the open back door. He looked at Stiles, who had taken up a good prone position behind the woodpile with the semiautomatic extended and ready.

Jim gave him a thumbs-up sign. Kerney pushed the gas can into the kitchen, crouched low, and ran like hell to the woodpile. He jammed his shoulder on a log as he flung himself next to Jim. Stiles cranked off two rounds, and the can exploded. Kerney took a quick look. Fire ate across the kitchen floor.

Eugene Cox rolled out of the hall into the kitchen and stopped as the fire moved toward him. Kerney pulled his head in. A burst of automatic fire tore into the woodpile.

"Shoot back," he ordered.

Stiles held the pistol over the top of the woodpile and squeezed off two rounds. The spent cartridges bounced off Kerney. The AK-47 fell silent.

"Did you hit anything?"

"I doubt that I even hit the fucking house," Jim replied.

The heat of the fire grew. Kerney took another look. The back of the house was engulfed in flames, and Eugene was nowhere to be seen.

"What now?" Jim asked.

The staccato sound of the AK-47 firing at the front of the house came before Kerney could respond. He waited to hear return fire. Two more shots came from Edgar Cox.

"Time to join the party," he said.

Bent low, they used the picket fence for concealment and stopped at the corner by the front yard. The porch was empty. Through a window, they could see flames blazing, flash-burning the curtains and peeling off the wallpaper. Thirty yards away, Edgar's truck was parked at an angle to the house, slightly to the rear of Gatewood's police cruiser. The patrol car had taken bursts from Eugene's AK-47 through the hood and front tires.

Kerney couldn't see Edgar, but Cody was running across the open field with Karen hard on his heels. Molly and Elizabeth stood exposed at the edge of the pasture. All of them were well within range of Eugene's AK.

"Holy shit!" Jim spat as he spotted the women and children.

Ammunition started to blow up inside the burning building. Eugene rolled out on the porch just as it caught fire and flames whipped up to the roof. He jammed in a fresh clip and started firing. Bullets chewed up the ground, sprayed across the police car, and shattered the windshield of the truck.

Jim steadied the semiautomatic to take Eugene down before he hit one of the women or children. Edgar beat him to it. The muzzle flash came from under the truck, and the bullet took Eugene in the chest. The wheelchair wobbled backward as Gene slumped over and dropped the AK.

Nobody moved until Edgar crawled out from under the truck. He stood rooted to the ground. Karen covered Cody from danger with her body, and Molly was hunched down with Elizabeth wrapped in her arms. Karen picked up Cody and started running toward Molly and Elizabeth.

Edgar didn't move an inch.

Kerney's eyes followed Karen. She checked Elizabeth to make sure the girl was all right before turning to take another look at the blazing fire. Then she walked with Cody in her arms and Elizabeth and Molly at her side to cut off Doris Cox and her children, who were running full-tilt across the pasture. With Molly, Karen held Doris back and herded everybody away.

Stiles and Kerney joined Edgar. He said nothing until the porch roof caved in and Eugene's body started to burn. The second story blazed. Heat stung their eyes and blew hot against their faces.

"I can't believe what I did," Edgar finally said.

"You did the right thing," Kerney replied.

"There were women and children to protect," Edgar said softly.

"I know," Kerney answered.

Edgar's blue eyes snapped back to the burning house. Images sixty years old blended with the sight of his dead brother burning in the fire. "No, you don't know," he said in a bitter voice. "You don't know the half of it."

"Maybe I do," Kerney responded. "Eugene told me a very interesting story."

Edgar stared at Kerney for a long time before he broke eye contact. "Good. I'm glad. It's time everybody heard that story."

"Mind telling me?" Jim inquired.

"After I talk to my daughter," Edgar replied.

"Fair enough."

Edgar dropped the Winchester, turned on his heel, and walked away.

Jim and Kerney moved back from the intense heat. The structure burned like a massive, billowing bonfire. Small-arms rounds randomly exploded inside the house.

"Where is Phil?" Kerney asked.

"If Edgar's truck still runs, I'll show you."

"What happened to Karen?"

"I'll fill you in on the way."

They cleaned the glass off the seat, and Kerney drove. The clouds lifted from the top of Mangas Mountain, and a dim red light flashed from the lookout station. Whoever was up there probably had every piece of fire equipment in the district rolling. The wail of sirens carried by the breeze confirmed it.

Jim looked at his arm. Blood soaked the sleeve where the stitches had given way. The adrenaline rush had ended, and the wound throbbed like hell.

"Karen is no lady to mess with," he began, grimacing in pain.

"Tell me about it," Kerney replied.

13

After Jim's briefing and a quick check of Phil Cox, who wasn't going anywhere, Kerney took control of the arriving fire crews. He posted two Forest Service firefighters with rifles on the hill above the ranch to keep spectators away. Then he called Carol Cassidy by radio, gave her a quick rundown on the situation, and asked her to send every law enforcement specialist from the Luna and Reserve districts as backup until the state police arrived. He wanted no repeat of the Elderman Meadows fiasco, and enough cops around to keep the locals at bay, especially any militia members who might show up and cause trouble.

He left Jim with a paramedic and went looking for Karen. He spotted her hurrying across the horse pasture from Phil's house.

"Are you all right?" he asked when she reached him.

"Fine. How about yourself?"

Kerney smiled. "I'm okay."

"You're limping badly."

"It will pass."

She smiled grimly. "My father told me what happened between him and his brother at Elderman Meadows. He said you heard something about it from Gene. Is that true?"

"Gene told me one hell of a story, and I believed every word of it."

"What do you know?"

Kerney recounted what Eugene had told him.

"It's quite a family I've got, isn't it?" Karen said.

"The part of it I like seems pretty solid."

She smiled with her eyes, stood on her tiptoes, and gave him a quick kiss. "Thanks."

"I should be the one thanking you."

"We can sort that out later. I need your help."

"What can I do?"

"Work with me on this," she replied, pointing at the burning remnants of Eugene's house. "I need a smart cop at my side."

"What you need is a special investigator," Kerney replied, smiling down at her.

"I've got one. You."

"I resigned, remember?"

"I never officially accepted your resignation."

"That puts a different spin on it," Kerney admitted.

Karen took him by the arm. "You're on the payroll. Ready to go to work?"

"Why not?" Kerney answered.

IT TOOK FIVE DAYS, working eighteen-hour shifts, before Kerney, Karen, and Jim had everything sorted out. Phil Cox caved in after learning that his father was dead. He confessed to murder, attempted murder, and a host of additional felony charges. Karen offered to drop some of the lesser charges if he rolled over on the militia, and without the iron will of Eugene Cox to shore him up, Phil capitulated.

Following Phil's directions, Kerney searched his house and found records that identified the militia members who had built the bombs that had been scattered around the wilderness, as well as the device used to kill Doyle Fletcher. Alcohol Tobacco and Firearms agents took the ball and ran with federal indictments against the bombers, while Kerney worked on state felony arrest warrants.

He also came away with the militia membership list and a scrawled note from Eugene to Phil with his recommendations for targets of assassination. Kerney was number one on the list, followed by Charlie Perry and Jim Stiles.

Doris Cox snapped as a result of the shoot-out at the Slash Z and had to be hospitalized with severe depression in Silver City. Kerney interviewed her just before she was discharged. Tonelessly, she told him of sexual assaults and physical beatings by Phil that made his stomach turn.

She took the children and left for an extended visit with her sister in Idaho. With Karen, Kerney saw her off. PJ looked desperately in need of a good therapist. Completely shut down, the boy refused to talk and had an angry belligerence stamped on his face.

All of Gatewood's deputies were militia members, along with six seasonal Forest Service employees from the Luna and Reserve offices. The deputies were suspended and Karen arranged for a contingent of state police to provide law enforcement protection during the investigation. Carol Cassidy placed the Forest Service workers on administrative leave and started an internal probe.

Amador Ortiz was found in San Diego, hiding out with a cousin, and brought back to face charges. He corroborated Gatewood's role in setting up the Padilla Canyon ambush.

Scooped up by the FBI for his complicity in the Leon Spence–Steve Lujan case, Ortiz was bound over in both federal court and state district court on accessory charges.

Kerney and Jim coordinated the interviews and interrogations, using state attorney general investigators and state police agents to do the leg work. They concentrated on the militia leadership, a group of twelve men that included a county commissioner, several lesser officials, prominent businessmen, and two of the biggest ranchers in the county. Because they had authorized the plan to kill Kerney, conspiracy-to-commit-murder complaints were in the works on all twelve.

Kerney handled the Eugene Cox and Omar Gatewood shooting-death investigations. He took the evidence to a hastily convened special grand jury. Jim Stiles was quickly exonerated, and the panel ruled that the killing of Eugene Cox by his brother was justifiable self-defense.

The night before the grand jury met, Kerney attended a Cox family discussion where Edgar, Margaret, and Karen debated publicly disclosing the sixty-year-old crimes of rustling, homicide, and Edgar's assault on his brother.

The family decided to empty the closet of the skeleton that had haunted them for years.

Under Karen's orders, and with Edgar and Margaret's consent, Kerney arrested Edgar for the 1930s crime of attempted murder of his brother as soon as the grand jury recessed and Edgar walked out the door.

Karen had turned the case over to her boss in Socorro. The DA had traveled to Reserve to depose Edgar personally and then conducted a press conference. He cited Edgar's military record as a career officer, his public service to the community, and his success as a rancher who had started from scratch and built his spread after retiring from the Army. He finished with a summary of Edgar's deposition of the murder of Don Luis Padilla and announced that no legal action would be taken.

Predictably, the headline in the Silver City newspaper read:

RANCHER SHOOTS TWIN TWICE IN SIXTY YEARS

The story, along with sidebar editorial pieces on the shoot-out at the Slash Z, remained at the top of the nightly news for several days. Kerney made copies of Edgar's deposition, the newspaper articles, and Molly's historical research on the Padilla land swindle and mailed them off overnight express to Dr. Padilla's daughter in Mexico City. Leon Spence had fingered Steve Lujan as Hector's murderer, and Kerney included that information in a hand-written note to Señora Marquez. She called the next morning to say she was thinking of retaining an attorney and suing the United States government and Eugene Cox's estate for damages.

THE ONLY DECENT FURNITURE in Jim's living room was an eight-foot sofa, an overstuffed easy chair, a floor lamp, and a framed T. C. Cannon poster of a somber Indian in full regalia sitting in a wicker chair. The rest of the room was taken over by an exceedingly large work table fashioned out of plywood and two-by-fours that Jim had slapped together. What Jim used it for Kerney couldn't say. It held mostly old newspapers, junk mail, empty drink containers, and an assortment of stuff that needed to be put away.

Kerney had been bunking with Jim since the day after the Slash Z incident, and he was home before sunset for the first time in what seemed like weeks.

Stiles found him stretched out on the couch, dead to the world, and shook him awake. When Kerney opened his eyes, Jim flopped down in the easy chair with a shit-eating grin on his face and a paper sack in his hand.

Kerney groaned in disgust and sat up. Sleep-deprived, he had hoped for a solid eight or ten hours of rack time. "What is it?" he snapped.

"I've been promoted," Stiles announced in a rush. "You're looking at the new area supervisor for the Game and Fish Department."

"That's great. You deserve it. Where is home base going to be?"

"I'm setting up a new office in Silver City. I'm going to move down there."

"Molly will like that."

Jim's grin widened. "We're getting married."

Kerney got up, pulled Jim out of the chair, and pounded him on the back. "Now, that is very good news," he said, grinning back at Stiles. "When?"

"Next month. We'd do it sooner, but Molly wants me to heal up a bit more. She said she doesn't want wedding pictures that make the groom look like he'd been beaten into submission."

Kerney laughed.

"Do me a favor?"

"Name it."

"Be my best man."

"It will be my great pleasure."

"You'll do it?"

"Absolutely."

"Great."

"Now can I go back to sleep?" Kerney asked.

Stiles pulled a bottle of whiskey from a paper sack. "Not until we celebrate."

"Thank God I don't have to work tomorrow," Kerney said as Jim cracked the seal and handed him the bottle.

"MOM, CODY IS BEING A JERK again," Elizabeth called out from the kitchen. "He's teasing Bubba."

"I'm just playing with him," Cody yelled.

Bubba yelped.

"Leave the puppy alone and stop acting like a jerk," Karen said as she entered the kitchen.

"I'm not a jerk," Cody retorted, his eyes hurt, his voice quivering.

Karen knelt down and hugged her son. "No, you're not. I'm sorry I said that."

Cody sniffled and nodded his acceptance of the apology.

"Did you finish the geography lesson I left for you this morning?"

"Yes."

"Let me see it."

He got his spiral notebook from the kitchen table and plopped down on the floor, eagerly leafing through the pages to find his work.

Karen sat with him. Bubba ran over and crawled into Cody's lap, his tail slapping happily against Cody's leg. Elizabeth, standing on a low stool at the kitchen sink, returned her attention to the dinner dishes.

She went over the lesson with her son, praising his good work and pointing out his misspellings. She decided the next set of lessons would have to be on penmanship and spelling, two areas where Cody was having difficulty. Elizabeth could help. She was excellent at both.

Karen let the children stay up a little later than usual, mostly for her own sake. She had seen them only in snatches during the last five days, as she ground through the investigations with Kerney and prepared the cases. But the crunch had finally eased. Her boss had assigned another ADA from Socorro to help, and had reassigned all of her pressing trial appearances to other staff.

She got the kids tucked into bed, went into the living-room, and curled up on the love seat. With the day off tomorrow she could turn her full attention to the children and her parents. All of them, including Karen, needed to get over the Slash Z fiasco and put things back together again.

While Mom had sailed through surgery, she needed help at home during the recovery and adjustment. Dad, still in shock over killing Eugene, hadn't purged all the guilt he felt, although going public on Luis Padilla's murder had certainly helped.

Karen sighed. And then there was Cody, who had become more emotional and wired since the Slash Z debacle. He would need a lot of attention.

Only Elizabeth—dear, sweet, beautiful Elizabeth—seemed able to take everything in stride. Karen had watched her daughter closely since arriving home from work, and could find no trauma or suspended reaction to the events they all had witnessed. She hoped it was true. She needed someone in the family besides herself to be on an even keel.

The thought of stability turned Karen's attention to Kerney. If anyone was solid as a rock, he was. She had liked Kerney when she first met him, and over the past week she had added feelings of respect and an appreciation of his abilities. Mingled in with it was a pleasant feeling of arousal that passed between them every now and then during their long days together. Nothing had been said, but Karen knew it was mutual.

She smiled as the thought of some well-deserved, healthy lovemaking crossed her mind. She had arranged for Kerney to draw a salary through the DA's office until everything was wrapped up. Maybe she could organize a way to keep Kerney around for a while longer, just to see what developed.

INSTEAD OF a traditional bachelor party hosted by the best man, Jim asked Kerney to organize a picnic. The guest list would be limited to Molly and Karen. The destination was Elderman Meadows, and it would happen on everybody's next day off.

Kerney agreed. The day before the event he made a special run to Silver City, where he bought every picnic delicacy he could think of, and an expensive hamper complete with utensils, plates, and all necessities—which he planned to leave behind for Jim and Molly when he moved on.

They rode in on the horse trail and reached the meadows just in time to see an elk herd moving into the trees. Nobody spoke until the last animal disappeared from sight.

"It's too early to eat," Jim announced.

"What do you propose as an alternative?" Molly asked.

"Let's find Mexican Hat," Jim answered.

"Let's!" Molly exclaimed.

"Find what?" Karen inquired.

"That's where José and Hector Padilla were going when they came to the meadows," Kerney explained. "I know where it is."

"How do you know that?" Jim demanded.

"Instinct." It was a better answer than bringing up the events at the Slash Z again.

"This I've got to see. Lead on," Jim ordered.

He took them up the middle finger of the meadow and into the forest. Jim sniped that he was lost, until they broke cover at the edge of a crater that slanted into the mountainside.

Sunlight poured into the hollow. The sheer drop-off was shallow, rocky, and barren, but the cavity glistened with the color of mahogany-red and yellow coneflowers.

"This is it?" Jim asked, shaking his head in disbelief. "It doesn't look like a hat to me. Not even an upside-down hat."

Molly and Karen started laughing.

"What's so funny?"

"Tell him, Kerney," Molly said, still giggling. "If you know, that is."

"See how the flowers are shaped?" Kerney replied. "Like a sombrero. Mexican Hat."

"I knew that," Jim said sheepishly.

They tethered the horses and climbed down into the hollow with the picnic hamper, the cooler, and a blanket. Kerney acted as host and served up lunch, which was greeted with delight.

When the meal was finished and the conversation lapsed, Jim and Molly disappeared for a walk in the woods. Karen stretched out on the blanket, her head propped up in her hand. In jeans, a pullover top, and boots, with her hair loose around her face, she watched Kerney as he repacked the hamper.

He closed the lid and looked over at her. On the blanket next to her was a small gift-wrapped box.

"Open it," she said.

"What are we celebrating?" he asked.

"New friendships."

Carefully, he unwrapped the present. Inside was an exact duplicate of his rodeo buckle, accurate right down to the inscription and the date.

"It's wonderful. How did you manage to do this?" he asked, grinning like a kid.

"I tracked down the manufacturer. They keep all their molds of official award buckles. After I explained the situation, they were very happy to oblige." She handed him a business envelope.

"More?"

"Maybe."

Inside was an offer from the county manager asking him to serve as the sheriff until a special election could be held. The contract would pay Kerney a nice chunk of money.

"Is this for real?" he asked.

"You bet it is," Karen replied. "And you get additional fringe benefits to go with it."

Kerney turned over the letter. It was blank.

"Such as?"

"For one, free housing. You can stay at Jim's place."

"Molly and Jim know about this?"

"As do my parents and Jim's. It was a group decision."

Kerney smiled broadly and stuck the letter into his shirt pocket. "I'll see the county manager in the morning. What else?"

Karen smiled shyly. "Dating privileges. Can you two-step with that knee?"

"I can."

"Can you hold a decent, intelligent conversation with a woman in a bar over drinks?"

"It's been known to happen."

"And eat an occasional home-cooked gourmet meal?"

"I believe so."

"Need I say more?" She held out her hand.

"Are there any more benefits?" Kerney asked as he took her hand in his.

"It all depends on how you define the term," Karen answered, pulling him closer.